BY JOSEPH CALDWELL

In Such Dark Places

The Deer at the River

THE DEER
AT THE
RIVER

THE DEER AT THE RIVER

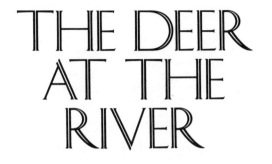

JOSEPH CALDWELL

LITTLE, BROWN AND COMPANY · BOSTON · TORONTO

FIRST EDITION

The author gratefully acknowledges the following for per-
mission to reprint previously copyrighted material:
"The Municipal Gallery Revisited" from *Collected Poems of
William Butler Yeats*. (Copyright 1940 by Georgie Yeats,
renewed 1968 by Bertha Georgie Yeats, Michael Butler Yeats
and Anne Yeats.) Reprinted by permission of Macmillan
Publishing Co., Inc., Michael Yeats and Macmillan London
Limited.

LIBRARY OF CONGRESS CATALOGING IN PUBLICATION DATA

Caldwell, Joseph, 1928–
  The deer at the river.

  I. Title.
PS3553.A396D4   1984   813'.54   83-26778
ISBN 0-316-12438-9

FIC
CAL

BP

Designed by Jeanne F. Abboud

*Published simultaneously in Canada
by Little, Brown & Company (Canada) Limited*

PRINTED IN THE UNITED STATES OF AMERICA

CI

TO DON, RON, ROD AND ANTONIO
TO EDDIE, TO LEO, TO JESS
TO DIFFY, HOWARD, JAMES
AND VAN

*"Think where man's glory most begins and ends,
And say my glory was I had such friends."*

WILLIAM BUTLER YEATS,
"The Municipal Gallery Revisited"

". . . and take upon's the mystery of things."

WILLIAM SHAKESPEARE, *King Lear*

THE DEER
AT THE
RIVER

I T was getting dark. The trees at the back of the yard seemed to be reaching upward as if to join the descending night and form a wall, cutting Noah off from the river, the woods and the solitary mountain beyond. The deer he was waiting for would have to come from there.

No lights shone from the house on the other side of the hedge and none from Noah's own house rising up behind him. He settled himself more firmly on the cement step that led to his back hall and propped his shoulders against the screen door. A slight sifting of rust fell onto his neck and along his spine, but he made no move to brush it off or move away.

He was naked and the cement under him was coarse, like hard pebbled sand. The slate flags of the walk that led to his workshop at the back of the yard were cool under his muddied feet and an evening wind stirred the hairs on his legs and chest, freeing them from the muddy smears that pasted them to his skin. A stinging on his right cheek told him he probably had a few cuts. In his mouth there was a taste of earth.

Noah set his elbows on the doorsill behind him and rested his hands loosely on his lap. In the deepening shadows the old stable where he had his workshop had changed from white to pale blue and was now becoming a dirtied gray, the color of smoke. Its windows, gleaming like black ice moments before, had become dried and drab as if the ice had melted not to water but to dust.

Noah worried that he might not have turned off the power on the band saw; then he remembered that it didn't matter anymore. A memory of having cut some shelves too short one day last week — the kind of mistake he hadn't made since he was a boy — crossed his mind, but he let it go.

He was looking past the lower branches of the catalpa tree into the bushes and bramble that grew down the bank to the river, to the Nubanusit. The leaves stirred slightly and a few branches nodded down and up again as if to taunt him, as if to suggest that something was about to emerge, perhaps the deer.

Noah was prepared to be patient. He was under sentence of death by order of the richest man in town, his wife was mad, his children were gone, and he wanted to do nothing more at the moment than sit and mourn and remember. And wonder why these things had happened.

He let his eyes survey the yard. At the side of the garden shed was a child-sized football that looked like a leathery egg laid by a brown cow. One of the shed windows was broken and had been stopped up with a Wisconsin license plate he'd found in the river. A girl's bicycle was lying in the driveway near the hedge. Next to the handlebars was a watering can tipped over.

On the grass a khaki blanket formed an arrowhead as if it had been picked up at the center, dragged along and then dropped. Toys trailed out behind like the debris of a falling star, plastic blocks, beads and rattles, a soft-furred monkey and a carved wooden dog Noah had made himself, with a head that moved up when the tail was pulled down. A mixing bowl with a large wooden spoon was set in the middle of the path that separated the grass from the vegetable garden. The onions were flowering and ready to go to seed, but the tomato plants looked sturdy and the small pumpkin patch was a good thick tangle of vine that crawled along the ground like flourishing worms that had sprouted leaves and blossoms from being in the open air.

Noah looked long at the garden trying to remember the days last spring when his wife, Ruth, was putting in the vegetables, how she had called to him through the open stable doors, talking about her hope for the peas, her despair over the squash; he remembered her pleased surprise when she'd unearth an old root from last year or from years before, sometimes recognizing it like a found friend, other times puzzling at its presence in her garden, uncertain if it had done her some service or not.

Once she'd found a 1935 buffalo nickel and he'd had to stop work and come out and look, another time a piece of a plow blade. Horseshoes she found all the time for the first three years, then none, then one again last spring, so small it must have been for a pony.

What Noah remembered most as he looked at the garden now was Ruth on her knees, the seeds dropping from her hand into the open ground. Her back was bent, her head bowed. She would move backwards, away from the house, silently, like a penitent performing some harsh propitiatory rite.

The wind became cold and Noah gave a sudden shiver as if he'd just come out of the river after a quick swim. Next to the step where he sat was Ruth's green linen dress he'd been wearing. It was rumpled and torn. He considered putting it across his shoulders but it looked so weary lying there, so defeated, that he felt he ought to let it rest. After looking at it a moment, he reached down and drew it across his lap, not to ward off the chill or even to cover his nakedness, but because he felt it was wrong to just leave it there as if it were no more than a muddied rag.

He let his hands, palms open, hold the dress to his thighs. He was ready for the deer to come. He would wait, remembering, gathering, holding the memories one by one, beginning with the crackling sound of flames, a fire starting in the woods down along the river. That he remembered first.

Noah, in bed, still half asleep, had lifted his head from the pillow. It came again, the sound through the open window, nearer, the sharp snap of limbs and bark, the fire chewing the timber before devouring it.

"Ruth!" he whispered, shoving his wife's shoulder. Ruth muttered something in her sleep like "Let's have a little decorum." Noah jumped up from the bed, now wide awake.

"Anne!" he called. "Danny!"

Joel, the baby, was already in his arms, hugged against his chest, and he was halfway to the door before he realized that no reflected red played up and down the bedroom wall opposite the window. And the noise of the flames had stopped. He called out again, "Ruth!"

Ruth murmured a quizzical "Hmmmn?" into the pillow on his side of the bed.

"Get up. The woods. I think there's a fire." For this his voice was a whisper as if there were an added danger in letting the fire know that he suspected it was there.

With a sound of sleepy protest, half grunt, half sigh, Ruth nestled her face in the hollow where his head had been, then shifted her body, a lazy rolling that became first a stretch, then a curling, as she settled at last into the warmth he'd left behind.

This meant she was still asleep but knew he'd gotten up. He'd seen it many times, this complaint that seemed to Noah so filled with sleepy yearning that more often than not he'd slip back beneath the blankets, stretch out at her side and draw her to himself. Then he would feel along his flesh, along his bones, her slow uncurling, and feel the slow flow of her body as it filled any emptiness that might ever have come between them.

But he didn't slip back beneath the blankets now. Instead he shook her shoulder and called again. The baby, without waking, rubbed his face into his father's shoulder, testing for a familiar smell before deciding whether to wake up or not.

Noah heard it again, the fire, like the amplified crumpling of wrapping paper, the sound breaking against the cold morning air. Just as Noah was about to yell "Fire!" it stopped. He turned toward the window. There was no smoke, there were no flames. In the early light, with the sun still below the line of trees high on the far side of the river bank, he could see the sky, still more white than blue, the pines almost black, with only the oak and birch beginning to green. The snap of the fire came again, fainter, then stopped.

As Noah stepped to the window, Anne, his ten-year-old daughter, came into the room. Too sleepy to raise her head, her eyes still resting shut, she assumed a familiar reason for the summons. "Joel's bottles are on the stove. Momma said boil 'em."

Danny, Noah's five-year-old son, followed, wide awake, expectant, but whispering because this was still the hour of sleep. "Did Momma have another baby?"

Ruth, propped on her elbow, opened and closed her eyes, then opened and closed them again, trying not to take in more than one gulp of light at a time. Her words pained with interrupted sleep, she said, "What's everybody doing up for, for godsake?"

Noah answered quietly. "Come here to the window and look." He backed away so that Anne and Danny could stand in front of him, then he turned Joel around and tucked him into the notch of his elbow so that, should the baby open his eyes, he too might see. Ruth dropped the props out from under her head and flattened out on the bed. "It's not *morning*. I can *tell* it's not morning."

Danny spoke, a barely restrained whisper. "Come see in the yard, Momma."

"I don't *want* to see in the yard. I want to *sleep*." With that she got up, wrapped herself in a blanket, and waddled to the window.

Noah moved aside to give her room. "See?" he said.

At the back of the yard, just inside the thicket that covered the slope down to the river stood an old deer munching the spring lettuce. Its head was lowered to the ground, its antlers rising from the taut skull like escaped memories turned to bone.

"Is he eating the lettuce?" Ruth asked, her voice demanding nothing less than the absolute truth.

"Daddy, make him lift up his head," Danny said.

"Don't talk. Just look."

But at Danny's words, the deer slowly raised its head and stared at an old clothesline post that had survived the installation of a dryer more than seven years before.

Its hooves planted in the soft soil of the garden, its tongue licking in the last of the lettuce it had tugged up from the ground, the deer blinked, then raised its head still higher as if an adjusted view would help it remember what the clothespost was and what it meant.

The long hair on its breast, gray and dry as if powdered with dust, hung down from its neck like a beard fallen from the chin, unmasking a grave and ancient face. Slowly it lifted its right foreleg, held it there, suspended, then lowered it again, touching the earth with a hesitant tenderness, all as if it had recognized in the worthless post a forgotten totem and had now paid it a half-remembered homage.

"Can we keep him?" Danny asked.

"He is. He's eating it. He's eating the lettuce," was Ruth's reply, nothing less than the absolute truth she'd demanded before.

The baby didn't wake and Noah let him sleep, his head fallen forward like a spectator more in need of rest than entertainment.

The deer blinked once more at the post, then went back to nibbling. Noah watched, and the others too, until Anne, making steam marks on the window with her breath and drawing pictures in them with her finger, said, "Momma, tell Daddy he doesn't have his pajamas on yet."

Noah didn't move. He simply held onto the baby that much tighter as if it might be covering enough. "He wanted you to see the deer," Ruth said, then added with her flattened voice, "eating the lettuce." She raised her fist to rap on the glass but Noah stopped her.

"Why?" she asked. "It's going to eat the whole world if you let it." But when she saw that Noah wasn't going to say anything, she lowered her arm straight down to her side to indicate that it was only with the greatest restraint that she could stand there and watch her garden disappear down the gullet of an old buck deer, and one that belonged back up on the mountain to begin with.

"Let him eat what he wants," Noah said.

"But why?"

Noah didn't answer because he couldn't. He could only watch. His feelings made no sense nor did his thoughts.

Ruth sucked in a quick breath and swallowed it, quite the opposite of a resigned sigh. The deer had begun to show an interest in the beans.

A truck on the road to Jaffrey backfired. The baby woke up with a startled jerk and the deer bounded off into the thicket and down toward the river. The fire-sounds of exploding sap and snapped branches receded into the distance and were silent.

"Okay," Ruth said. "Show's over. Everybody back to bed." She took the baby into the blanket she was wearing, nuzzled the tip of her nose lovingly into one of his eye sockets and started toward the crib. "And close the window. It's freezing." She gave an exaggerated "brrrr" that vibrated against the baby's cheek and made him squeal with pleasure.

Anne closed the window and erased what was left of her drawing with her bare arm. Noah reached over to the chair near the bed, picked up his pants and was putting them on.

"What're you getting dressed for?" Ruth asked.

"I'm not getting dressed."

"Oh." Ruth shrugged and brought the baby's blanket up to his chin and tucked it in around his shoulder.

While Danny was still staring down into the yard, Anne went to her mother and asked in a quiet voice as if the subject were secret and intimate, "Can I go ride my bike?"

Danny turned from the window. "Can I go play with the Cooper's puppies in their yard?" Without waiting for an answer he began to run out of the room, but Noah headed him off at the door.

"It's too early to go waking people up." He tried to look reasonable, even authoritative, but when he saw the wonder in his son's eyes — as if they beheld at that very moment a vision of four puppies crawling all over him in the morning grass — Noah had to draw the boy close to himself and kiss the top of his head.

"It's too early to get up," Ruth said as she got back into bed and flopped the blankets on top of her.

"But we *are* up," Anne whispered as if no one was supposed to know.

"We are all going back to bed," Ruth announced, arranging the blankets neatly around her, setting an example for the restoration of routine and order. "I'm the first one gets up and I'm not up. See? I'm in bed." She rolled onto her side making murmuring noises.

"I can't sleep," Danny said.

"Well, try," said Noah. "Try for fifteen minutes and if you're still awake you can get up."

"If I count to sixty fifteen times I can get up?" Without waiting for this to be confirmed, Danny ran out counting.

Anne, at the side of the bed, asked, "Can I take Joel into my bed with me?"

Before Ruth could answer, Danny was back in the room. "Can I take Joel in bed with me?"

"Anne asked first," Ruth murmured, the murmur genuine this time as it worked its way up from a half-sleep.

Without protest Danny picked up his count, the numbers clipped and quick, the sounds clicking away with him down the hall.

Anne gathered the baby, blankets, bottom sheet, pillow and all, into her spindly arms and left the room, a soft rustle of cottons and flannels and the smack of bare feet along the wooden floor.

Ruth, asleep by now, moved her arm over to Noah's side of the bed, brought it up to his pillow and there she let it rest.

Noah started toward her but stopped at the window and looked out at the woods. Now the sky was beginning to blue and the pines to show their green. But the yard showed no sign at all of a dawn visitation. Of course it was hunger that had brought the deer, but Noah couldn't let it go at that.

It was, he told himself, the early hour. Perhaps an interrupted dream intruding on this waking vision, the sensations of his sleeping state imposed onto the simple sight of a deer eating lettuce in his wife's garden. He felt himself blessed, and his family blessed. Never had he realized until now that it was his particular fate to be happy, to be content. He undressed and slid in next to Ruth and took her in his arms.

"Ummmmn," Ruth said.

And Noah marveled all over again that the deer had come to them not only down along the mountain rocks and through the thicket, but it had come to them through fire.

2

Noah had fallen in love with Ruth Strunk on a Saturday morning in autumn twelve years before when he was twenty and already making his living as a carpenter and cabinetmaker. He was not, however, many women's first choice for a husband and a father, nor even the second choice or the third. Noah Dubbins was the man who'd killed the blind girl's pig. And his reputation went back even farther than that.

When he was five, his mother ran off to Leominster with a man named Rademacher who'd come to Mattysborough to open a bookstore. Thomas Dubbins, Noah's father, seemed to have gone into mourning rather than into rage and he pretty much stayed there, numbed by his dull and boring job at the ball bearing factory and by alcohol, and consoled from time to time by a Mrs. Malone who lived near Jaffrey Center with a senile aunt.

This left Noah if not to himself than to housekeepers more interested in television and talking on the telephone than in taking care of a fierce unruly child who didn't hesitate to slug it out when he was opposed and to use every foul word known to the playground of the Mattysborough Consolidated School when he felt like it.

In class he was absentminded and considered dumb. He fought a lot and usually won, as much out of fury as from strength. He terrified his opponents by the viciousness of his attack, and they surrendered.

He was known to have cried only once: when his seventh grade teacher, Miss Loomis, had said, "What would your mother think of you? She'd be ashamed." After Noah had wiped his tears on his sleeve, he punched Miss Loomis in the nose.

Another year, walking home the mile and a half from high school — he was a sophomore then — he decided he'd wade his way along the river with his shoes and socks on. This was possible for only about half a mile but he was sufficiently soaked up to his knees to feel it had been worth while. Lucille, the housekeeper of the moment, would be in despair.

He did this at least two or three times a week until, after a month, he noticed that the old Colbert Carding Mill on the far side of the abandoned railroad tracks had been empty for as long as he could remember. There were twelve panes of glass to each window, ten windows up and eight windows down on both front and back, with five windows up and four windows down on the sides. It would be an achievement to break every one, especially if he tested to see how far back he could stand and still hit his mark.

He got no farther than the two upper windows on the north side before his arrest. For his sentence he was told to replace each single pane — even though the building was scheduled to be torn down in the spring — and to do it without help from either his father or his friends. (Which was just as well. His father would be drunk, his friends too busy, and besides, he liked to work alone.)

That he enjoyed replacing the windows more than he'd enjoyed breaking them puzzled him but he forgot all about it when the job was finished.

That summer he began driving his father's Ford LTD, two years before he would be eligible for a license. He would drive to Keene where there were more traffic lights than in Mattysborough and see how many red ones he could drive through without being stopped. It was almost a week before he got a friendly warning from a state trooper who neglected to ask for his nonexistent license.

He became more selective but more daring. He'd run a red light only when it would terrorize the other driver who'd had the right of way. He was stopped twice: first by two policemen who punched him up a little, took the three dollars he had in his wallet and let him go with a warning to stay out of their territory; then, finally, by a patrol car in Jaffrey where he had to appear with his father in front of a judge. His father dozed off during the proceedings and was reprimanded. Noah himself was put on probation but he drove anyway, still without a license and still terrorizing drivers who had the right of way. Only now he did it in Hancock and operated more cautiously because he felt sorry for his father who had to pretend he didn't notice what his son was doing.

All this was recorded in the town chronicles, a history more in the oral than the written tradition, but enduring nevertheless.

About this time he mended an old kitchen chair for the Costellos, a sprawling Irish family itself a prime source of interest to the keepers of the local Doomsday Book. The Costellos saw in Noah a brother equally subject to undeserved curiosity. Their numbers alone nominated them for peculiarity; there were eleven, three near Noah's age, and each in turn was making his contribution to the ineradicable record being so dutifully kept by their betters. To some Costellos, Noah was mentor; to others, pupil. And now, to all, he was an astonishment. He had taken the chair, replaced rungs and spokes, reglued the whole thing and corrected its age-old wobble. Noah considered it nothing special; it had been done almost by instinct. The Costellos, who tended to have more energy than skills, considered it a feat worthy of wonder and respect.

Of course Noah was, to them, different to begin with. To have a father with no mother or brothers or sisters was odd indeed. And the house where Noah and his father lived had no carpets, only linoleum on all the floors, and the rooms were always neat. Also, Noah had pitch black hair, a throwback to his mother's ancestry which was sometimes said, especially since her departure for Leominster, to be part Algonkian. The Costellos were also fascinated by the severity of his features, the high cheekbones and dark, dark eyes, the large straight nose, the mouth brought forward slightly by a small oblong mound of flesh, a mounting for the lips, and then the strong but narrowing jaw. They liked to think of him as part savage even though the families of both his parents had populated the cemeteries around for over a hundred and fifty years. His skills they considered further evidence of his supposed savagery; they were skills of the hands and not of the mind. Also, when they went swimming or when they peed together, Noah was uncircumcised, another peculiarity, another primitive characteristic.

Noah fixed a second chair and then put up some shelves. He became a hero in the household. Mrs. Costello made him cinnamon toast. He could eat and sleep there whenever he wanted; there would always be room. He stopped driving the LTD without a license. He built a bench around two sides of the Costello kitchen table to save wear and tear on the chairs. It was so sturdy the younger ones as well as the three teenagers Noah's age could jump up and down on it — which they all did, at his invitation.

Then the Costellos moved away to Houston, Texas. That's when Noah stole a truck and drove it to Rindge. But he made a wrong turn and got stuck trying to shift into reverse. When the truck jolted forward it crashed through a fence and hit a pig. As God would have it, it was a 4-H pig being raised for the summer fair by a girl who'd had two eye operations. That both operations had been successful did not count. The pig died and Noah was known henceforth — and shunned — as the boy who'd killed the blind girl's pig.

He was put on probation again and told to pay for the pig. But no one would give him a job. He'd killed the blind girl's pig. Two Saturdays later, his father, leaning against the refrigerator, proposed a woodworking shop in the back storeroom just off the kitchen. It could be a way to pay for the dead pig. And, his father must have hoped, keep him out of mischief.

To Noah this sounded enough like a prison sentence for him to accept it without complaint since he felt genuinely bad about the pig. And besides, he was grateful that he'd be left to himself with no one to bother him.

And so it was there, in the back storeroom, that he started to make his own living; it was there that he went to grieve for the lost Costellos, and it was there that he would temper his savagery into patience and nurture his loneliness into solitude.

Noah was walking west on Federal Street on his way to buy the new electric drill he'd been saving for when a girl came around the corner riding on the back of John Scott's Honda. She waved, called out "Noah Dubbins!", looked back, waved again and disappeared where the street swerved right toward the bridge that crossed the river. Her hair flew out behind the way a girl's hair flies out only on clear autumn mornings.

Noah wanted to call back but he'd forgotten her name. He'd seen her only once before and even then they hadn't really met. He'd returned a mutt puppy to her mother after it had been announced on a local television that a ginger colored mutt was reported lost by Mrs. Blanche Strunk of Star Pond Road.

Noah had the puppy. It had gone padding past him on High Street two days before and Noah had greeted it by saying in recognizable English, "arf, arf," while continuing on his way. By the time he reached the bridge Noah realized that the dog was following him, as if with the "arf, arf" he had inadvertently spoken an actual dog language and the puppy was taking him at his word, whatever that word may have been. An invitation, perhaps a promise of food. Possibly companionship. Noah didn't know but he let the dog follow him home.

It wasn't hungry and in its trailings it seemed not so much eager for companionship as for the fulfillment of the promise or the proposition made by the "arf, arf." Noah threw sticks for the dog to retrieve, but it would take its eyes off him only long enough to acknowledge the flight of the stick. Then it would look up at him again, questioning.

Noah petted it and scratched it and rubbed its belly. The dog submitted, willing to indulge Noah, but not wanting to be distracted for too long from the promise previously made.

Noah tried talking to the dog. He repeated the "arf, arf," letting it grow to a real bark, then a growl, then a whine, then a whimper, then the "arf, arf" again. The puppy looked up at him, puzzled, concerned perhaps for Noah's sanity and well-being.

Noah tried ignoring the dog. Still it followed him around, its tail, its eyes, its opened mouth making the old eager demand that Noah now despaired of ever deciphering.

On the second day of the dog's stay, Noah's father, looking into his coffee cup as he stood next to the sink, said "You got yourself a dog, huh?" This was his first acknowledgment that the puppy had been with him and his son, in his house, for two nights and over one day.

"He's lost."

"Lost? How'd he get lost?"

"He was on High Street."

Noah's father nodded his huge head, accepting this as the explanation of everything, then finished his coffee and went off to work at the ball bearing factory where they didn't seem to mind his drinking and where he was now a foreman and entitled to wear a suit coat on the job but not a matching suit or a tie.

Noah had just poured some of his coffee into a saucer for the dog when it was announced on TV after the morning news, among other community concerns, that Mrs. Blanche Strunk of Star Pond Road had lost a ginger colored puppy that answered to the name of Noah.

Noah put the saucer down in front of the dog and said "Noah." The dog sniffed the coffee and began to lick along the edge of the saucer. "Noah?" Noah asked. The dog went right on licking the rim of the saucer, avoiding the coffee itself. Noah stirred in some sugar then said, "Noah."

Now the dog was lapping up the coffee and only when it was finished did it look up, expectant as always, wagging, inviting Noah into fields of play that didn't exist or that could probably never be found.

Mrs. Strunk's house at the end of Star Pond Road was a shack, or rather a series of shacks, one joining the other, almost a little village of rectangles and cubes of varying heights and sizes, each built, it seemed, to accommodate a haphazard impulse as much as to fulfill a need for added space and room. Some sections were clapboard, one was sided with asbestos, another was made of unfinished pine placed vertically and sealed with strips of cedar.

There was a large vegetable patch in front filled with the refuse of a fall harvest, remnants of cabbage and bean, a few pumpkins still ripening. At the garden's edge was a rocky pasture that sloped upward to a wood of pine and birch. Directly in front of the house was a cut lawn that led down to the shore of what must be the Star Pond that had given the road its name. It was a lake really, the water a clear green and, except for the house and lawn, it was closed in completely by aspen and birch, then oak and pine.

When Noah pulled up near the pond at the edge of the lawn, seven yelping dogs from nowhere leaped and fell and leaped again against the door of his car, mutts of such intricate crossbreeding that they seemed the result of an experiment in dog genetics, a mix of browns and blacks and whites and rusts, a variety of sizes and structures, as if the bloodlines of every known breed had been distilled down to these final seven hounds.

They bashed themselves against the car as if the infliction of self-injury were the only polite form of welcome they'd mastered so far. Inside the car, the puppy stepped up onto Noah's lap and looked out, cocking its head this way and that, no more than mildly curious as to what all the fuss was about. Soon bored, it returned to its side of the seat and faced forward as if ready for the ride to resume.

Now the dogs ran around to the puppy's side and made their welcoming attack all over again like a mob maddened by its zeal for common courtesy. The puppy looked over at Noah, then up toward the windshield, then at Noah again, as if wondering why they weren't moving on.

Noah decided that's exactly what he'd do, drive on and take the puppy with him. Mrs. Blanche Strunk obviously had enough dogs already. But just as he reached forward to turn on the ignition, the puppy climbed over his arm, stood up on his lap and looked out the window. Its tail began to wag, then its whole behind. Its head began to bob, looking down to see if the door had been opened so it could jump out, then looking up again, out the window.

A whimper, a bark withheld because the moment was not yet right, strained up through its nose, a testing of the vocal mechanism to make sure it could deliver when the right moment came.

It raised now one hind leg, then the other, still wagging, stumbling, trying to find an equilibrium on Noah's lap without surrendering its view out the window. It had, in effect, begun to dance, the first time in Noah's life he had ever seen a creature literally dance for joy.

A girl of about eighteen, a young woman, was coming toward the car from the house, the seven dogs leaping and yelping around her. She was reading a book as she walked. The puppy had somehow danced one leg into the spokes of the steering wheel and Noah had to yank it up and out before it broke any bones.

The girl was skinny and about a head shorter than Noah's six foot two. She was wearing not blue jeans and a T-shirt or sweater but a sort of old-fashioned peach-colored cotton dress with a white belt of imitation leather pulling it in at the waist. The short sleeves puffed out a little as if to compensate for the small breasts that poked out in front. She had only the slightest suggestion of hips, the suggestion mostly the flare of the belted dress rather than a rounding of any flesh beneath.

Halfway to the car she stopped, closed the book and bent down into the maelstrom of dogs. Her long hair fell forward, a flow of dark rich brown like the graining of the best walnut. To Noah it seemed that she's sensed his evaluation of her breasts and hips and had decided to rebuke him with this display of one of her better features, her hair.

She was now down among the dogs, cuffing them, scratching them, driving one of them into such a frenzy that it raced all the way to the pasture and back again three times. The puppy meanwhile wet on Noah's lap.

The girl came to the window of the car as the dogs clawed at its side, hoping they'd be allowed inside if that was where the girl was going. Noah saw little pink pimples across her forehead like a light rash and noticed that a tiny nick in the shape of a perfect rectangle had been chipped away from her right temple as if she had once been made of something other than flesh. Her eyes were green like Star Pond and she was laughing at the found puppy, a laugh that lifted her cheeks upward and outward so that Noah no longer thought of her as skinny. And besides, her lips were full and not thin and bloodless as Noah had expected them to be.

"Come on, Noah. You're a bad dog. Bad bad bad."

The puppy squeezed through the upper part of the opened window before Noah could roll it all the way down and the girl was rubbing noses with it, or trying to. The animal itself squirmed in her hands and licked her on the eyes, on the nose, on the chin, on the lips. The girl laughed and the puppy whimpered, scrambling with its back paws, trying to gain a foothold on her breasts. And the breasts themselves seemed more rounded now as if filled out by the girl's squeals and laughter.

With the puppy held high over her head like a trophy won, she turned and started back toward the house with all the other dogs following in clamorous procession. The puppy squirmed its plump little body in an effort to reach down for a few last licks and finally freed itself from her hold. Down it jumped into the common pack, setting off a new round of yelping, each dog begging its chance to be held aloft and carried in triumph into the house.

But the girl merely stooped a little and let her arms stir among them all without special favor, shepherding them closer and closer to the door.

Noah had wanted to be thanked. He had also wanted a better look at the girl's behind and at her legs. He had the habit, going back to the first fevers of puberty, of seldom rejecting outright any female he saw, in school, on the street, in the pizza parlor, riding by in a car, anywhere. He would look at the form and features and if his desires didn't flare, he'd go to work immediately, revising, reshaping, adding or subtracting years if necessary, enlarging, diminishing. This girl with ten pounds more, that woman twenty years younger, this one four years from now, that one with larger breasts, another with slightly less nose and no acne.

He resculpted and repainted, he dressed and undressed as his need demanded. He gave them flesh and took it away, he performed miracles of cosmetic transformation and, after he himself had matured a little, he even provided them with changes of temperament: less giggly, more lively, deeply passionate, smarter, rabidly sexual, dumber, cool and inaccessible, secret, tender. Whatever was needed to qualify them for his lust he freely gave, allowing very few to escape the reconditioning that would gain for them the ultimate approval of his id.

Gradually the habit — or the will — left him and he began to draw in the circumference of his focus to women nearer his own age, women who provided with less effort on his part (or preferably with no effort at all) the stimulus for desire. But now, for the sake of this particular girl, he found himself reverting to the old generosities.

He got out of the car and purposely left the door open so the slam wouldn't make her turn around before he'd seen her legs and her behind. But before he took his second step he felt the sting of the dog's pee on the inside of his thighs. He looked down. A stain that no one would believe had been made by a mere puppy darkened his crotch almost to the knees. He took the second step anyway, and a third.

Even though the girl seemed to have little in the way of hips, her buttocks were certainly well formed, making it seem that the faded peach-colored dress was filled with more than just sticks and bones.

Noah went to work quickly. Taking her buttocks, her hair, her eyes, mouth and laugh for his basic material, he fashioned from the rest of her a young woman who could fill his every need and in the process renew it, replenish it, even expand it to dimensions that would make him dizzy or, if he were lucky, demented. In his mind he kissed, but gently, the small breasts and realized they weren't so small after all.

Noah took a fourth step, ready to call out to her, ready to tell her she wasn't as scrawny as she looked. But the door to the house had opened as if to the word *sesame* and the girl and all the dogs passed through without even the puppy giving Noah a backward glance.

It was finally the book that brought Noah Dubbins and Ruth Strunk together. Just before Noah reached the highway at the other end of Star Pond Road he began to wonder what had happened to the book the girl had been reading. She wasn't carrying it when she went into the house. He turned back and found it on the grass, an old green hardcover copy of *O Pioneers!* by Willa Cather. The girl's name was dutifully written inside in a careful but looping hand.

Noah mailed it to her with the explanation that he'd found it on the day he returned the mutt puppy named Noah. He signed it "Noah Dubbins" so that on the day Ruth rounded the corner on the back of John Scott's Honda she knew what name to call.

"Noah Dubbins!"

Her hair flew out. He raised his hand and she was gone. But not before Noah had fallen absolutely in love with her.

Within the first years of their marriage — she had seemed unimpressed with his having killed a pig — Ruth accomplished what Noah himself had been able only to imagine. She fleshed out and toned down, she hardened in some places and softened in others, her forehead cleared, her bosom bloomed, her hips mellowed, so that her hair, her eyes, her mouth and her behind were no longer special in themselves but simply proportionate parts of her now (to Noah) perfect beauty.

At moments Noah thought all this had come about because of him, that his hands were powered with the sculptor's gift, that his caresses and his touches had molded her to conform to the vision he'd created of her on that first day when he'd seen her circled by hounds.

At other moments he acknowledged that Ruth had simply matured and that was all. In any event, his talents were not without limits. She had terrible trouble with her teeth and his gifted sculptor's hand hadn't done much to raise the level of her arches to the necessary height and keep them there, especially during her three pregnancies.

3

ON the night Ruth went insane, Noah worked late in his shop putting the last brass fittings onto a chest of drawers. It would be ready for delivery at eight-thirty the next morning, on time to the promised minute.

He washed at the big tub sink in the corner of the stable so the running water in the house wouldn't wake Ruth or the children. When he cupped huge handfuls of water against his face he felt he was washing with the water of contentment. He liked being a carpenter; he liked knowing he was a good one and that he had been able to make it his living.

He turned off the workshop lights by switching off the power. With young children who might want to see some of the tools "go," it was best to throw the main switch whenever he left. He locked the sliding doors of the old stable and walked through the quiet yard. It was good to be weary, to catch only vaguely the weed-smell of the tomato plants, to come into the back hall where the odor was must and salt, of things not quite dry, muddy garden tools, sneakers, swimming towels.

The kitchen and the dining room smelled of bananas, the living room like dried figs as if the old carpet were really Persian after all and in its disintegration had released home-scents that had been locked into its weave long years before.

The upstairs hall was an overlay that didn't mix, soap that

smelled like raspberry Kool-Aid and uric acid from the baby's diapers. The door to Anne's room was closed because she was ten now; Danny's door was open just a crack because he was only five. The door to his and Ruth's room was closed so that when Joel cried it wouldn't wake the others.

Noah went in and shut the door behind him with a quiet click. The room was stuffy and smelled of old milk. It was completely dark. He couldn't even make out the window next to the crib. The shade was down, which was odd. There was never a need to pull down the shade. The room was visible on that side only to passing birds or to someone who'd bother to perch himself high in the branches of the maple tree outside. Even on the darkest nights some light came through, from the moon, from the street-lamp on the corner or in winter from the reflected snow.

He was annoyed. He didn't want to turn on the light. It would wake him up completely and probably wake Ruth and the baby too. He started toward the window next to the crib, further annoyed because he didn't see how he'd get the shade up without a noise. He was passing the foot of the bed when he heard Ruth's breathing, short rapid breaths through her nose.

"Ruth? You there?" he asked, knowing she was, but feeling that the rapid breaths and the lowered shade required an explanation that should begin at the beginning. Ruth didn't answer.

"Ruth? You okay?"

Noah began patting around the blankets with his hand, trying to find her, to touch her, but her feet must have been pulled up. He could even sense that she had brought them up more, avoiding his touch.

Noah went back to the door and slapped the wall until he found the light switch.

Ruth was in the bed, propped up against the headboard, the blankets pulled up around her neck with her hands inside. Her knees were raised, her eyes staring down at them as though something there was making her recoil. The rapid breaths continued as if breath were the only weapon she had to hold off whatever it was she saw.

Before Noah could call her name, before he could rush to her, he realized what was happening. She was having the baby. He began lowering his hand from the light switch when he remembered. She'd had the baby two months before. But it had been so like this, Ruth propped rigidly against the headboard, her knees raised. But there'd been little sweat then and her breathing had been calm. It was late in the afternoon and Anne had come to the shop to tell him Momma wanted him upstairs.

The door to their room had been open. Ruth, he remembered, had licked her lips, wetting them before telling him to close it. Noah hadn't really heard. He assumed it was time to take her to the hospital. He started back out the door.

"I'll bring the van to the front and then come back and help you downstairs."

"No," Ruth said. She arched her back, straining harder against the headboard. Her voice was low and even. "It's here, under my skirt."

Noah closed the door and went to the bed. There'd been no blankets then and he saw, poking out from under the hem of her dress a single tiny foot like a hairless mouse, gray and shining as if it had been coated with the melted tallow of a smoking candle.

Ruth clutched at the sides of her skirt and began gathering it up over her knees. "It got turned around and the feet came out first. You have to get the head out for me. I can't bend down." She didn't hurry her words.

There the baby's body lay on its stomach, puckered and wrinkled like a deflating balloon. The arms were stretched out as if it had tried to free its head and failed.

Noah reached out toward Ruth's face to take it in his hands. "No," she said, turning away. "The baby."

He stopped his hands and began reaching down. Ruth started to close her legs, then she spread them wider. "Get your hands in around the head. Push me aside. I'll be all right. But cup your hands around the head and make sure the neck is free so it can breathe."

Noah looked at the baby's gray flesh and drew back his hands.

"Now," Ruth said. She took a deep breath and looked over her right shoulder.

"You don't think I should get an ambulance?"

"There's no time. Reach in and get your hands around the head. Don't tug. Bring it out inside your hands. Just force me away."

Noah put the tips of his fingers just inside the vagina, pressing the soft labia aside.

"Hurry," Ruth said quietly. Then, as if it were a form of permission, she looked down to watch.

Noah reached farther inside, careful to push against the sides of the cervix so that he wouldn't clamp the baby's neck.

"It's all right. It's all right. It's all right." Ruth kept repeating the sentence at measured intervals as if it were the first time Noah was penetrating her and he'd agreed to stop at the first sign of pain.

He could feel little scraps of flesh, one on each side, the baby's ears. He reached in more. Now he could feel a certain roughness. Hair. Holding his breath, he formed his hands across the top of the head until the tips of his fingers almost met. With a slow pull toward himself, his hands cupped protectively, Noah began to withdraw. He took long deep breaths as if to instill them into the lungs of the emerging child.

Ruth was silent. Then, turning again to the right, she looked out the window. "It burns," she whispered. "It burns."

Noah felt the head slip free, part of his fingers still inside his wife. He drew them out, then quickly grabbed the baby by the ankles and held it up.

There the gray thing hung, no sound at all. Noah slapped it on the buttocks because he was so afraid.

"A boy," Ruth said, her voice firm, definite.

At that the cry came out, at that the ribs expanded, contracted, and expanded again, inflating the wrinkled body and coloring the gray to pink. Noah raised him high as if in offering, then turned him toward himself, the crabbed upside-down face on a level with his own, the cord from the little round belly looping limply down, brushing the tip of Noah's nose. The baby howled louder as if he objected to being hung up and looked at.

"I can take him," said Ruth. "Hand him to me." She took him against her chest and tugged at the neck of her blouse.

"Here, let me," Noah said, reaching up. It was only then that he saw the blood on the back of his hands.

With a quick jerk, Ruth ripped open her blouse. She pulled at her brassiere, trying to free her breast. "I have to be unhooked. I wasn't ready." She leaned forward and Noah unfastened the brassiere, smearing blood on the smooth skin of her back.

Ruth moved the baby over to her left breast and pressed his nose gently to the nipple. Like a little snail, the mouth worked its way up and began to nurse. The only sound Noah could hear was the baby breathing, air forcing its way past flaps of mucus in his nose.

With her free arm, Ruth raised first one of the baby's arms and then the other, counting fingers. While she was counting the toes of the left foot, she suddenly gasped as if she'd been jabbed. Then she let go, a long relieved exhalation.

"I better go call the hospital," Noah said. "You're bleeding."

Another held breath, then Ruth expelled a glob of brown blood, the size of a fist, with what looked like veins on its surface. Noah's first thought was it was a kidney, but when he saw the other end of the umbilicus attached to it, he felt foolish. It was the placenta.

Kneeling at the foot of the bed between Ruth's legs, his knees sunk unsteadily into the mattress, Noah could feel the warm blood soak up into his pants.

"All I was doing," Ruth said, "was ironing." She sounded bewildered, as if wondering why ironing should have given her a baby. "Call down and tell Anne to pull out the plug."

Noah looked at Ruth now, the raised knees, the shoulders braced against the headboard, the head pressed against the wood. She was making fun of him for being so frightened after Joel was born. There had been the claim that he'd fainted in the waiting room after he'd taken her to the hospital.

Noah agreed that one moment he was standing and had heard the doctor tell him that all was well, then the next he was sitting on the floor with his back against the wall. The doctor said he'd fainted, but Noah knew he'd simply fallen asleep. When he told Ruth about it, she sided with the doctor.

"You fainted," she said. "I used to do it all the time when I first started having my periods. There's nothing wrong with a good faint."

Noah insisted he'd fallen asleep. He'd even had a dream. But Ruth said you dream when you faint too, and they're always pleasant. At least hers had always been. Noah felt if he could just remember the dream he could convince her, but he never remembered.

But she wasn't mocking him now and he knew it. She was terrified.

"What happened?" he asked. "What's wrong?" He went to the bed and lowered himself at the foot, never taking his eyes off her. "Are you cold?"

He knew it was more than a chill, but thought if he started with the simplest fact he could ease her toward telling him what was wrong.

Ruth said nothing. She began taking in longer and deeper breaths, clutching the blanket that much closer to her throat. Noah reached for her forehead but she jerked her head away and held her breath.

"Ruth, tell me. What's the matter?"

At first Ruth didn't move. Then slowly she began to inch her head back so that she could look directly at him. In her eyes there was a pleading that he must not touch her. Then her breathing began again, the long deep breaths.

Noah put his opened hands on his thighs, a signal that he was not going to touch her. He looked at his hands, then up at Ruth.

Her lips were parched and even from where he sat Noah could catch the scent of her breath, a metallic smell, as if she'd been sucking on pennies. Her face was flushed and steamed, her hair hung in damp strands, curling at the ends, the way it did last year when she'd been putting up jellies or canning or this spring boiling baby bottles. The raised chin could almost be an attempt to escape the steam.

Noah watched, then began to lean forward. Again her breathing stopped. Noah pulled back. She began breathing again.

"You're afraid," he said. "Of what?"

Slowly Ruth brought her knees together under the blankets then spread them again, never taking her eyes off Noah. She tried to smile, but it was the smile of someone hoping to deny pain. Her hands let go of the blanket and it fell down at her sides. She was naked and Noah could see her shudder in the sudden cold. He reached toward her cheek, but Ruth had begun to raise her left arm. Sweeping it across herself, she drew the blanket aside, turning her head away as if what she revealed was for Noah alone to see.

Between her spread legs was a doll Noah had made for Anne when she was a baby, its head inserted into her. It was Joel that Noah saw, then he knew it was the doll. He had carved it from a single length of walnut and Ruth had made different sets of clothes for it. Stripped now, it lay stomach down, one buttock larger than the other, its legs too short, its feet too big, because Noah was a carpenter and not a sculptor after all.

First Noah saw the doll as a mockery of Joel's birth, then as a parody of their lovemaking, Ruth inviting him now to some sexual adventure, loveless and punishing. It aroused him and he knew himself susceptible to it, but then the terrible desolation he'd been holding off came over him. It emptied him, taking the bones from his arm and the heart from his side. Something terrible was happening to Ruth, to his wife.

Noah decided he was supposed to remove the doll, that if he participated in her horror, she might be able to tell him what it was. He reached for the doll, holding out his hands almost as if he was about to fold them in prayer. Gently he placed them on the sides of the doll and looked up at Ruth. She seemed to be looking at him in disbelief: surely he could not do what he was about to do.

"Tell me if I'm doing what I'm supposed to do," he said quietly.

When she didn't answer, Noah moved his hands up along the sides of the doll until the tips of his fingers were touching her. It was then that he heard the baby's muffled cry. His hands sprang away from the doll, open and in front of him. He held them there until he heard the baby again, stifled and struggling.

"Where's Joel?"

Noah had jumped up. The baby wasn't in his crib.

"Where is he?"

Noah opened the closet door, then heard the sound somewhere behind him. He turned. A dresser drawer had been left open a few inches. When Noah pulled it toward himself, he saw Joel down among Ruth's silken slips and underclothes, waving his arms and beating his plump little legs in the air. He seemed surprised to see the light and his father's face.

Noah knelt down and started to take him into his arms, then almost dropped him when he felt the blow on the side of his face. He crouched over the drawer, the baby held underneath him as Ruth clubbed the wooden doll against his back, his shoulders, his head, making the slurred hissing sounds of someone trying to speak with a swollen tongue.

Noah brought one arm up to cover his head so he wouldn't be knocked out, then simply knelt there, bent over the baby, letting the blows fall.

Finally the beating stopped, but the thick hissings continued, sounding like someone trying to tell what it had been like to drown.

4

For reasons that no one could discover, Mount St. Michael, the hospital where Ruth was sent, had lost none of its elms during the time of continental blight. The pestilence that had unleaved whole towns and robbed the most luxuriant avenues of their grace had passed over these one hundred and twenty-seven acres without even pausing to explain why.

This gave Mount St. Michael a hushed notoriety, creating a murmuring superstition in its powers to cure. And understandably so. The elms after all proclaimed the presence of mystery in the world, the possibility of exception, the suspension — however limited — of a universal curse.

Inmates were maneuvered by their relatives into positions under the trees as if they provided some radiological therapy for their ills. And when a patient said he preferred the sun along the lake or the solitude of the path that led to the dairy, this was interpreted as a reluctance to get well, a resistance to treatment.

But for Noah the trees and their myth were not only to be ignored but avoided. Not that Ruth couldn't use massive doses of benignity, whatever its source. Her needs were as desperate as anyone's there. But for Noah the force of mystery proclaimed by the trees was so arbitrary and imponderable that he was wary of it. Ruth's madness was mystery enough. He preferred that he and his wife no longer be the object of such attentions. After all, who knew what the response might be once these mysteries had been roused on their behalf? They were best left alone. Let the elms arch over the path that led from the manor to the gym, and let anyone sit or wander in their shade if that's what they wanted. For Noah and Ruth the lane lined with white pine was enough, or the bench above Fern Lake presided over by nothing more than a horse chestnut of the most common kind.

And so he sat next to Ruth now on the wood-slatted bench, trying to tell her that on his last visit he had stolen her purse but had brought it back. He would start saying the words in just a minute, but first he wanted simply to look out over the field of fronds that was called with only half accuracy Fern Lake. It was all ferns and no lake.

As one of the grounds-keepers had explained on one of Noah's early visits, the actual lake, when the old Varner estate became a hospital, was considered dangerous, not just for potential suicides but for the generally disoriented. So the water was drained, the springs piped into a harmless creek, and the ferns that had prospered on the far shore were allowed to advance unchecked into the mud depths, claiming for themselves this new and fertile land.

As Noah watched, a breeze crossed from the other shore, bowing the fronds to each other, stirring the leaves, as though some piece of news or gossip had been borne to them on the wind and must now be exchanged, discussed and elaborated upon. Noah saw the conversation rise then die as the breeze came up the hill past him, past Ruth, whispering nothing until it reached the pines at the top of the slope where again the news was eagerly taken up and found now to be a cause for long sighs and general mourning.

Noah waited to hear himself begin to tell Ruth about the purse, but no words came. It was, he told himself, because he was too tired to say anything at all. The baby had kept him up for two of the six hours he allotted himself for sleep. Because of the hospital bills, which he couldn't possibly meet to begin with, he had taken on contract work for a carpenter in Keene named Nelson Sheerin. He was making replicas of dry sinks that could be sold as "handcrafted" and he'd promised to deliver a certain number before the summer's end. He needed the money. Desperately. He'd go back to work of his own design when Ruth was well, which had better be soon.

He was still getting by without hiring helpers, even though it meant he had to work that many more hours and that he was doing some work that could readily be trusted to less skillful or experienced hands. But he needed his solitude more than he needed the help.

The one concession he made to this need to be alone — and it was more a pleasure than a concession — was to take Joel with him into the shop during most of the day. Noah had forgotten that he had the habit of singing out against the sound of the band saw until one afternoon he happened to see Joel waving his arms and legs and smiling as if he was being tickled or teased. At first Noah thought the baby was just entertaining himself with his four favorite toys, his hands and feet. Then he realized he'd been singing and the baby had heard.

He sang louder and noticed that the waving increased and the smile became a laugh. Letting out long-sung oooh's and aaah's, he would become operatic, going from baritone to bass to tenor to falsetto and back again, with the saw itself singing through its nose, a serious rising and falling that refused to be either amused or distracted by Noah's exultation.

After an especially long cutting, Noah would go and stand over the baby's playpen and encore a few phrases. Joal would squeal and wave his arms in a quick and complicated semaphore that his father had no trouble understanding. Noah would poke the baby's belly button with his forefinger and Joel would squeal louder and Noah would remember, just in time to keep himself from absolute joy, that Ruth was in the hospital, insane, and that he'd stolen her purse.

Noah turned and looked at Ruth sitting next to him. She was wearing her favorite coat even though it was July, the one she'd bought at a rummage sale six years before when she was pregnant with Danny. The coat would have had the feel of wool if it weren't interwoven with tiny splinters of what felt like horsehair, some chemical probably that helped it shed the rain and snow, keep its shape, and wear like armor.

Brown and green plaid with an intersecting grid of wheat-colored yellow, it looked like a perfect camouflage for the woods on the other side of the river that ran in back of their house. Ruth had bought the coat for its pockets. Slit into the sides, they could hold books, bottles, apples, toys, lunches, a change of shoes and once an earth-clodded rose bush from her mother's, ready for replanting. This kept her hands and arms free, not only for the children, but for any job along the way, pulling a three-foot boneset weed from the privet, retrieving a bicycle from the driveway down the block, giving a quick clap of the hands to warn a dog or a child out of her path.

The coat was buttoned tightly around her neck and because she wore no stockings, only her sandals, Noah couldn't help wondering if she was wearing anything underneath. The thought came to him that maybe she'd gone off into some strange eroticism, flashing her naked body to the doctors or the male attendants, to other visitors, or, what seemed worst of all, to the grounds-keepers.

Or perhaps not flash it, but expose it slowly, her smooth rounded flesh, secretfully, needfully.

Noah could see her in the coat, standing at the turn of a wooded path just beyond the gym. He saw the broad back of a grounds-keeper in a green denim jacket moving toward her.

Noah jerked his head as if to shake off a fly. Had he fallen asleep and had a dream? He didn't know, but he was awake now and the vision was gone. "You've got your coat on," he said. Then he added, "Looks nice."

Ruth said nothing. So far, this was one of her nontalking days, and even when she did talk on the other days, it was usually gossip and anecdotes about the other patients or the staff. How Jack Jaffe from Corridor C had a pair of glasses with a false nose and moustache that frightened Ginny Bonito when he took them off; that old Doctor Corrado, Ruth's doctor, always wore bright orange socks; how Margaret Gavin kept sneaking home by telling someone in the parking lot she was a visitor and her car'd broken down — it was that easy if anyone really wanted to get away; that a Mr. Culp was a millionaire hiding from his creditors; that Deborah Rutland, claiming to be the Angel of the Annunciation, had stepped off the roof of the dairy barn and hurt one of the cows.

The time had come to tell her about the stolen purse. "Ruth?" Noah said. "I've got something I want to tell you. Are you listening?"

Ruth turned her head and looked directly at him, one of the few times since her illness that she did. What Noah saw stopped him from going on. It was Ruth's face, but emptied of divine grace; it was as if all blessings and gifts had been withdrawn and left behind this desolate remnant.

Her eyes, slack with loss, drooped as if the strings and sinews that held them firm in the skull had been loosened and they had begun to sink wearily, helplessly, down behind the bones that ridged her cheeks.

As for the face itself, it seemed she had given her flesh a release, a permission to go where it wanted to go so long as it let her alone. It had chosen a downward course, sagging off the bones, too exhausted to hang on any longer. Her slumped cheeks formed shallow draws along the sides of her nose, natural ravines for tears whenever they might come.

Jowls had begun to form, weighting down the corners of her mouth, thining her lips, making them bloodless and cold.

At the chin, however, the downward course was halted. Never really lowering itself, it seemed to take on the full weight of the descending flesh and forbid it to go any farther. And if the eyes chose to look down, as they often did, the chin automatically raised itself that much higher as if to counter the head's impulse to follow their lead. And so the most dejected look became, at the same time, the most imperious. It was that of a deposed monarch mourning a kingdom lost, yet scornful that it had once been her possession, a look at once arrogant and pitying, as if she despised even the object of her grief.

"Oh, Ruth," Noah said, his voice hoarse and near a whisper. He moved his hand up to her cheek. When she didn't pull away, he left it there, knowing that if Ruth were to tilt her head sideways, just a little, so that her cheek would settle into the cup of his palm, if she were to brush her soft and haggard flesh against the coarse grain of his opened hand, he would feel that all the yearnings of his life had been fulfilled and he would be satisfied forever.

But Ruth raised her head higher and turned away, leaving his hand suspended near her throat. He held it there, then lowered it to his lap. After looking at the hand a moment, he let it slip down between his legs and left it there.

"I found your purse," he said. He wished he'd been able to say, "I stole your purse" or at least "I have your purse." After all, he hadn't found it, he'd taken it.

Ruth said nothing. She looked out over Fern Lake at the woods on the far side, her eyes moving from tree to tree, from branch to branch, as if she were following the course of a bird or animal visible only to herself.

Noah looked up at the sky, hoping to see something he could

comment on while waiting for her to say something. But the sky was clean and its color too pale for him to even say, "How blue the sky is." So he waited, then said, "Your purse, it's on the front seat of the van if you want to walk me over and I'll get it for you."

Ruth made no sign that the subject interested her or that she'd even heard. Then she said, "Mother thinks all of you should go live with her while I'm here. At least the children."

Her voice was tentative, not quite sure where it wanted to go, or if it was going to be allowed to go there. Before her illness it had always been direct, but now the simplest statement, like the one she'd just made, had an undercurrent of questioning: "Am I saying what I wanted to say?" "Is it all right if I say it?" "Am I saying it the way it's supposed to be said?"

What the voice had lost was its delight in itself as the instrument of an alert, amused and agile mind. What had been a fine edge, cutting through nonsense, through uncertainty, was rounded now and slowed, as if it had grown a soft fur. The furred sound was in the tone of her voice and her words curled back onto themselves like a small animal seeking safety and anonymity.

Noah didn't want to go into the subject of the children or of Ruth's mother. He knew he should be grateful that Ruth had spoken at all, and that it was about something that concerned the family, but he wasn't. He wished she'd continued her silence. But still he had to say something. Silence from Ruth was allowed, but not from him.

Maybe he'd distract her by telling her that he had been praying for her. *That* should certainly surprise her. Even though he was a nominal Catholic he'd never had the habit of prayer, not since his mother'd left. But he prayed now. He'd tell Ruth that he prayed kneeling on his knees, his head bowed, in their room, at night, not leaning against the bed or the nursing chair, but unsupported, between the crib and the dresser, not in mortification but to make sure that he was seen, that he was heard. He asked that Ruth be made well, that she be relieved of her suffering and that she come home to him. He prayed for it more passionately than for anything, ever, in his entire life. On his knees. His head bowed.

But it might embarrass her as it embarrassed him. As it probably embarrassed God. Maybe that's how it would work: God would grant his petition just to rid them all of the spectacle. Noah decided he'd talk about the children after all.

Still looking at the sky, he asked, "What should they go live with your mother for?"

"She didn't say."

"We're all right the way we are."

"I told her."

"Told her what?"

"I don't remember."

"You told her we're all right?"

"*Are* you all right?"

"Sure we're all right."

"Then that's what I told her."

Noah paused, then said, "I'll talk to her."

Of course they were not all right. He was getting too little sleep. And the commodities he thought he possessed in endless supply, his patience and his strength, seemed to be giving out.

It seemed to him almost a judgment that they should. Right after Ruth got sick, on his way back from his first visit to Mount St. Michael, he had felt almost euphoric. He looked forward to taking on all the tasks that would now be his. Here was an opportunity for heroism, and he welcomed it. In all his pride he welcomed it. He would care for his children; he would keep his home together. He would be faithful to his wife and help her get well. The idea that he would be easily equal to the challenges ahead elated him. He was about to become the man he knew he was capable of being: sufficient to all things, to all circumstances, no matter what.

Then sleep began to go, money began to be more urgently needed, work began to increase, and work hours along with it. Strength began to weaken and patience to dissolve. And it wasn't just the baby's waking him at night that gave him trouble.

Danny and Anne had found ways to exasperate him, and ways that were all the more effective because they were so well intentioned, gallant and doomed attempts to be good and to be helpful because their mother was ill. They brought Noah near to rage even as they — or because they — broke his heart.

Danny's contribution was an endless string of homilies, so earnest and so obvious, yet completely contradictory to the actualities being dealt with.

At breakfast, nodding gravely beneath the weight of his own wisdom, he'd say, "If I don't eat the yolk I won't get the vitamins and iron I need to keep strong." The yolk then would be undisturbed and Danny would have disappeared from the house.

In the evening, he would say, "Anne and I mustn't watch too much television because it isn't good for your eyes." And then he would have to be dragged from the set and made to go to bed an hour after his appointed time.

Among other sage sayings were "Joel has to cry because it helps him develop his lungs. Otherwise he won't be able to breathe when he grows up." Soon afterwards the howling baby would have been surreptitiously punched or a casual attempt made to smother him.

"We can't have a dog because it might bite the baby and get caught in the saw." Noah would then phone Ruth's mother — unofficial dispenser of dogs for Mattysborough and all the towns around as far as Hancock — and alert her to an imminent plea for a dog and beg her not to give in, whatever the arguments.

"You're not supposed to look in the Driscolls' window because they don't like it when they're supposed to be going to bed."

For this last, Noah gave Danny a firm shake of the shoulder, a stern warning and had him sent to the guidance counselor. Mrs.

Shearer, the guidance counselor, suggested that Noah allow Danny to see him getting dressed and undressed, going to the toilet and taking a shower.

Noah complained that those were the few times he had to be alone now, then grudgingly agreed. The result was that Danny now pursued him everywhere, saying things like "The lawnmower is not a toy to play with," meaning he'd taken the wheels off to try to make a skateboard. Or "You shouldn't go swimming in the river with your shoes and socks on," which meant that his soaked shoes and socks were probably in the back hall downstairs at that very moment.

Noah, however, did tell Mrs. Driscoll next door to be sure to let him know if Danny was ever a "nuisance."

Then there was Anne, always insisting she could do everything, when she couldn't do anything.

"I can clean the bathroom!" And then there'd be a dusting of cleanser all over everything including the toilet seat and the windowsill.

"I can make the meat!" And then the hamburgers would be burned to something as dry and crumbled as granola.

"I can vacuum the rug!" And then all the apparatus would be left in the middle of the living room with the baby sucking on one of the brushes.

And she never mentioned her mother.

Ruth looked down at the ground and said, "Mother thinks even if you don't want to go there yourself to live, maybe the children at least, and she'll take care of them."

"What's wrong with me? I can take care of them. They're my kids."

"That's what I told her."

"I'll talk to her myself."

"I told her I just finished fixing up Anne's room and Danny's last winter. They can't go live with her when I just finished fixing up their rooms. Even the ceilings, I papered them, didn't I?"

"Yeah. They're beautiful. And not easy either. To do, I mean."

"I told her. They have to stay at home. I just fixed up their rooms."

"I'll talk to her."

It crossed Noah's mind that if the children were to go to live with Blanche, with Ruth's mother, he himself would be free to go to see Esther Overbaugh whenever he wanted to. He hoped he wouldn't go to see Esther Overbaugh, but that didn't mean he didn't want to. Still, he was determined not to go. It would be unfair to Ruth and to Esther as well, but his greater reason was that it would smudge the image he had of himself as hero. And more than that, there was his notion that his fidelity to Ruth, his sacrifices on her behalf, would make her well, that her return to health would be a reward for his own good conduct, that what would happen to Ruth depended largely on him, and he must not fail her. He also knew that this reasoning was complete nonsense. Still, Esther came often to his thoughts and once into his dreams.

Ruth said, "Are they all right?"

"They're fine. I told you, they go to day camp until just before school starts."

"I mean the ceilings. Where I fitted the edges together so it matched. It didn't come apart?"

"No. It still looks beautiful. Just the way you did it."

"I'm so worried it might come apart and I'll have to do it over."

"It won't come apart."

"I did it so it wouldn't." Then, following a thought sequence all her own, she added, "And besides, Mother has all those dogs."

Noah touched her coat just at the knee. She tensed at the touch, but Noah left his hand there until he'd finished saying, "Don't worry. Not about anything. Okay?"

At that, Ruth jumped up. "Someone, they stole my purse! I

need it. It's gone. I can't find it. Someone took it." She searched and slapped her pockets like someone who'd just been robbed.

Noah stood up facing her and made short pressing motions in the air with the palms of his hands as if trying to hold back her voice from the air itself. "I found it. I've got your purse for you. It's in the front seat of the van. Walk me over and I'll get it for you."

Ruth looked just past his shoulder. Tears began to form in her eyes. "You stole it," she said.

"I found it."

Ruth looked up at the sky so that the tears rolled sideways across her cheeks away from the natural runnels her madness had made for her. She wiped the tears with her finger tips, then held out her hand to see what they looked like. After nodding what seemed to be approval, she rubbed the tears back into her cheeks like an unguent.

Noah took her by the arm and began to lead her away. For the first few steps, she looked straight ahead, then began to glance down slightly as if disdaining all the objects in their path. She let loose a long litany of obscenities, words she seldom used before her illness, and then only one at a time. It was as though she were cursing everything along the way, trying to wither it with a searing malevolence.

Then Noah thought it might be otherwise. Perhaps she was only trying to protect them both, to ward off, to hold back, whatever harm might be waiting to spring out at them.

When they came to the edge of the parking lot, Ruth let her obscenities trail off into silence. She looked warily at the cars, about twelve of them, placed in the various spaces like colored tokens on a game board. To Noah it seemed she was trying to figure out the game, to guess its rules, to determine what moves might be expected of her.

He tried to lead her to the van, but she refused to move. He left her there and went to get the purse.

It lay on the seat, tan leather, the flap open, making it look like a deflated basketball. Noah pulled it toward him, strewing its contents out along the seat, the handkerchief, the small bottle of hand lotion, a Bic pen, a plastic rain hat, two pennies and an electric bill with a grocery list on it. He paused a moment, then picked up the purse, threw back the flap and began to pitch everything inside.

When he'd finished, he spread the opening wide and looked inside to satisfy himself that he'd given it all back. He brought the flap over and closed the purse, then realized he didn't want to return it. He wasn't ready to. He had no idea why he wanted to keep it, any more than he had any idea why he'd stolen it in the first place. All he knew was that he must give Ruth back her purse. He would simply take it to her and hand it to her.

Noah began sliding out the door of the van. Just as his right foot touched the ground, he tossed the purse onto the far side of the seat. It lay, folded over itself, like a sleeping puppy.

"I left it home," he told Ruth.

She looked at him, not suspiciously or even with disappointment, but with resignation. She simply nodded her head, acknowledging what had been said, accepting what she'd been told. The purse had belonged to her but had been taken away, and she resigned herself to the loss as if it had been fated, inevitable. It had been hers, but now she had to let it go.

On the drive home, Noah had to stop on the road that led from the highway into Mattysborough because he'd started to sneeze. Without looking, he reached into Ruth's purse, took out the handkerchief that had a tiny bouquet of violets embroidered in one corner and flipped it open. He was annoyed that it was so small, as if women had smaller noses or fewer nasal needs.

Holding the handkerchief to his face, he continued to sneeze, then realized, when tears came to his eyes, that they weren't sneezes at all, but sobs that he couldn't let loose. He was crying, but all that was allowed him were these little squeezed eruptions, these pinched explosions, as if his grief were only an allergy and his sorrow was lodged in his nose.

5

Over the whine of the bench saw Noah could hear the high-pitched notes darting in and out of the rafters of the workshop like a newly arrived lark looking for a place to perch. Cory McFee, in his boy-soprano voice, was singing yet another Beatles' song, but which one, Noah couldn't tell. Noah finished his cutting and looked over to the far side of the shop where he'd put the boy to work sinking nailheads and filling in the holes of the dry sinks he was making for Nelson Sheerin in Keene.

Gangly and angled as a picked cornstalk, the boy was singing away for all he was worth as if the wood he was working on needed these sounds to tame it and hold it in place. Oblivious of itself, the song rose and fell like a bright lament that reveled in its grief.

Noah regretted all over again taking an apprentice into the shop. He knew he needed someone to help relieve the day-to-day pressure but he still wasn't convinced he'd gained more than he'd lost. To begin with, it compromised his solitude. But then it also provided a free assistant who eagerly did the sanding, oiled the machinery and put in the screws, who worked the hand clamps for gluing up and who would perform the hundreds of other dull and dirty chores that defined a servitude reaching back to the great carpenter guilds of the Middle Ages.

In return for this, Noah was supposed to train him in the carpenter's sacred skills, initate him into a brotherhood blessed by the patronage of St. Joseph himself, and qualify him as a master himself who could, in turn, enjoy his own solitude — until some whistle-voiced kid, some *apprentice*, came along and spoiled it all.

Cory's arrangement with Noah was a somewhat special elaboration of the old codes. His sister, Tally, had been Noah and Ruth's baby-sitter but, as a fifteen-year-old living in Mattysborough, she'd decided to devote her summer to more arduous good works than baby-sitting. Off she'd gone to be a volunteer swimming instructor and Cory quickly begged for her old job. He was younger than Tally by two years, but he was a boy and tall for his age, compensations he thought more than sufficient. But, in payment for taking care of Joel and sometimes Anne and Danny as well — when they weren't at day camp — he asked to be rewarded not in coin but with the privilege of working with Noah in the shop under the honorable title of apprentice.

Noah patiently pointed out certain inequities in the arrangement, but Cory insisted on his own formulations. He had pondered them over and over again with all the strict scrutiny of one who's received the true call. He pleaded his cause with a firm rationality. And besides, it was not unknown in ages past for the apprentice to do tasks unrelated to the profession itself. A master's bidding was presumed to be enough.

Noah liked the idea of historical precedent legitimizing the boy's indenture, but he didn't like the idea of anyone hanging around his shop, especially someone who could exhaust him in an hour's time with his endless enthusiasms, to say nothing of exasperating him with his constant warblings. When he'd mentioned his dilemma to Tom Resek at the hardware store, Tom snorted and said who'd want a prissy kid like that on the premises; the boy'd come to Noah only because practically everyone else in town had already turned him down even if all he wanted to do was work for the summer, for nothing if that's the way it had to be.

Melvin Cooke, who had the Ford franchise out on 202, suggested they all chip in and buy the kid a feather duster. That decided it. Noah knew what it was like to be the boy who'd killed the blind girl's pig. They were treating Cory McFee in pretty much the same way even if it was for different reasons. Noah took him on.

As Noah fed another board into the saw, the song stopped. A respite was at hand and Noah was grateful. Then he noticed someone was standing in front of the bench saw. Without looking up he could tell it wasn't Cory. Cory was lanky and wearing a blue T-shirt with cutoffs. The man standing in front of the bench saw was fat and wearing dungarees with a cowboy jacket to match.

After he'd run the pine through, Noah looked up. Hippolyte Thibideau was standing there, his head cocked to one side as if he were yet another apprentice being taught how to cut a piece of pine. Even after Noah shut off the power, the huge man kept looking at the saw itself, his gaze released only when all movement had stopped.

"You're working in pine," he said. But before Noah could confirm the obvious, the man went over to the playpen where Joel was sleeping, his massive shoulders leading the way, first one, then another, like a vain and shy celebrity forcing his way through an adoring crowd. He bent over the playpen, his cheeks and jowls slung down like two weights holding his head in place, the shining black forelock that usually curled toward his left eyebrow looking now like an inverted question mark sprung from his brain.

Wagging his jowls and swinging the forelock, he reached a finger down and tickled the air about four inches above Joel's back as if scratching an itch that hovered just above the baby's spine. Satisfied that these attentions were enough, he stood up and looked out through the screen door as if trying to remember why he'd come. The sight of Ruth's vegetable garden seemed to remind him.

"You need some money?" he asked. His voice, as always, was high and strictured as if his bulk had forced his lungs up into his neck.

Noah jerked his head so he could look directly at him. His first thought was that he was being accused of stealing Ruth's purse. The line of detection was direct. The purse was Ruth's. Ruth's best friend since the first grade was Jean Thibideau. Jean Thibideau (born Dundee) was Hippolyte Thibideau's wife. Ruth had told Jean, Jean had told her husband, and now Hippolyte had come to confront him with the facts and discuss possible procedures for restitution.

"Money?" Noah asked.

"Yeah. Money," Hippolyte Thibideau answered.

Noah looked at the man's face. What did he know about the purse? Nothing. There was no accusation there, only the bland stare of someone waiting for a simple answer to a simple question. Noah didn't know what to answer except yes, but he wasn't ready to say that yet, so he looked down at the last button on the man's white shirt. The button couldn't hold on much longer. The shirt was stretched and strained across the man's stomach. The button would pop off at any minute and hit Noah right in the eye. He looked at the pockets of the cowboy jacket, then at the shoulders, then back at the face. He couldn't help thinking of what Ruth had once said. "Poor Jean. On her wedding night she went to bed with a god and woke up with a gorgon."

Hippolyte Thibideau had been the handsomest man in Mattysborough. Then, after he married Jean Dundee, everything changed. While he never lost his thick dark hair with the fetching forelock, nor did his blue eyes ever lose their kinship to the sky, he did, practically on the morning after the nuptial night, begin to turn to beef right before your eyes. His face started to jowl and blotch, he bellied out like a blowfish and his hands, once almost as strong and sinewed as Noah's, became pudgy, the puffed backs looking like unbaked biscuits, the fingers plump now like pork sausages.

His feet, however, seemed to have shrunk and his tread became lighter, almost dainty, as if he was aware that his new bulk was an added burden to the earth and that he had to make some compensation. Also, with his pudgy hands, he touched more gently, almost delicately. And his temperament, in an adjustment to this new delicacy, had gone from hearty and assured to thoughtful and distracted, as if he was trying most of the time to remember what he had been like before.

(Jean, according to Ruth, didn't mind the changes at all. Making no bones about it, she told Ruth she loved "Polly" — the name the man had been given in his crib — for his money. Which worked very well since Polly was sole heir to the town lumber mill that had flourished on the banks of the Nubanusit since the eighteenth century, making him the richest man in Mattysborough.

That said, Jean insisted on a crucial distinction. She did not love his money; she loved him *for* his money. She argued that it was equally legitimate for a woman to fall in love with a man because of his money or to fall in love with him for his — as she put it — eyes, ears, nose and throat.

Ruth had agreed. It made sense. And hard common sense was one of the several characteristics that Ruth and Jean, as best friends, shared, the others being a capacity for exasperation and an almost beligerent ability to cope with whatever had to be coped with. The two of them could dwell for hours, mostly by telephone, on the follies of the world around them — Jean with her marriage and her money, Ruth with her children, her husband and her home — each encouraging the other to greater and higher heights of exasperation that would lead them to the lofty conclusion that nothing could be done, it was all impossible, competely idiotic. No one could possibly cope. They would then hang up and immediately proceed to cope, quite handsomely, and with a spirited gruffness that ignored the enormity of their task and the splendor of their achievement.)

Polly Thibideau had turned away from the screen door. "You're going to get good squash," he said.

"Pumpkins," said Noah.

Polly nodded, giving approval to the change.

"We're eating the beans," Noah said.

"Good. Good. They're best fresh."

Noah still didn't know what to say about the money. He could see Polly's hands come together, make a fumbling attempt to join, fail, then finally hold halfway down the rounded slope of his stomach.

Once before Noah had had the experience of owing Hippolyte Thibideau money. It hadn't been a loan, but a large, very large, lumber bill owed the mill, six months overdue. Polly had asked to see him.

The office was at the top of a long flight of wooden stairs that led up from the hangarlike room where the new lumber was fed for drying into the kiln. Because the ascent was actually two flights to accommodate the height of the kiln, the builder had thought to put a landing halfway up and, to give the climber an excuse to pause, he'd put in a window that looked out over the bend in the river and onto the rocky hill that rose up behind the mill itself.

Noah caught a quick glimpse of the frozen river and the snow-buried rocks on the hill, but he didn't pause. He did notice, however, that the steps were less worn higher up as though not everyone had been able to complete the climb. He'd prepared his explanation and had gone over it with Ruth. It had been a mistake for him to make six highboys out of solid mahogany — with all the slow, painstaking work he would put into them — and not to have sold them in advance. Now three had been taken, but were unpaid for, and he had hopes, faint he would admit, for the others — once they were finished. He hoped Polly would understand and be patient.

In the office, Polly was sitting on a swivel chair at an old rolltop desk, both inherited along with the mill. An array of different colored vitamin pills was spread out in front of him like a track of jelly beans dropped by an Easter bunny. A half-peeled orange served as a paperweight on a stack of flyblown, time-dried papers at his elbow and a quart of Pellegrino Mineral Water, unopened, stood on an unplugged hot plate. On the wall the pendulum clock said, accurately enough, ten to eight. The winter sun still hadn't come over the hill just outside the windows so the lights were on, two bare bulbs at the ends of two long cords, looking like enormous drops of dirty water leaked through the roof, gathering weight, getting ready to plop, one on the desk, the other on an old leather daybed shoved against the wall away from the windows.

An electric heater was trained more or less toward the daybed, but was actually tilted upward as if to warm the picture of a female nude kneeling over the neat columns and rows of the outdated calendar beneath. The woman's right hand was raised, reaching behind her neck and held under her waved and abundant hair, all on the apparent assumption that the most appealing part of her anatomy was her armpit. The rest of the room was freezing and the smell of the half-peeled orange made Noah think of popsicles.

"George mentioned you wanted me to stop by," Noah said. He knew that to call George Bananos, the mill's manager, by any name but Banana-nose was rather formal, but he thought the seriousness of the event required it.

Polly put a vitamin pill into his mouth, swallowed it without water and waited as if expecting some immediate result. When nothing happened, he took another one and said, holding it on his tongue, "What would happen if I told you I needed that bill paid?" He tilted his head back so the pill could slide unaided down his throat.

Noah found himself embarrassed, not because he was being asked for money, but because Polly seemed to need it. For Noah to need money was usual and acceptable. For Hippolyte Thibideau to need it was awkward and embarrassing. He was embarrassed for Polly, not for himself.

Trying to sound optimistic, Noah explained about the highboys and the sure money in the not-too-distant future. Polly listened, bent over his vitamin pills, turning them over to see if there was anything tucked underneath as if he was playing a shell game all by himself. When Noah finished, he picked up a blue pill and put it into his mouth. Without swallowing, talking like a child with a marble in his cheek, he said, "I don't see how I can wait that long," his voice rising as if one more appeal for the payment and he would be required to speak either through his eyes or through his ears.

Noah cleared his throat so he wouldn't talk at the same pitch. "I don't know what to tell you except what I already said." He cleared his throat again, worried that one more time and Polly would take it as a criticism. "I can't go to the bank. They're already financing a new Rockwell planer cost almost three thousand."

"A Rockwell planer? You're pretty far up in the world."

"Saves time. Time's money." When Polly didn't say anything, he added, "And what it can do to a board — plane it as smooth and clean and true as anything." Still, Polly said nothing. Noah had tried first wisdom and then enthusiasm. Now he spoke the worst. "Of course you could always get a lien on it."

Polly swiveled his chair around and looked Noah up and down as if he'd been asked to guess his weight. He was wearing, as usual, the dungaree outfit he'd adopted his sophomore year at Amherst in the late sixties and hadn't been able to relinquish. It made him look like a beer drinker, an additional disguise since he seldom had anything but the Pellegrino and sometimes Saratoga Vichy. He was looking at Noah, thinking. He put a yellow pill into his mouth, then opened the bottle of mineral water, poured some into a coffee mug and drank it down. "Maybe you could do some work for me and we'll call it even. That interest you?"

"Sure, but I don't know when I'd do it. I'm already into a fifteen-hour day and I've got back-orders into spring. Would summer be okay? Execept I'll be able to pay up by then."

"No, I don't mean do *your* kind of work for me, I mean do *my* kind of work for me."

"Like what?"

Polly looked him up and down again, then swiveled back and began tossing the pills into his mouth like peanuts, a yellow dust falling from his fingers down onto the front of his white shirt. Suddenly he stopped and spun the chair around. "Oh, I'm sorry," he said. "I'm not being a very good host. Would you like a vitamin? An 'E' maybe? Good for curing cuts."

At first Noah was inclined to refuse because he owed the man money. Then he decided acceptance might signal some kind of accord between them, an agreement that the matter was on the way to amicable settlement. He accepted the pill and swallowed it without water. It tasted like old library paste.

"What I was going to say was, do you know how to use a gun?" Polly asked. "I mean aim it at someone and mean it?" He sounded no more curious than if he was asking Noah if he knew how to operate a double-clutch stick shift.

Noah felt a quiver of interest. The prospect of using a gun, of committing a crime, seemed to excite him the way a lewd suggestion could expose a hidden sexual urge. His excitement surprised him more than the question itself.

He felt the pull of his adolescent rebellions, the gleeful enactments of his youthful rage. The idea of robbing a filling station flashed through his mind, something he'd been meant to do a long time ago, but had forgotten. He'd accepted too quickly his prison sentence to the workshop just off the kitchen. He'd surrendered his rage too soon, too easily. The tasks he'd set out to do he'd never accomplished. Breaking windows, running red lights, stealing a truck, they'd been *his* apprenticeship, but he'd never achieved the masterpiece he'd been training for. He could feel for one swift moment the heft of a gun in his hand. Power and calm met in his grip. He could do it.

He saw Polly watching him, carefully thoughtful, with the disinterest of a doctor testing the reflexes and responses that would be used to inform a later diagnosis. Noah decided he'd set it all aside, the gun, the filling station, his forgotten ambitions, for the time being anyway. He wanted to know more of what Polly had to say. To find out, Noah asked in as casual but direct a manner as he could summon, "Use a gun for what?"

Polly only smiled and shook his head, pleased, as if Noah had just revealed some peculiar facet of his character, one that Polly alone had long suspected and that was now verified. The pleasures of vindication changed his headshake to a nod.

"I told Jean," he said, "I told her you hadn't become so nice like she thinks you have. I told her you could probably turn pretty mean again if you had to. Well, it's OK. I won't tell her about just now. It'd break her hard little heart."

"Tell her what about just now?" Noah asked. Of course he knew exactly what. That he had a mild criminal streak in him — and was probably quite capable of using a gun for other than honorable purposes. But he tried to sound ignorant anyway. "What would you tell her?"

"Never mind the whole thing. I was only joking. I shouldn't make fun like that. What I really wanted to tell you was not to worry about the bill in case you had it on your mind. You'll pay it when you pay it."

Noah shrugged his thanks. Polly hadn't been serious about the gun. Noah wasn't sure if he was disappointed or relieved. Both, he guessed. He wasn't going to be returned to the old defiances after all. He'd continue to be what he'd become, what his work and what his wife had made of him. In his mind, however, he tested once more the heft of the gun. Then he set it down.

But when he saw Polly still smiling, still nodding his head, he became enraged. His honest worry about the debt had been used to titillate some secret susceptibility, to expose to himself as well as to Polly a readiness to wield a gun, to see it as a way of rebelling against his troubles, of canceling his stupidity in running up the bill, a way of getting even for the harassment of money owed.

He'd been tempted and he knew himself not all that ready to resist. Polly had summoned up the specter, made it actual, right in front of him, and then had sat back and seen it all, watched it all, smiling, overfamiliar and knowing.

Noah wanted to tell Polly, to spit it right out into his fat face, that his wife Jean, two years before, had told him that even though she was Ruth's best friend, Noah could fuck her — the word was Jean's — anytime he wanted to. He didn't want to and never would. Maybe he'd tell Polly that too. That he wasn't interested in his wife, that he didn't want to fuck her, a greater insult than if he did.

But he didn't tell Polly that. Instead, he said, "Thanks. I'll pay as soon as I can."

"Of course you will. No problem." Polly reached up and

slapped Noah's arm, then swiveled back to finger his hoard of vitamins.

Noah looked at the piece of pine he was sawing. He hadn't answered Polly's question. He needed money, and he was going to need more. Even if he had Ruth transferred to the state hospital at Concord, he still couldn't afford to pay for the treatment she'd have to have. And besides, he'd vowed he'd keep her here, where she could see him, be with him, talk to him. He still considered himself part of her cure. He had to keep her at Mount St. Michael.

There was the Rockwell planer, the one he'd been buying with the bank's help when he owed Polly the lumber debt. He figured he could get about two thousand for it now, if he could find a buyer. Not having it would mean longer hours and harder labor, but if it had to be done, it would be done.

Then the table saw, the new one. He still had the old one, and the new one, sent back, would return over a thousand. After that, for a couple of hundred, there was the sander, the power router for cutting grooves and shaping edges, and the smaller tools like the saber saw and the doweling jig. He'd prepared himself to let them go one by one, like a destitute dowager selling off her jewels. But if Ruth didn't get better — fast — it still wouldn't be enough. Of course there was always the house.

Still, he did not want to be in this man's debt. But it would be foolish to refuse. It was for Ruth, to help her get well.

Noah tried to hold his thinking to this particular path so it could lead him safely to acceptance. But there was, along the way, that slight distraction, that stirring in the brush, something he should turn and look at. The last time he'd owed Hippolyte Thibideau money, something wrong had suggested itself. Noah thought he should examine that whole previous event before making up his mind.

But he didn't. There was no time. For Ruth's sake, it had to be done. And the sooner the better.

He turned the power on so Cory wouldn't hear the conversation. Over the whine and snarl of the metal disk grinding its way through the wood, he said, "To tell you the truth, yes, I could use some money. And if you can help —" The cutting was complete. He looked up. Polly wasn't there; he hadn't heard. Noah turned off the saw.

Polly was over in the corner, talking to Cory. "You're the kid sings, am I right?"

The boy nodded a modest yes. Cory, aside from being a baby-sitter and an apprentice carpenter, was known to be the best boy soprano in Mattysborough, much in demand for weddings and banquets despite his reputation for being "prissy." For weddings he would sing the "Ave Maria" and for banquets he would sing Beatles' songs. Because the Beatles' songs were sung in pretty much the same way as the "Ave Maria" some people thought they too were hymns and admired the boy's piety. Others snickered.

Cory's passion for the Beatles dated from the death of John Lennon. What had appealed to him was the great mourning crowd outside the Dakota, people holding candles in Central Park, crying in public. He'd never heard of the Beatles before, but now he wanted to be a part of all that sorrow. He took up the songs, singing them in his sweet reedy voice, each an elegy, intense, all the rhythms smoothed into melody alone, each a sung prayer addressed to those silent crowds he wanted for his admirers.

"Didn't I hear you at the gym, for the basketball team, the banquet?" Polly asked. "You did 'Eleanor Rigby,' am I right?"

" 'Penny Lane,' " the boy said quietly. Then he added, "They laughed."

"Not everybody. And besides, why pay them any attention? What do they know except how to throw a ball through a hoop?"

"My mother was there."

"I'll tell you what," Polly said. "Sing me a song. Right now. And I'll stand right here and listen."

"You'll laugh." Cory was looking down at the tap hammer and nail punch in his hands.

"No, I won't." When the boy didn't say anything, Polly went on. "Why would I laugh?"

"My mother said I'm too serious."

"What's wrong with being serious? Go ahead. Sing me a song. Right now."

"You'll laugh."

"I'll prove it to you. I won't laugh."

Cory glanced from Polly to Noah. Noah couldn't be sure if the boy wanted the permission or would prefer to have it refused. Also, he didn't want the boy to be the object of Polly's "playfulness."

"I'm supposed to sink nails," the boy said. "I'm an apprentice."

"Just a couple of verses. Any song you want. The Beatles, they're my favorites. Noah's too. Huh, Noah?"

Noah nodded and Cory, taking this for permission, looked out the upper window of what had been the hayloft of the old stable and, as if addressing himself to the top branches of the catalpa tree, began singing "Eleanor Rigby." The piped notes darted again around the shop, rising to the rafters, swooping, soaring among the beams, the words themselves reverent and rapt. The song became a hymn of unspeakable yearning. Noah could see in the boy's eyes the reflected light of all those candles and he could hear the attendant pleas that at least some of all that silent awe be given to him.

The voice piped even higher, the slightly aspirate tones ardent with fluttered desire. Noah turned away so he wouldn't see, pretending he could concentrate better if he didn't look. He, too, stared out at the catalpa tree, then lowered his head so he could see Joel still asleep in his playpen. But the song forced him to look back.

The boy was singing now as if to ward off the lure of his own needs, an uncertain supplication that he be both spared and fulfilled. His huge round eyes were glazed with a reckless courage. Skinny as a plucked chicken, tall as a cattail, he sang away, his song filled with a frail despair and an even frailer hope. It made Noah uneasy.

The song ended and Cory looked at Polly. Polly was solemnly nodding his head. The boy bent over his work and began tapping the punch onto the nailheads, sinking them into the pine.

"That was very beautiful," Polly said sternly as if he expected the boy to disagree. He touched Cory's shoulder, obviously his favorite form of tribute. The boy nodded his acknowledgment and thanks. "And I didn't laugh, did I?" asked Polly.

The boy paused at his task, thought a moment, then shook his head no.

"See?" Polly said. "I told you I wouldn't."

Cory nodded again and went on tapping.

Noah was relieved. Polly had been genuinely interested and genuinely touched. Noah had misjudged him. He was a kind and feeling man. Noah wouldn't hesitate to accept the loan.

Polly stepped in front of Noah at the bench-saw. There, clamped onto his mouth, was a suppressed smile and he was shaking his head in disbelief. He'd been making fun of the boy after all. Quickly Noah glanced over at Cory to make sure he wasn't looking.

He was. He'd seen the smirk, the shake of the head. He stared first at Noah, then at Polly, then returned to his job, tapping too lightly at first. He tilted his head a little to the right to show that he was concentrating on his work and had nothing else on his mind.

With an exaggerated grimace to indicate that it wasn't an easy thing to do, Polly worked the smile off his face, but not completely. "Well?" he asked. "You need some money?" His high voice sounded as though he was holding down a laugh that might burst out at any moment, especially if Noah said yes.

"No," Noah said. "We're all right. But thanks. I . . . I appreciate the offer."

Never would he accept money from this man.

Polly, lowering his pitch a little, exacted assurances from Noah that this was the truth, then reminded him that he could always change his mind. Noah thanked him again.

Polly went over, scratched the air above the baby's back and went out, letting the screen door slam behind him. In the yard he stopped and looked up at the house as if concerned for its prospects, then made his way through the vegetable garden, careful to walk between the rows, delicately, daintily, like an ape doing a high-wire act.

Noah fed another board into the saw, then shouted toward the screen door, "Jean said I could fuck her any time I wanted to!"

"What?" Cory yelled.

"Nothing!" said Noah.

6

Noah heard an ambulance, the siren blaring down the street outside. It was coming for Ruth. No, Ruth was already gone. It was coming for him. If he could wake up before it got there, they wouldn't take him away. Or was it the children they'd come for? It was getting closer, screaming, almost a human voice, trying to wake him up. The ambulance stopped in front of the house, the siren at full cry, except it had gone from a cry of warning to one of terror.

Noah struggled to wake up, but he couldn't move his legs except with the most arduous effort and then it would be for only a few inches. His eyes refused to open more than halfway. He tried to call out names, but he couldn't form the words.

The siren sounded now like a cry for help, a cry filled with despair that rescue would ever come.

Noah raised one arm from the blanket. "Ruth!" he managed to say, but it was no more than a whisper. Then, as though he'd said his own name, he raised his head from the pillow and held it there like a cautious animal, his whole body stiffened by the sudden awakening.

It was Joel crying in his crib. Noah dropped his head back onto the pillow and listened. "Awah! Awah!" It sounded as though the baby had found one word and had been condemned to say it over and over again until some human touch would free him from the spell.

Noah groaned over onto his side, forcing one ear deep into the pillow and crossing his arm over the other. This made the baby's cry sound as though it were coming from inside his head, a muted reverberation through the hollows of his own skull. He raised his arm from his ear and let the arm fall over to his side. The pull of it turned him flat onto his back. Without modulation or change of rhythm the cry continued.

Maybe it would wear itself out like an alarm clock running down. Maybe the repetitions would lull the baby back to sleep, or maybe Noah could hear it as a crow's call or the revolutions of a stalled motor that wouldn't catch, sounds he could do nothing about.

Or better still, maybe Anne would hear it and stumble into the room, moving through the tangle of clothes on the floor, to the crib. She might even have a warmed bottle with her. Noah could pretend to be asleep and Anne would place the bottle on a propped pillow, drop into the small upholstered chair next to the crib, Ruth's nursing chair, fall asleep for a few seconds, then jolt herself awake and leave the room as if she'd been summoned to some other duty in some other part of the house. He'd seen it happen.

But Anne didn't come and Joel's cry continued, no longer a plea for release but now an angry protest that he'd been put under the spell to begin with. Noah realized he'd have to give Joel to Blanche. But as soon as the idea formed in his head, he responded with a violent "No!" He wouldn't do it.

It would signal to Blanche and to himself that she was winning the war of attrition that would end with all his children safe within her care. Repeatedly Noah had had to ask himself if that would be such a bad thing. Blanche Strunk was a good woman who loved her daughter and her daughter's children with a gruff and asthmatic affection. That much Noah could admit, but then he balked. Blanche had never been able, he felt, to get it into her head that they were Noah's family and not hers and Ruth's alone.

Blanche was fond of Noah, that much he knew. She admired him and was grateful for the many kindnesses he bestowed on Ruth and on Ruth's children. But she seemed unable to consider that Noah had any role beyond that of a vaguely defined bene-factor. His inclusion in family affairs and family matters was not a recognition of him as husband and father; it was a reward of gratitude for his benevolence. He assisted Ruth and Blanche by carrying some share of their burden with the children. He was a sort of amiable and attractive volunteer that Blanche readily ac-cepted because she believed in her heart that the privilege was all his, that he himself knew this, and that he would never dream of making claims in his own right.

When Ruth went to Mount St. Michael, Blanche included among her necessary adjustments the assumption that the children would now pass to her by title of lawful succession. It startled her when Noah said no — and so insistently. But rather than be adamant on her own behalf she was touched by his pretension. It moved her that this man could respond so generously to her daughter's calamity. In her sorrow and worry about Ruth she was willing to indulge him. He was kind and faithful. And he would soon enough bring the children to her as a matter of course, once he'd satisfied his need to make some contribution, however un-necessary, to the present situation. She could wait. And it would allow her time to give Ruth the greater part of her concern dur-ing these bewildering days of her early illness.

So easy was Blanche's assumption about the children's coming to her that Noah found himself considering it a legitimate issue. Then too, it received support from his own recurring fear that went back to his first days with Ruth: his marriage, his house-hold, his happiness could all be taken from him simply because he treasured them and cherished them with a love that would become at times a physical ache, like a yearning made flesh.

He feared that what he was experiencing in his home and in his daily living was nothing more than a temporary respite from the long solitude of his earlier life. Sooner or later he would be returned to the empty rooms and solitary meals of his childhood like an obedient and compliant convict who'd been allowed a single day in the open among green fields and under the blue sky, but must now resume his real and former life.

The effect of all this, however, was to strengthen Noah's resolve never to surrender his children, not one of them. He would give in neither to Blanche's assumptions nor to his own fears. It was a vow, sacred to himself, and he would keep it.

"Awah! Awah!" The continued cries seemed to challenge, to mock Noah's promise, to defy him, to dare him to stick to it. He heaved and shifted himself until he was sitting on the edge of the bed. He was still drunk. Or at least the drugged heaviness of a hangover hadn't set in yet. Which meant it couldn't be too close to morning.

Noah listened, and then contradicted himself. Yes, he'd give the baby to Blanche. He had his own sanity to protect. Things couldn't continue the way they were. Ruth's diagnosis remained uncertain. Outright schizophrenia — probably incurable — or post-partum depression — possibly curable. Not even Dr. Corrado would say anything for sure.

His debts were mounting. Some of them got paid, some didn't. The Rockwell planer had disappeared from the shop and Cory didn't sing for two days after its departure. Noah discovered he preferred the boy's singing to his silence. Meanwhile, Noah began, some of the time, using the old bench-saw, preparing himself for the imminent departure of the new.

Then, that evening, he'd knocked Danny out of his chair at the kitchen table when he said he wouldn't eat the lamb chop Anne had burned. After Danny got back up, Noah dumped everything on his own plate into the garbage and jammed the plate itself in after it. He'd heard no sound from either Anne or Danny as he pulled on his jacket and slammed out the front door.

When he came home they were both upstairs probably asleep since it was almost midnight. Hungry, Noah ate the sandwiches Anne had made for his lunch the next day. He crumpled the wrappings and tossed them toward the garbage pail, missing. After the fourth miss, he dragged the pail closer and tried again. Another miss. He kicked the pail over, sending the garbage across the floor from the sink to the refrigerator.

He started bending over to right it, but found himself giving it an even more vicious kick, spinning it, so that the garbage whorled out around it, potato peelings, eggshells, apple cores, crushed wads of paper towels, coffee grounds, and his own uneaten dinner. Some of the gray overcooked peas rolled under the stove, the rest of them scattered over the linoleum like seeds thrown onto worthless ground.

Satisfied he'd made his feelings known, he clumped up the stairs and went down the hall toward his room. Anne had left her door open so she could hear Joel if he cried before her father came home. As quietly as he could, Noah closed it.

The door to his own room was open too. He didn't want to go in. He stood at the door. In the shadow of the shaded night-light he could see Joel in his crib. But he also saw Ruth asleep on her side of the bed, her back to him. He stepped into the room.

Quietly, very slowly, saying nothing, he undressed, giving Ruth time enough to prepare for him in mind and in body. And he, too, wanted to savor the stealthy movements that would transform the ordinary tugging, pulling, unbuckling and unbuttoning into a thing of grace, a ritual that led in an unbroken flow into the act of love itself.

When the neck of his sweater got caught on his nose he didn't yank it over his head, but continued instead the gentle pull, forcing the tip of his nose painfully upward so that the warm air he exhaled was immediately inhaled again, bringing back the whiskey scent of his own harsh breath mingled with the odor of his body trapped inside the sweater's wool.

Free of it, he unbuttoned his shirt, giving each button its moment of consideration, still watching Ruth on the bed. When he realized he'd forgotten to undo the cuffs, with the shirt already hanging down behind him, he patiently brought it up again, unbuttoned the cuffs, then shed the whole shirt easily with a slow backward hunching of his shoulders.

His high-laced work shoes were his greatest challenge. He made tentative bends, but when that threatened to topple him forward, he allowed himself to lean lightly against the dresser. His pants, his shorts he slipped off without any trouble at all, able now to balance on one foot, then the other. With a wide proud gesture, as if revealing at last his full nakedness, Noah reached over to the side and placed first his pants and then his shorts onto the top of the dresser.

He looked at the bed. He could feel his flesh taut and muscled along his bones. He gave himself a moment of awareness, a few seconds' sense of his own body, its fineness, but only so that he would know all the better what he was offering to Ruth now.

He went to the bed and reached out to put one hand on her head, the other on the mounded blankets where he knew her thigh would be. He let the hands hover for a moment, then slowly he lowered them. The bedclothes sank at his touch, as he'd known they would. Still, he groaned, first in pain, then in accusation.

He'd given Ruth a chance to be there, he'd given her all that time and now she wasn't there.

Noah pulled the blanket up in front of him, trying to tear it but it wouldn't give. He jerked harder, throwing himself off balance. Face down, he was sprawled across the bed. A pillow lay bunched against the headboard on Ruth's side. He stretched toward it but it was out of reach. He turned on his side and arched his back, then slid his hips up toward the head of the bed, bringing the rest of his body along. He clutched the pillow in his fists and tried to pull it apart. It wouldn't tear. He drew it closer and tried again, but the strength wasn't there. He pulled it against his stomach and punched it again and again and again, then let go.

Joel stopped crying. Noah jumped up and, after steadying himself with his knee against the mattress, went over to the crib to find out why he'd stopped. Without wasting time on a glance, he picked the baby up just under the arms and pressed him against his chest. Then he held him out and looked at him.

Joel squirmed as though trying to find out what had happened to the solid world that had been supporting him only moments before. Even in the half light Noah could see the open eyes, more curious than frightened by the sudden change. The legs were raised then lowered, treading air, trying either to touch bottom or adjust to the freedom of sudden space. One fist was held to his mouth as if he couldn't make up his mind to say what he was going to say. After looking to one side then the other, he decided to say nothing at all.

The eyes closed, then opened, then closed again, the head slumped to the right and he was peacefully asleep, dangling down from his father's hands.

Noah was tempted to shake him awake. He wasn't ready to let him sleep. What he seemed to want was an admission of guilt from the baby, a recognition that he had done something wrong by crying, in being so determined to impose himself, his will, his needs, on his father.

Before Noah could forget the whole thing and just put the baby back into his crib, he began to rage. Joel was a tyrant, intolerable in his arrogance. He had set himself over his father's power. What Noah wanted was an acknowledgment of that power, and a submission to it. He wanted repentance from Joel for his ignorance and he wanted the sense of blame to come from Joel himself, a self-accusation that would both humble and restrain him, that would breed a healthy fear and an awed respect for his father. Given this, Noah might then allow, even encourage, a growth of love between them.

Noah shook the baby slightly. Joel raised his eyelids halfway, saw his father, then closed them and slept again.

When the alarm went off in the morning, Noah lifted his head from his chest and without opening his eyes started to reach for the clock. He felt his hand come away from something not himself. He listened to the alarm, then opened his eyes. The clock was over next to the bed. Noah was in the nursing chair next to the crib.

He started to get up but felt a weight against his chest. He looked down, his chin touching soft hair. Joel was sprawled across him, one arm curled around his father's arm, the other lying out across his father's chest. Still holding the baby against him, Noah got up and went for the clock. Something checked his stride. He got to the clock and switched off the alarm. By now Joel was awake, rubbing his nose against the white flannel of his father's sleeve.

It was when he was putting Joel down into the crib that Noah remembered that he was wearing one of Ruth's nightgowns. Joel had cried again during the night. Noah had gotten out of bed, gone to the bottom drawer of the dresser, taken out the nightgown, put it on, picked up Joel and held him in the chair to quiet him. Then apparently they had both fallen asleep.

Noah slipped the nightgown over his head and dropped it onto the rumpled bed. After he got dressed he picked it up again and examined it as if a closer look would explain to him why he'd done what he'd done, as if the answer were woven into the cloth and could be read if he'd only try. Then, as if it might help him toward some understanding, he put the nightgown back on, tugging the skirt down when it got caught on the buckle of his belt.

He stood still for a moment, thinking, considering the experience, but came to no conclusions. He went back to the crib, lifted the sleeping baby and held him in his arms. Again he paused, wondering if what he was doing now would provide some clue as to why he'd put on his wife's nightgown the night before. Nothing occurred to him. He sat down again in the nursing chair, holding Joel against him.

At first, nothing. Then the thought came to him that it was softer for Joel to lie against the flannel of his mother's nightgown than against the hair on his father's chest. Noah considered this, then accepted it because he could think of nothing better and it was getting late.

He put Joel back into the crib, realizing that he had already reversed again his decision to give him to Blanche. It had been a nighttime aberration. There seemed no need to even consider it. In spite of a mild hangover, he felt himself somewhat restored, his patience somewhat renewed, his strength revived. Perhaps all would be well after all.

He took off the nightgown and started for the door. Again he stopped. He went back and hung it on the inside of the closet door. Again he started out and again he stopped. This time he went back, carefully folded the nightgown and put it into the bottom drawer where he'd found it. Then he closed the drawer slowly, quietly, so no one would know.

7

HIPPOLYTE and Jean Thibideau lived on a hill just inside the town limits in a red brick Georgian house. Their neighbor on the north was Toddman Spencer who owned the bank; their neighbor to the south was Ronald Fleming who owned the newspaper and television station. Theirs were the only houses on the hill.

Two streets away, just beyond the Mattysborough boundary, was a development of ranch-style houses built on eighty acres of the old Tyson farm. The development was called Thibideau Estates, but the people of Mattysborough — gleefully — called it Tyson's Spite. Toddman Spencer had refused farmer Tyson a loan for new equipment and dairy renovation, and finally even for seed money. Hippolyte Thibideau, as an officer of the bank, confirmed the decision, and Ronald Fleming declined to bring the farmer's plight to the attention of the public. Jean Thibideau, on the other hand, quietly introduced the farmer to the developer, then sat back and watched it all happen.

The proximity of the development to his house on the hill was annoyance enough to Polly, but the name provoked a sullen unappeasible wrath. Still, he could do nothing about it. A generation earlier, his father had persuaded the county commission to honor his good name by changing Dovecote Road to Thibideau Street. (He originally asked for Thibideau Avenue but since the road was at that time only a hayrick wide, he was persuaded to settle for the lesser designation.) But what had been a sign of private distinction for the father now become a public embarrassment to the son. One generation's sweet-scented rose had become the next generations sharp-barbed thorn and it stuck not in Polly's ribs but in his pride. The development had been named for its main street and he could make no claim against it.

There was, of course, a buffer between the hill mansions of Mattysborough and the bland bungalows built on the plains below, but this back acreage was subject to constant invasion by the children of the development dwellers. They explored and foraged through its strip of woods, fished in its deep but narrow stream and, with their inevitable dogs, occasionally used the broad lawns of the backyards as their public park. (Some of the dogs had been poisoned. Jean had long suspected that her husband had a secret malevolence in him, but since she'd never been the object of it nor had she any other palpable evidence beyond the way he looked in his sleep, she never made any accusations or asked any questions. She did, however, make a point of saying after each incident, "Who ever would do a thing like that should be strung by his thumbs from a sour apple tree." She'd then wait to see if Polly would take a quick look at his thumbs. He never did.)

Meanwhile, Toddman Spencer, Ronald Fleming and Hippolyte Thibideau were known only to growl and spit. As for Jean, she said nothing about the development itself. But she was known to be a woman who often smiled for no visible reason. These days she smiled more than was usual.

And she was smiling now, with all the heroic charm of a wealthy hostess cornered by a lowly guest, listening to George Banana-nose who was thanking her drunkenly for having his retirement party in her very own beautiful backyard and gracing it with her very own beautiful presence. Noah, too, was listening, standing at Jean's side, waiting impatiently for him to finish so he could talk to her.

Banana-nose, however, had apparently accumulated through the years over a thousand praises and he was determined now to speak each one.

"You're aces," he was telling her. "Aces." Barely did he manage to stop his jabbing finger just before it poked her in the collarbone.

Jean was holding a stack of dirty plates. She'd been on her way from the great table spread out under the copper beech to the kitchen when Banana-nose on his way back from the bathroom intercepted her. She shifted the plates from her right to her left arm. Noah shifted his weight from his left foot to his right.

Noah hadn't been invited but he was there anyway, looking for Cory who was nowhere in the yard. He'd wait until Banana-nose was finished, then ask Jean where he was. Noah looked again across the great expanse of the lawn toward the copper beech and the barbecue pit but saw only the mill workers and their wives, about thirty in all, most of them clustered around Polly who seemed, at the distance, to be lecturing them on a subject of grave importance. (It turned out later he'd been giving them his recipe for barbecue sauce.) Cory was nowhere in sight.

Jean, her smile immobilized by the length of Banana-nose's harangue of praise shifted the plates back to her right arm. She seemed ready to hear herself lauded for the rest of the night. Noah looked directly at her, hoping to get her attention by the intensity of his stare, but she went right on smiling, right on listening.

"I was in the pew just behind you last Christmas Eve. That was me. Right behind you. I could hear you sing. That was me. Listening to you sing." He spoke as if these were tidings of great joy and Jean nodded, accepting them as such.

Jean Thibideau was considered, by general consent, the most beautiful woman in Mattysborough. Granted, her skin was only peaches and cream — a complexion common in these parts — but here the peaches were in the most delicate phase of their ripening

77

and the cream was the richest, the smoothest to be found in the county around. She had red hair going toward chestnut, green eyes with enough flecks of hazel to keep them from being too pale, high cheekbones that were rounded to keep the face from seeming too sharp, a wide mouth perfectly proportionate to her somewhat squared jaw, and a delicate, lightly dimpled chin that brought the whole face to a highly refined conclusion.

To Noah she'd always looked like an owl. To him, her face was flat, and the nob-cheekbones, the unbent nose and the delicate chin failed to improve sufficiently on the essential design. He was able to concede that she was beautiful, but he meant beautiful for an owl.

That Jean herself subscribed to the town consensus about her looks was evident in the way she dressed: as sloppy as possible. She seemed to believe that there was no degree of dishevelment that could disguise her basic beauty. Challenge it how she might, with uncombed hair, baggy pants and wornout sweaters, it was, to her mind, forever triumphant.

For Banana-nose's party, she'd made no exceptions. She was wearing a V-necked sweater made appropriate for summer wear by the moth holes that aired it front and back. (She'd said to Ruth on another occasion, "It's a hand-me-down from Saint Sebastian.") Her white pants were Polly's old flannels held up around her waist by a silk necktie; the bottoms were rolled not just to accommodate the length of her legs but to show as well the custom cross-stitching of the seams. Her feet were bare, splotched with dried paint the color of the cast-iron furniture scattered about the lawn. Her hair was pulled every which way, away from her head, as if its red were actual flames and had been scorching her scalp.

Her one concession to accepted grooming was the care she gave her fingernails. As usual, they were manicured to perfection, finely shaped and buffed to a soft shine. She apparently gave to them all the attention she denied to the rest of her presentation and whenever boredom or unpleasantness threatened, Jean would look to her fingernails and find in them the needed relief or repose.

Noah watched as she held out her free left hand at arm's length to see if the excellence of her nails could be improved by being seen at a distance. She seemed to think so. She then wriggled her fingers as if getting ready to play the piano, a further testing — successfully passed — of their ability to survive any given gesture.

Banana-nose was now telling her, with slightly slurred speech, that she would be welcome at any time to come over to his house and watch the color television he was being given for a retirement present. What was his was hers, and always had been. Did she know that?

"I'd love to come over," she said, abandoning her fingernails to their own sublimity, "but you know how jealous Polly gets. For your sake, I'd better not."

Banana-nose, impressed, said in a low voice, "You're right. I hadn't thought of that. I guess you'd better not." Shaking his head sideways he repeated, but now in tones made melancholy by loss, "You're aces, Jean Thidibeau. Aces," then walked away, still shaking his head in awe and disbelief that he, Banana-nose, had come so perilously close to getting Jean Thibideau in trouble with her husband.

"I came to get Cory," Noah said before Jean could continue toward the kitchen.

"Cory? Oh yes. Cory. The skinny one who sings." She started away but Noah followed. "Well, you'll have to wait," she said. "He hasn't sung his song yet."

"And he's not going to," said Noah.

Jean ignored him. "Eat some chicken. It's ghastly," she said, still walking, concentrating on the sight of her bare feet moving through the grass. Noah wondered if she did her toenails the way she did her fingernails, but stopped himself from looking down. "Better still, take these plates to Melissa in the kitchen and tell her to give you some of the bean soup I made the day before yesterday. Phenomenal." She gave Noah the plates and wiped her hands clean on her sweater, using the movement to bring the sweater taut over the mound of her breasts. She then licked her fingers clean with the tip of her tongue and dried them on Noah's shirt-sleeve, rubbing the cloth between thumb and fore-finger as if she had an intention of buying a yard or two.

Noah accepted the plates and paid no attention to the fingers. "Come on, Jean," he said. "You don't want him to sing. Leave the kid alone."

"It was Polly's idea and it's Polly's party. I let him do what he wants."

"All he wants is to make fun."

"He's paying him ten dollars. For one lousy song. The kid's thrilled."

"He works for me and I don't want him making a fool out of himself."

"Ah," said Jean. "The truth at last. It's ourself we're thinking about. Disgrace by association." Pleased with the insight, she looked again at her fingernails, examining them with an apprecia-tion most women reserve for their diamond rings.

"If you say so," Noah said.

"Well, you're too late. He has to sing. He's already eaten two whole chickens, six corn on the cobs and washed it all down with enough Pepsi to pollute the Nubanusit from here to there. You've heard of 'sing for your supper'? Well, if he leaves now, he gets a bill."

"I'll pay it."

"You can't afford it. Not with the price of Pepsi what it is today."

"I don't want him singing."

Jean stopped walking. Apparently she was ready to take a stand.

"Oh, stop being so stubborn. Relax. Nobody's going to think you've 'gone Greek' with firm-bottomed boys just because your precious apprentice happens to have the highest notes this side of the Boston aviary." She looked at him, sucking in her cheeks and pouting her mouth to indicate possible suspicion. Then, relaxing her face, she added, "You haven't, have you? 'Gone Greek,' I mean."

Noah tilted his head a little to the right. "You never know, do you?" He managed to glare right at her.

Jean, too, tilted her head. "*I'd* know," she said.

"Oh?"

"Mm-hm. No question about it. After all, that's not exactly the odor of sanctity you give off every time you get within five feet of a woman. Believe me, I'd know."

"Then I guess *you'll* tell *me*. If I 'go Greek.'"

"Don't worry. It's a promise." She held his gaze and let her smile soften. The stiffness left the tilt of her head and a soft languor began to take its place. Noah was tempted to change the conversation to Ruth, to Ruth's illness, just to remind Jean she was his wife's best friend. But then he saw her eyes deepen, leaving their usual mockery behind, moving toward sadness, and he decided not to. He looked down at the plates, then at Jean, then again at the plates.

"You shouldn't worry about other people so much," she said. "Why not think of yourself once in a while?"

"I do," Noah said. "All the time."

He turned his head and looked toward the house, checking the direction he was about to go and the distance he would have to travel before he could deliver the plates safely into Melissa's hands. Cory was sitting on the second step leading down from the back door. He was looking off to his right at a stone birdbath to show he hadn't been watching them.

"Come here and take these dishes," Noah called. The boy,

after all, was his apprentice and Noah was required to assert his authority. Cory got up and came toward them, but warily, almost sideways, as if he was expecting a punishment.

"They asked me to sing," he said quietly, hoping his words might stay the hard hand that was about to knock him on the side of the head. "Except not to tell you because they said I'm not supposed to work for anyone else when I'm an apprentice. Is that true?"

"Whoever said that is full of shit," Noah said, holding out the dirty plates to Cory.

Jean reached for them. "Why don't *I* take those in before Melissa has conniptions," she said. "I think Polly's about to be discussed and I don't want to be here to defend him." She took the plates and headed toward the house. "Melissa sweetheart," she called, "is the Brown Betty ready? I want to show these locals what class is all about." With her elbows, feet and one little finger, she maneuvered the screen door and disappeared inside.

"She has paint on her feet," said Cory. He'd been watching Jean rather than look at Noah.

"Are you sure you want to? Sing here I mean?" Noah asked.

Cory shrugged. "They're going to pay me ten dollars they said."

"They? You mean Polly?"

Cory nodded yes. "Mr. Thibideau."

"And you *want* to sing? Here? For him? For them?"

"He promised me he wasn't laughing the other time. He said he was just smiling because he couldn't believe how good I was. And he said these people, they said they wanted to hear me. He said Mr. Bananos asked especially." Cory paused and looked at a leaf lying on the lawn. "They're giving him a TV." He lifted the leaf with the toe of his shoe then said, still not looking at Noah, "Mr. Bananos is drunk." He paused again, then looked up.

"I talked to him about what I should sing. I guess he forgot he asked for me especially." Cory returned his attentions to the leaf, trying again to lift it to see what revelations might lay hidden underneath. "I don't care some of them make fun so long as my mother isn't here." He concentrated on lifting the leaf, then continued, "Except now — well — they said you weren't going to be here either." His voice had gradually lowered almost to a whisper. He stopped troubling the leaf and let it lie gently on the grass. "I didn't want you to see them if they laugh at me. That's why I didn't tell you."

"Come on, let's go home." Noah said abruptly. "You don't have to do anything you don't want to do."

"But I do want to," Cory answered. "Except I don't want you to see me." He paused again, then: "They're giving me ten dollars."

Noah was silenced. He didn't have ten dollars to match Polly's offer. If he gave ten dollars to Cory it would mean ten dollars he should have spent on Anne and Danny, both of whom were outgrowing shoes and blue jeans at the rate of one inch an hour. He looked over toward the barbecue pit. The mill workers had been given enough to drink so that now they could start telling jokes in front of their wives. The women had also been given enough to drink so that, at the moment, they were shrieking in raucous embarrassment at something Jim Smith, the man in charge of the drying kiln, had just told them.

Noah had envied these men, the workers at the mill. Their camaraderie, their boisterous play, the insults they exchanged so easily, their sincere if intermittent concern for each other's fate. But he had a fear of them too, and a fear for that part of himself that had yearned to join them. Going to the mill for lumber over the years he'd come to sense the price they paid for the camaraderie: a never-ending search for a common denominator, often the lowest, at which they could meet, each leaving behind whatever the others might suspect was superior. Intelligence, compassion, an admitted tenderness toward women, privacy, independence. Lust was allowed but not yearning; discontent but not striving; pain but not anguish. Skills were accepted but not enterprise. Disdain was permitted but not ambition, appreciation but not passion.

Day by day, hour by hour, moment by moment, they had to reassure each other that they would neither covet nor kill, that they were not to be feared, that they were harmless, agreeable, even amiable. Which they were. Which they had become. They had tamed themselves into a fraternal acceptance of each other and could remember only at moments what had been sacrificed, hints of what had been lost, some show of striving or passion, some evidence of yearning or tender regard.

As a boy, Noah had longed to be one of them. These, he had thought, were the men who would bestow on him his manhood. Now he'd come to know, through the strengthening of his solitude, that it was they who would have taken it away. Or, worse, he would willingly have made it an offering, handed it over to them, and they, in turn, would hand it back in small and harmless doses as though it were a dangerous drug, not to be trusted and certainly not to be taken freely.

His youthful rage had saved him. His outcast status had preserved him. Their judgment of him — the killer of the blind girl's pig — had kept him free. The rebellion inspired by his parents' desertion — his father off into alcohol, his mother off into Massachusetts — had separated him and kept him whole. This was his parents' legacy, this was the gift they'd unwittingly given and that he'd accepted long ago with gratitude and forgiveness.

But now these people would be subject to Cory's somewhat special brand of passion and yearning and, in self-defense, they'd find some way to impress on him that yearning was a shame and passion a disgrace. Eager and ignorant, the boy would hear the smug snickering and think it came from some profound source and must therefore be the truth. He could say now he didn't care, but Noah had already seen the bewilderment and hurt. Still, he had no right to stop him, especially when ten dollars was at stake. Noah paid him nothing.

"You really want to sing then?" Noah asked.

Cory, too, looked over at the millworkers, at the wives, grouped at the barbecue pit and nodded yes. "I told Mr. Thibideau I would. He won't like it if I don't."

"OK then. Go ahead."

The boy thought a moment, then nodded again.

"But," Noah said, "I'm going to stay."

Cory quickly turned to look at him. His mouth opened to say something, but he said nothing. He closed his mouth and gave another nod.

Cory sang "Strawberry Fields Forever." Noah had apologized to Polly for coming uninvited, explaining that his "apprentice" was going to sing and he didn't want to miss it. Polly said he understood and Noah was offered chicken and beer, both of which he declined. He did, however, ask that he be allowed to introduce Cory to the guests since he was his apprentice. Polly hesitated, then said yes of course.

"Cory McFee is going to sing for us and he sings very well. As you probably know, Cory is learning the trade of carpenter and cabinetmaker and so it's my honor to introduce him to you." Noah wondered if there was more he should say, but couldn't think of anything. He'd never spoken in public before but told himself it was about time.

The crowd seemed unsure about how to react to what Noah had said and how they should respond to what was about to happen.

Were they supposed to take Cory — and Noah — seriously or not? Jean gave them a hint by applauding politely and, when everyone turned to look at her, showing them a face of implacable interest.

Noah stepped back behind Cory and leaned against the copper beech. He folded his arms and looked directly at the spectators.

The boy sang with an inspiration approaching ecstasy. Awkwardly angling his body, widening his eyes, and twitching his arms and legs in uncontrollable spasms, he stared relentlessly at the ground in front of him, singing "Strawberry Fields" as if it were an exhortation to the ants and worms and any other insect creature that might crawl within the sound of his voice.

Noah gazed straight ahead, glancing from face to face, and if anyone returned his look, he immediately shifted his eyes in Cory's direction to correct their focus. Only Jean refused to obey. She kept her eyes on Noah, noncommittal and appraising at the same time.

Noah looked over to check on Banana-nose. The old man was the most intent of all, as if trying to figure out, with all the intelligence at his command, why he was being subjected to this particular spectacle. Some poor boy was having a fit in front of them and Noah Dubbins was forcing them all to watch. Which George Bananos obediently did.

The song ended on a high-held note of passionate appeal, not for applause, but for acceptance — and not the crowd's acceptance but God's. Stunned, the audience continued to stare. Noah initiated the applause, intensified it, speeded it up, then tapered it off. Cory bowed, jerking his head up and down like a chicken pecking for seed.

As the audience began shifting, getting ready to move on, Noah said, "Sing another one." Everyone looked at him. He looked back. The shifting stopped. Noah continued his casual stare into the crowd as Cory, this time looking up, darted his way through "Yesterday," depositing his notes high and low, intended obviously more for future discovery than for present enjoyment. Upward and downward he sped, onward, a winged messenger who'd taken unto himself the business of angels. The final word, the last note, was placed proudly at the audience's feet like a divine reprieve brought back from on high and everyone had to recoil slightly to escape the touch of its grace.

Noah orchestrated the applause, then, leaning back against the tree, said, "Sing another one." The shifting lasted a few seconds longer than before but soon died down. Noah began to feel he was being cruel. These people had done him no harm. They, too, had their despairs. The party was their time of respite. For this one evening they were being allowed to feel welcome on the earth, to believe their lives were better than common, to feel assured that they'd become at last who they were meant to be, people bright, witty, beautiful and wise.

And now Noah had confused them, and in the confusion all the certainties of the evening were called again into question, with only unacceptable answers given. He had wronged them.

But these thoughts came too late. Cory, almost spastic with elation, was singing "Penny Lane." The call of children's voices came to them from nearby Thibideau Estates, barking dogs and the sounds of television sets and transistor radios. Cory heard none of it. He poured out into the growing summer dark not only his voice but his heart, his soul, and the very light of his dazzled eyes.

Banana-nose was given his Sony TV — which he kept calling a Toyota — and the evening ended. While Cory was in the house being paid off, Jean came and stood next to Noah, the two of them side by side, both watching the back door to the house.

"Am I allowed to say you were magnificent?" Jean asked. But before Noah could answer, she said, "No, wait. First tell me, am I allowed to be sincere?"

Noah looked over at her but said nothing. He wasn't sure if Jean Thibideau knew what sincerity was. Probably what she'd meant was: am I allowed to *act* sincere. That, Noah suspected, was the best she could do, so he let her go ahead.

"You were wonderful," Jean said. "Do you know that?"

"You'll get used to it."

"I'd *love* to."

Speaking to no one in particular, Noah said, "Come on, Cory, let's go."

As if in obedience Cory came through the back door of the house, his left hand jamming some money down into his pocket. Noah knew now why he'd come. Not just to rescue Cory, but to give Polly the chance to repeat his offer of money so Noah could accept without having to ask for it himself. But Polly'd made no mention of it. Which is why Noah'd punished everyone with two extra songs.

Noah hated them all. Polly, Jean, Cory, Banana-nose, each and every one of them. He was the man who'd killed the blind girl's pig and he was glad of it. They had it coming. The pig had it coming. The girl had it coming, blind or not blind. He wondered what it would be like to send a wrought iron lawn chair crashing through the Thibideau sunporch.

Jean's hand was on his sleeve. He looked down at it, at the finely trimmed and shining nails. Before he could shake it off he heard her say, "You want to know something?" She was looking over at Cory. "Some people don't deserve you."

Noah moved his arm away. "I know." He paused, thought, then said it anyway. "Too bad you're one of them."

* * *

On the ride home, with Cory's bike propped up inside the van by a completed dry sink bound for Keene in the morning, the boy said to Noah, "Mr. Thibideau, he's really nice after all. He said everyone thinks I could go on TV and he's going to ask me again sometime, to sing he said. He gave me twenty dollars instead of ten. Because I sang the extra, I guess." After a moment, he added, "Mrs. Thibideau, she looks like a witch. What a mess. I can't imagine anybody going for her." After another pause, he asked, "Can you?"

Noah didn't answer.

8

Wₕₑₙ Noah heard the creak of the second step from the top, he pulled back into the shadows of the kitchen doorway. He wasn't sure how long he'd been waiting. He'd been listening to the old kitchen clock, its tiny pink-pink-pink like the warning signal at a train crossing far off, the repeated strikes sounding impatient as if trying to hurry a freight that lumbered along dumb and indifferent.

With the creak of the stair he realized that no trains had come within calling distance of Mattysborough since he was a boy. The warning signal became the clock again, its measured tick releasing the seconds into the air, springing them into being, each having its quick existence before being absorbed back into the unmeasured time from which it had come.

Noah pulled back farther into the dark of the kitchen and swallowed hard to clear his ears. The creaks in quick succession told him that Anne was down almost as far as the stairway landing. He swallowed again, not hard this time, dipping his chin and raising it as if the motion completed to the very last detail his disguise.

He pulled down on Ruth's wig — the one she'd bought on a shopping spree with Jean and never worn. He wanted to make sure it fit tight against his skull. For a moment, it gripped the sides of his head but then slipped back up, pulling along with it the hair just above his ears. The sound was loud, like the rub of sand against bone. He patted the top of his head to make sure the wig hadn't risen to a peak like a dunce cap, then pressed its sides so the hair didn't bulge too far out over his ears. He should have got a haircut.

After he folded the lapels of Ruth's bathrobe over the top of her nightgown, he cinctured the cord in closer so it wouldn't come open. The flaps of the lapels fell back so he held them closed with his right hand. He wanted to be tucked in as much as possible. The least unfolding, the slightest opening in the entire apparatus would be, both figuratively and literally, his undoing. Both the robe and the nightgown fitted too closely under the arms but that was all right with him as long as the seams didn't give. He imagined a rip would be as loud as a screech.

The smell of Ruth's rosewater on his fingertips clogged his nose but he didn't want to sniff. He rubbed his nose with the back of his left hand and then, in reflex, sniffed anyway. He wanted to clear his throat, to cough — just a small single-spasmed cough — but he thought he'd better not. Silence was an absolute necessity.

He'd considered showering with Ruth's soap, but he didn't want to leave any trace of her scent in the bathroom to puzzle the children. Then, too, he didn't want to bring the smell of Ruth quite so close, to rub it on his flesh, to shower it into his hair. The rosewater on the tips of his fingers would have to be enough.

His plan was simple. While Anne was coming down the five final steps from the landing, before she could start toward the front door, he would walk past her at a distance of a few feet, go to Joel's playpen, pick up the stuffed skunk he'd made sure was there, then stop in front of the TV for Danny's shoes and socks and Anne's book, then take Joel's hooded sweater from the lamp stand and a baby bottle from between the cushions of the couch. He would, dressed as Ruth, make Ruth's nocturnal move through the room.

The book he would put on the table near the window, Danny's shoes and socks he'd tuck under his arm along with the skunk, Joel's sweater he'd put in the notch between the newel post and the stairway railing so it could be taken upstairs on the next trip, and the baby bottle he'd take into the kitchen. If Anne had not yet turned around and gone back up to bed, he'd wait in the kitchen doorway and decide what to do next.

Anne had started walking in her sleep three nights after she'd seen her mother at Mount St. Michael. She'd sneaked into the back of the van just before Noah left the house, hiding under the quilts he used to wrap furniture for delivery.

He was sitting with Ruth on the bench above Fern Lake, reading Willa Cather's *My Antonia* out loud to her, the part about the Bohemian dance at the church. It was one of the days when Ruth sat not next to him but at the far end of the bench, alone. He tried not to mind and when she said yes, she'd like him to read to her, he took it as a compensation, perhaps even an apology for her need to be aloof that day.

While he was reading, he heard a noise like a gagging in Ruth's throat and looked over at her. She had started to stand up, but then she sat down quickly and began brushing something from her lap.

Noah was about to go back to his reading when he saw Anne walking along the far side of the lake. She was looking up into the trees, swinging her arms to show how casual she was, how un-extraordinary it was for her to be there. Noah took one glance at Ruth who was now rubbing her legs as if to soothe an ache the brushing might have caused. Her hand slowed but began to press harder as if she were trying to clean her palms of something sticky. She was not looking at Anne.

Noah put the book down on the bench, careful not to move too fast. "I'll be right back," he said. "I left something in the van."

Anne was pretending to study the berries on a bush when Noah got to her. Without breaking stride, he took hold of her arm and began steering her away, tearing a branch of berries from the bush. At first Anne said nothing, just skipped alongside trying to keep up. When they reached the path, she began to pull back.

"Can't I just see her?" she said quietly.

Noah said nothing. Anne stopped and Noah had to tug at her arm. "All I want is to see her," Anne repeated, only louder.

"You can't." When he tried to yank her along, she refused to move. "Some other time," he pleaded. "Maybe sometime soon. But not today. All right?"

As Noah began forcing her along, Anne started to pull in the opposite direction, laughing in short spurts as if to persuade him they were playing a game. Over Anne's shoulder, Noah saw Ruth at the bench, standing, watching them. At that moment, Anne broke loose and began running back toward the lake.

At first, Noah considered just letting her go. She had put herself through so much to get there. But what if Ruth was cruel to her, or tried to hurt her? And should she see her mother the way Ruth looked now?

Noah ran a wide arc, putting himself between Anne and the lake. Anne had begun to tire and Noah had no trouble turning her around. He held her close to keep her from seeing Ruth. Hugging her, he led her back, away from the lake. She tried to pull loose, but he held on that much harder.

"Why can't I see her? All I want is to see her. Then I'll go home."

She pulled away enough to be able to look up at her father's face. Noah had no way of knowing what she saw there, but it stopped her struggles. She said no more; she walked calmly at his side to the parking lot.

On the ride home, she leaned forward a little as if still not resigned. Finally, she spoke. "What I wanted to do is just stand there and watch when she came to be with you, when they'd bring her or whatever they do. Just so I could see her. I wasn't going to do anything. I wasn't even going to wave or anything. Why couldn't I wait until she came so I could . . ." Her voice had slowed; now it stopped.

She didn't move. Then she said, "That was Momma, wasn't it?"

Noah said nothing. Slowly, Anne eased herself back into the seat, still looking ahead out the windshield. Just before the turn onto the highway, she said quietly, "Do they do things to Momma there?" Again Noah didn't answer. And Anne never asked again.

Three nights later, just after midnight, she was brought home in her nightgown by a stranger, a woman who was driving through on her way to Concord. Anne was awake, but offered nothing by way of explanation or apology.

The guidance counselor said the obvious. "She's looking for her mother. Take her to see her as soon as you can. Meantime keep the doors locked at night so she doesn't hurt herself."

For the first night, Noah locked the doors and watched as Anne came to them and struggled to get out, waking herself with the effort, then crying in bewilderment because she was in the front hall instead of in her bed.

The second night, Noah tried gently to lead her back to bed without waking her. She began beating him with her fists, then woke up, terrified.

It was when Noah was working the next day, when he was sawing the side panels for the dry sinks, that he began to get the idea of Anne not so much seeing as sensing her mother's presence and being satisfied. He imagined Anne coming down the stairs. Then he saw Ruth, not distinctly, but among shadows. She was moving through the rooms, through the half light. Anne would come down the stairs and stop at the bottom step. Ruth's presence continued to move slowly through the rooms. Anne would pause. She would, even in her sleep, sense her mother, moving. She would wait, then turn around and go back up the stairs.

When it came to Noah that *he* must provide the presence, he dismissed it, ashamed that it had even come into his head. Then he realized that he himself wanted to sense Ruth being there, moving through the rooms. He wanted to have her there, even if only in shadow.

He made a sterner try to shake off the idea. It would be ridiculous, repugnant, him in Ruth's wig and bathrobe. Then he sensed again his wife in the darkened rooms, silent, working her way through the half light.

But this was not a thing for him to attempt, it was not for him to achieve. He wondered if he himself was beginning to go completely crazy at last, just to have thought of it. Then he was touched by the strangeness of it. He was being beckoned not to madness but to mystery. He was being invited into shadows that might hold in their depths revelations he must not refuse.

Again he dismissed the entire notion, appalled, even frightened that the idea could be so persistent. He ridiculed it in his mind, scoffed at it right up to and including the moment that he held up the bathrobe to see whether or not it would fit.

Anne was now on the steps leading down from the landing. Noah stepped out of the kitchen into the hall that led into the dining room. Why hadn't he planned to do something in the dining room? He couldn't just rush through. Ruth never walked from one room to another without doing something along the way: picking up, straightening out, examining, repairing. Or why hadn't he waited in the dining room to begin with?

In the light from the open stairway he could see the empty

rooms. Anne would appear at any moment on the far side of the arch that separated the dining room from the living room. Nothing stirred. The high-backed chairs had each been knocked into a different angle at the table, looking as though they'd been vacated by a group of panicked diners told the ship was sinking. He could straighten a chair or two on his way through as Ruth would have done. And possibly scratch a spot of food off an upholstered back. No, he wouldn't scratch. It would make a noise. There must be no noise, no sound at all. He must be a dream, a ghost, a memory.

Noah began his move toward the dining room, along the wall. Then he realized he shouldn't act as if he was trying to hide. He stepped into the middle of the passageway. For a moment, he simply stood there while his bare feet pressed themselves down onto the floor, a further resignation to whatever fate might bring.

He wanted to cover his face, to pull the wig all the way down to his chin, but he forced himself to raise his head that much higher. He would not be afraid. All he had to do was walk through the dining room, straighten a chair, pass under the arch into the living room, pick up the stuffed skunk in the playpen, put a book onto the table near the window.

Anne had stepped into the living room. Her nightgown reached to just below her knees; she was growing taller. Some of her hair, separated into tangled strands, fell loosely over her left eye, shading it from what little light there was. A rip separated part of a sleeve from the shoulder of her nightgown and the pink ribbon that had been threaded through the sleeve's hem had come unlaced and hung down along the length of her arm to her wrist. Her eyes were open, not with the squinting resistance to light of the newly awakened but open with the puzzled gaze of someone wandering in important thought.

Without stopping, she went toward the window or toward the table in front of it, Noah wasn't sure. He began to straighten one of the chairs at the table. The bathrobe flapped open again at the throat. He clasped it shut and tried to shove the chair in with his knee. But that isn't how Ruth would have done it. He nudged it in with his hip, then continued toward the playpen, pleased with the accuracy of his gesture.

He passed behind Anne who was now looking not out the window but at it. He reached down into the playpen and picked up the skunk. Had Anne seen his reflection in the window? She stepped up to it and put her fingers against the glass as if to make sure there was something there between herself and the outside.

Noah stooped down and picked up Danny's shoes and socks next to the armchair where he'd been watching television. Danny'd gotten the habit of playing with his toes whenever he was concentrating; talking, watching television, playing cards, off would come his shoes, his socks and he would begin to fiddle with his toes, numbering them, as if it were a process by which he organized his thoughts or recorded his memories.

Because Anne had not yet started for either the front door or for the stairs Noah added a few things to his inventory of tasks. He picked up the newspaper from the floor and put it onto the couch. He quietly punched the center of one cushion. When he took the baby's bottle from the crevice between two cushions, he got a glimpse of Anne. She was turning away from the window as if she hadn't seen what she'd wanted to see. Without interrupting his predetermined rounds, Noah went to collect the baby's sweater, crossing her path silently as he did it, about eight feet away from her.

When he unhooked the sweater from the lampstand the cord of the bathrobe began to loosen. He pulled on it, but didn't want to take the time to knot it. A sense of stirring air told him Anne was moving, but in which direction he wasn't sure. He'd pull the sleeves of the sweater right-side-out, then look.

As he inched his fingers into the tiny sleeve, he started to hum. As soon as he heard himself, he stopped. Too abruptly he thought, so he started up again, very softly, then let the sound fade gradually as he pulled the sleeve through.

Slowly the wig began creeping up the sides of his head. The vibrations of his hum had loosened it. And the bathrobe cord that had held on as long as it could, as tight as it could, was now letting go. He was being abandoned.

The stuffed skunk, crowded out from under his arm by Danny's shoes, fell to the floor and after a slight bounce settled against his right foot, warming it a little. As if it were a scent given off by the skunk itself, a reek of rosewater suddenly clogged Noah's nose, causing him to pull his head back. The wig, startled, jumped up a little farther.

Noah's instinct was to stand as still as a fence post. But he knew he'd established a rhythm, a bit jerky and slightly off the beat, but as close to Ruth's as he could get, and he mustn't break it now. He was supposed to take the sweater and put it over the side of the playpen. That would take him across the room, away from the entrance to the front hall and away from the stairway too, so Anne would be equally free to go in either direction.

He turned and had taken a full step toward the playpen when he saw that Anne had stopped at the foot of the stairs and was looking directly at him. Had he waked her? Her face told him nothing. Her lips were parted and he thought he saw her eyes blink as though a quick flicker of dark would reveal to her what she wanted to know. He continued toward the playpen, clutching the sweater to him so the bathrobe wouldn't open. A shoe fell, but he kept on going.

When he got there, he spilled everything down into the playpen, the sweater, the remaining shoe and sock, the baby bottle. The wig had stayed in place when he'd leaned over, but the bathrobe cord had loosened completely. He brought his lower right arm across his waist to hold the robe closed.

His back was to Anne but he could see her reflection in the window, watching him. Slowly she moved her head from side to side as if to give herself different perspectives of what she was seeing, different verifications of its existence. He wanted to bend down again into the playpen and retrieve the shoe but he was afraid the wig would fall off. He contented himself by bending a little and surveying the mess heaped before him as if he were making sure everything was where it was supposed to be.

In the window he saw Anne start to turn, hesitate, move her head in a slow circular motion as if trying to relieve a crick in her neck, then go toward the stairs. He watched her climb. She did not look back. She made the turning at the landing, placing one hand on the wall to either steady or guide her, to remind her where she was. His only fear was that she might stub a toe.

Before she had disappeared up the stairs, Noah saw himself reflected in the window. It was the ghost of Ruth, disheveled and grotesque, peering at him from the far side of the darkened glass, astonished to see him there at such an hour and so strangely dressed.

Anne had gone upstairs and Noah moved through the archway into the dining room. He nudged another chair back into place with his hip then continued back through the hallway toward the kitchen as if to escape both Ruth's astonished gaze and her disheveled ghost.

But instead of going into the kitchen he went down the back stairs and into the yard. He needed the grass to cool his feet. He could think of no other reason for having come there. Then it crossed his mind that he'd come to present his action — his raising of the ghost of Ruth — as an offering to the deer, an act that he hoped would find favor for himself and for her.

Noah quickly pulled the bathrobe closer around himself so he would become less conspicuous and went inside.

9

IT was raining hard, a sudden midsummer storm that had come up across Mount Monadnock in just the few minutes since Noah had left Overbaugh's Bar and Grill. The windshield wipers of the van worked back and forth like straight razors shaving off the water only to have it grow back just as thick and heavy as ever.

Noah was grateful for the storm. It supported his sense of determination. There was nothing hesitant about lashing rain, and lightning wasted very little time on reflection. Noah hoped it wouldn't stop until he had the childen in the van and all their weekend clothes and belongings with them. He counted on the storm to hurry them, to justify his refusal to discuss anything. He should never have let them go to their grandmother's to begin with.

Lightning cracked against a tree on the side of Star Pond Road and Noah pushed down harder on the gas as if the lightning had been a whip striking against the flanks of the van. He was trying to escape from Esther Overbaugh.

He'd gone to Overbaugh's Bar for a beer on a summer Saturday afternoon, no more than that.

After half a beer and a few exchanged words with Esther who was sitting behind the cash register at the end of the bar, he conceded that he might have come not just to see an old friend, but maybe to test whether or not some of the solace Esther had given him in the old days might be taken in now by some incorporeal process, something like osmosis or photosynthesis: Esther would emanate tender satisfactions and he would absorb them, an innocent mating that could distress no one, including himself.

After the second beer and a few laughs at things that were funny because he and Esther wanted them to be funny, Noah admitted the truth to himself. He'd come here hoping to be overwhelmed, to be thrown under by a ravening lust, to be made helpless and therefore unaccountable. It was Jean Thibideau's fault, her hand always on his arm two weeks before, the way her fingers had fiddled around with his sleeve, the sight of her skin through the holes in her sweater. And he'd been rude to her. He shouldn't have been. It made him keep thinking about her. He wanted to go back and apologize but decided he'd better not. Instead, he decided to see Esther.

He'd played the ghost of Ruth for five nights straight. For the first three, Anne came down the stairs, asleep. He'd moved through the rooms, doing assorted and selected chores. On the first two nights, Anne had gone back upstairs with nothing to indicate she knew he was there. On the third night she came over to him near the window where he was tucking Danny's socks into his shoes. She didn't try to put her arms around him or touch him with her hands. She rested her head against his chest, keeping it there for only a few seconds, as if medically checking his heartbeat. Then she lifted her head away, turned and went up the stairs.

The next two nights Noah waited but she didn't come down the stairs at all. The next morning, after the fifth night, she began at breakfast to talk about her mother, freely, making plans for the present she was going to make for her birthday, a horse painted on the scrap of doeskin she'd found in a remnant sale at Derby's. (She considered being taken to a remnant sale her first adult experience.) Her grandmother had plenty of paint; she repainted her woodwork every spring because the dogs weren't allowed out in winter.

Possible visits to her mother were also discussed, forthrightly, without embarrassment or self-pity. Noah guessed Ruth's ghost had done its job and could be dismissed.

He looked down at his beer. Esther had been his first girl. She was a senior and he was a junior in the old high school just before the new one was built. His father had been sideswiped by a truck while walking along 202 from Rosie's Tavern. He was in danger of dying and in the month that the danger lasted, Noah found out what it was like to be held against the heaving expanse of a woman's bosom, even if the bosom was only that of a seventeen-year-old girl.

Noah was relieved when his father survived, but he was also bewildered when neither he nor Esther could find any new support for their affections and activities. Esther tried offering vague sympathies but there seemed nowhere Noah could apply them. And so they'd drifted apart.

He looked around the bar. Esther was at the door to the kitchen brushing something off her right shoulder. He got up to go talk to her. She was holding her left hand out, wriggling her fingers to free them from whatever had been on her shoulder. She was watching something float down to the floor. She was raising her head, turning it toward him.

Before Noah realized that a decision had been made, he was headed for the outside door. Bumping against the pinball machine, he set off a series of bells as if he'd tripped an alarm that warned not of his entry but of his exit.

"Noah!" he heard Esther call after him. "You're coming back, right?"

Noah leaned closer to the windshield so he could see out. The green of the trees appeared in front of him like sudden apparitions in the split second that the water cleared from the glass. The thunder seemed to come from rocks being bowled toward the van, hurrying it along the ruts ground down into the sides of Star Pond Road.

He did not look forward to seeing Blanche. He didn't know what he'd do if she insisted on the children staying. He'd fight, but he wasn't sure how. He had no weapons prepared, his decision to get the children home had been too sudden. And besides, Blanche could always disarm him, that look of amazed loss that would slacken her face.

He had seen it when she was taken to Mount St. Michael and saw Ruth for the first time. And he'd felt it gathering in Blanche's eyes and in the erratic twitch at the ends of her mouth when he'd told her that, contrary to her expectations, the children would stay with him. It was the true face of Blanche Strunk, a face of puzzled sorrow and defeated expectations, and Noah had few defenses against it, nor had he wanted any until now.

In a flash of lightning Noah saw a diagonal cut across the road. He braked to a halt and saw that a birch had fallen slantwise, blocking his path. He honked the horn, then banged the heels of his hands against the steering wheel. The tree didn't budge.

Noah started the motor and gently nudged the van down toward the base of the tree to see if he could force it aside. The wheels spun deeper into the gravel and Noah cut the motor. He clenched his fists to thump them down on the horn, then opened them and relaxed his hands without having made another sound.

Now he could go back to Esther. He started the motor again and shifted into reverse. He had done what he could. Once he'd realized that all that would keep him from going to bed with Esther was to reclaim his children and take them home, he'd tried exactly that. He'd left a half-finished beer on the bar. He'd come through strom, thunder and lightning. But now his way was barred. He had no where to go but back.

He started to shift again into reverse but felt he should wait just a bit. His resignation seemed to have calmed him. It seemed even to have led him into a new depth of himself where another strength, one he hadn't noticed before, was suddenly found. His submission to the inevitable had given him a fresh determination *not* to submit. Abject acceptance had given him the respite necessary for the mustering of new forces.

To clear the fallen tree, Noah braced himself under its slant at a height just below his shoulder. His head cramped under it, his knees slightly bent, with the right foot a little forward of the left, he placed his hands against the bark and began to straighten upward against its weight. If he could lift the top from the tangle of the tree across the road, he might be able to swivel it over to the side and clear his path.

Twice he strained but nothing moved. Water poured off him. How much was rain, how much was sweat he neither knew nor cared. After a short rest he put himself back into position, crouched under the incline of the tree, his hands opened onto the trunk. He paused, waiting to feel all the oppression he could — the tree weighing down on him, forcing his body to bend and stoop beneath it. Asking no more than that he be allowed to stand up straight, Noah pushed against the tree as hard as he could, then harder.

It worked. The tree was lifted free and, like the heavy grace of a giant arm gesturing majestically over the road, it was brought to the side, then rudely dropped into a waiting ditch.

When he got to the house, Noah stood outside a moment, his head raised, his eyes closed, letting the rain wash down on him. He opened his mouth, gulping in as much as he could catch, then wiped his mouth with his rain-soaked sleeve.

When he opened the door, the dogs were on him, crazed as ever. One crashed itself against the closed door behind him. Another hooked its paw into one of his pockets and one ran around him in circles as though a porcupine had been treed in his hair. The short brown and black one named Stubby clawed the wall as if it were a trick he had been trained to do, while Tinkle kept running to the far side of the room and back again as if to charge through the pack and get at Noah for purposes that were never made clear. Fibber simply sat at Noah's feet and howled while Willie kept leaping up as if desperate to deliver a message directly into Noah's left ear.

After he had unhooked Dink's paw from his pocket for the third time, Noah began to wade into the room. Still the dogs barked and howled around him, identifying him as the hard-sought quarry brought to bay at last. Blanche came in, retying the cord of her blue chenille housecoat. (Retying the cord was her equivalent of making herself presentable.) Onto her lower lip was pasted one of the special cigarettes she smoked for her asthma. As she moved through the dogs, she stroked their backs and patted their heads, assuring them they had done a good job; they had performed the honors of the house admirably.

"Yes . . . yes . . . yes . . . ," she said.

The dogs retreated to chairs, to sofas, to the rooms beyond; Stubby and Tinkle, growling and whining, tried to catch each other's necks in their jaws, while Dink stayed behind to sniff and root at Noah's shoes.

"You're wet," Blanche said.

"It's raining."

Blanche nodded agreement, confirming a sad fact they'd both have to learn to live with. Noah expected no spoken greeting, no hello, not for lack of courtesy but because it would have been anticlimactic. In this house the dogs did the welcoming. And why would he complain? He had been treated to extremes of excitement and made the object of crazed attentions. Where else could he find similar treatment? This in turn allowed Blanche to present herself as rescuer; he came into her company as into a refuge. She had tamed the wild beasts, restored order, and created a circumference of calm that now enclosed the new arrival.

And it could not be forgotten that trouble had been taken. Effort had been expended, extra adrenalin had been brought into play. Who would not be grateful? Some people perhaps. But for Noah entry here was an event that he never failed to appreciate. Even today.

"I came to take the kids home."

It was only for a moment that Noah looked right at Blanche. She'd taken the cigarette from her lip and her mouth was opened as if she were dumbfounded by his simple statement. To recover, she put her hand at her hip and hooked her thumb into the cord of her robe.

"They're drawing," she said as if the words demolished by force of irrefutable logic what Noah had just said. She coughed, a large gargle of phlegm in her throat, more a rearrangement of mucus than a release, as if the fluids had declared their discomfort and Blanche had obliged by shifting them and turning them over until they could settle down again with some degree of contentment.

Before Noah could say anything further, Danny called from far off, from one of the more distant rooms, "I found a wolf's head."

"It's not a head," Anne called, her voice coming through the same maze. "It's a skull."

No one came into the kitchen, no one appeared in the doorway.

"It's a *skull!*" Danny cried, pleased enough by such a ghoulish revision to relinquish his own definition. "I'm going to give it to Momma."

As Noah started through the rooms he heard Blanche mutter, "It's not a wolf, it's a dog. And Momma doesn't want it."

Noah walked straight through the dining room, then to his right to the sewing room, then straight ahead to the television room, then left toward the bedroom, almost feeling the need of the children's voices to lead him through the labyrinth.

When he'd first seen Blanche's house, Noah thought it was a series of shacks tacked one onto the other to accommodate a growing family or to celebrate a recent affluence. He soon learned, however, when he started going with Ruth, that each addition, even though it would be called dining room or bedroom or laundry room or sewing room, was, first, last and always, a new space for dogs. True, there was a table in the dining room, a cot in the extra bedroom, but these were signatures, nominal identifications that could just as easily have been made by a sign that read "Dining Room," "Sewing Room," etc.

Human life was confined pretty much to the kitchen and the closed-in porch. The television set had been moved into the kitchen after only two days in its appointed room, time enough, apparently, to give the room its name. The washer and dryer and ironing board were on the closed-in porch as were the sleeping cot and the sewing machine.

(The sewing machine would be brought into the kitchen for the cold months, like the move of a cow to winter quarters. So was the sleeping cot because that's where Ruth had slept and where Stubby slept now. In Blanche's house, spring was announced not by a calendar date or the planting of a crop or even the appearance of a finch, but by the return of the cot and the sewing machine back out to the closed-in porch.)

In the bedroom, Anne was coloring in the flowers on the wallpaper with a red crayon, careful not to go outside the line. Danny was drawing free-style with a purple crayon, in and out among the leaves and flowers on the wallpaper.

"What're you doing?"

"A dinosaur," said Danny, not lifting his crayon from the wall.

Noah pulled the boy's hand away. Danny looked up at him, surprised.

"Time to come home." Noah snapped the crayon in two and threw it onto the cot. There on the rug was Joel, gurgling and waving his arms as Stubby licked what looked like chocolate off his face.

"Get away from there!" Noah stomped his foot next to the baby's head and Stubby pulled back, wagging his tail. Joel's arms and legs jerked to a stop and Stubby moved in again to resume his licking. Noah picked the baby up and held him against his shirt. He smelled of burpings and needed a change as well. Stubby, tongue out, scratched at Noah's leg.

"Grandma *wants* us to draw," Anne said, not trying to justify herself but to show that she wasn't quite ready to accept the guilt her father was making her feel.

Blanche appeared at the doorway, puffing her cigarette. She cinctured her robe in tighter, then reached out for the baby. Noah, in reflex, started to hand him over, then pulled him closer to himself.

Blanche, looking not a Noah but at Joel, her arms still held out, said in the voice reserved only for babies, "Who's Mr. Pooh-pooh? Tell me, who's Mr. Pooh-pooh? You are. Yes, you are. You're Mr. Pooh-pooh. Grandma's Mr. Pooh-pooh."

Like Stubby, she wagged both her head and her behind as she went for the baby.

"I'll change him when we get home," said Noah, wiping his sleeve against the baby's cheek to finish the job Stubby had begun.

"But Grandma *told* us we could draw," Danny said.

Noah tried to flatten Joel's mussed hair as an excuse not to look at any of them. A wisp of smoke drifted over his hand.

"Yes," Blanche said, "I told them they could." But she too sounded guilty. Her voice raised just a pitch, she went on, the sound of someone trying to edge slyly away from a judgment, knowing the ax is going to fall anyway. "Just look how nice Anne's making those flowers look." She then let loose a cloud of smoke that completely veiled the flowers, making both appraisal and disagreement impossible. "And those mountains Danny's drawing there —"

"It's a dinosaur," Danny prompted, worried that an inaccuracy would discredit his grandmother's case and be used against them all.

Noah looked at Blanche who was raising and lowering her head, following the contours of Danny's drawn line, searching for some suggestion that could support his claim.

"I didn't mean you had to come home because you were drawing on the wall," Noah said. Then, trying not to sound as feeble as the reason itself, he added, "It's just that it's time."

"It's Saturday," said Danny.

Before he could expand the argument, Blanche spoke out. "Your father's right. He's the one knows when it's time."

Anne seemed about to take up her brother's cause, but Blanche kept right on going. "Anne, go wrap up the marble cake that's left so it won't go to waste. I can't take the chocolate part. Danny, get the swimsuits off the line so I can put 'em in the dryer before you have to go."

Adults had joined forces, further protest was futile. It was this idea, Noah thought, that depressed him. The injustice of placing a subject completely beyond appeal. Then he realized that it was the defeat of his own last wish that had affected him. He had still hoped to be talked out of it, to be convinced that the children should stay, so he could go back to Esther. His determination to put his children between himself and Esther had not canceled his passion; it hadn't even suspended it. If anything, it had intensified it. Each obstacle was fuel added to the flame; his desires were nourished by each new impossibility. But the more he wanted Esther, the more he wanted the children. And he saw no relief in sight.

He had tried to think of Ruth, especially in these rooms, to transfer his urges back to her where they could be, if not satisfied, at least assuaged to the frustrations of fidelity. But all he could summon was an image of Ruth's scorn, a scorn justified now by his need for Esther Overbaugh. Still, he would be faithful. And yet . . .

If Noah could have done at this moment what he wanted to do, he would have begged, he would have pleaded with his children to come home with him. And he would have begged, he would have pleaded with them that they stay right where they were and send him away. To Esther.

Danny had picked up the broken crayon and was examining it, thinking of ways it might be mended. "But tomorrow we were —"

Before he could finish, before Noah could indicate that he might relent, Blanche interrupted. She took hold of Danny's ear and gave it a tug as if that were the working mechanism that closed his mouth. "Now run along, son, like a good boy." She then gave his cheek a light tap, an affectionate hint of what he'd get in stronger terms if he disobeyed.

Noah was about to ask the boy to say what he'd started to say, but Danny's face had brightened. He obviously felt no need to continue his protest. It was as if his grandmother's tap had magically switched him into a completely different consciousness. "We can take the skull with us," he said, as if this were more than an overriding compensation for his thwarted plans.

The change in his expression had been like the click in a slide-show machine, one picture completely replacing the other. All regret had gone from the child's face. Whatever disappointments he may have felt were now nonexistent. Previously expectations were canceled and fresh hopes and prospects substituted in less time than it had taken Noah to blink.

He was appalled. Within the split second that the change had occurred, what accommodations had his son secretly made, what defeats had he accepted? Or to what treaties had he subscribed? On what terms had the surrender been made? What were its conditions; for what length of time did it apply?

Noah realized he was signatory to a bargain the contents of which he would never know. His son had written its terms in some hidden part of himself and in such a cryptic script that, should they ever be revealed, they would be recognized by neither of them.

Noah had done nothing, his son had done it all. What Noah had not been willing to negotiate, he had been forced to accept. And he did, knowing at least whose had been the victory and whose the defeat.

The boy had run joyfully from the room to get the swimming suits from the clothesline outside and Anne had gone to wrap the marble cake. Blanche was picking up the crayons scattered on the floor. Joel was studying the top button of his father's shirt, moving closer, then backing away, testing its changeability in relation to space and distance. Outside the rain was coming down steadily and the lightning and thunder seemed to have moved to the east. An even pattering against the window and onto the roof overhead sounded like distant horses galloping on grass.

"You understand, don't you?" Noah said.

Blanche stood up, holding the crayons like a bouquet of flowers whose heads had been lopped off. "They'll come some other time," she said, shrugging, blowing smoke down onto the crayons as if that might restore their bloom.

Anne and Danny made their dash for the van as if fleeing for their lives. The rain bowed their heads and they clutched their weekend belongings to themselves like refugees making for the border. There was a slight fumble as they fought for the trouble of opening the door, but by the time Noah got there with Joel they were both settled in the front seat. Anne took the baby onto her lap, squeezing him and rubbing her wet chin into his hair.

Noah started the motor and made the turn toward the road. Blanche was standing in the rain, an old slicker held over her head, her blue chenille robe reaching down into the wet grass. She let go one side of the slicker so she could wave. It flapped down over part of her face. Her hand moved from side to side in farewell, then lifted the slicker again so she could watch them go.

Danny waved back through the misted window and Anne yelled, "Goodbye, Grandma!," frightening the baby so that he began to cry. Again the slicker flopped down in front of Blanche's face and again she waved, looking like someone blind trying to wipe away the dark.

Just before they reached the highway, Noah reached one hand over and rubbed Joel's back through his blanket, hoping that some physical touch might take his mind off the twitching in his groin. Never had he wanted Esther Overbaugh more than at this moment.

10

THE only time Noah had wanted to be unfaithful to Ruth before now was when his father died. He and Ruth had been
married over two years, Anne was a baby and they'd just moved
into the old house near the river with the stable out in back.

Ruth had transformed Noah's father. The man had always been
quiet and private, even before the alcohol, but the first time he
met Ruth (Noah wanted to show her the workshop in the back
storeroom), his father did something unprecedented. He turned
off the television set, put down the newspaper he was reading — he
usually watched the one and read the other simultaneously — and
asked her to sit down. He offered her some whiskey. She accepted.

Never had this happened before, and Noah had shown his
workshop to at least four girls. His father told Ruth she must
come for supper on a night when he'd bake Boston brown bread.
Again she accepted.

At supper, his father told two jokes. Noah had never heard him
tell a joke before in his life. His father had heard of Ruth's
favorite writer, Willa Cather. He knew she was buried in the
cemetery near the Meeting House right over in Jaffrey. He asked
Ruth about her mother's dogs. How was the mutt puppy that had
spent two days under his roof? He was disappointed to hear that
its name had been changed from Noah to Tinkle. He liked the
name Noah. He thought he'd known one of Ruth's uncles.

Wouldn't Ruth like more stew, more Boston brown bread? Ruth would.

The next Saturday his father bought a rug for the living room. For as long as Noah could remember, every floor in the house was covered with linoleum only, all of it put down by his father. It was cold to the feet but it was practical. With no women in the house there seemed to be no need for a carpet. The following Wednesday a dark green plush rug was laid over the maroon and mustard colored linoleum, leaving only the borders around the walls showing, the urns and garlands that were its principal pattern.

The three last years of Thomas Dubbins's life were happy. Noah wondered if it hadn't been his own solitude, his own long hours working in the back storeroom at his carpentry, that had subdued his father, even more than his own wife's betrayal, that the man's respect for his son's solitude had made the man solitary himself, and silent. The opposite was generally assumed: it was the father's remoteness that caused the son's retreat, but now the assumption had become, to Noah, an open question — without an answer.

When his father died of a heart attack in the lunchroom of the ball bearing factory, Noah became very efficient. He made all the arrangements. He was a father himself now and capable of taking over. There was a wake with people from the factory he'd never met, and a funeral with mostly old people because it was a Thursday, a workday.

The weather was cold and some of the roads were still blocked with the snow from two nights before. Ruth bundled Anne in four blankets and brought her along, even to the cemetery. This was Anne's grandfather.

Noah worried about the ground being hard. Would Ruth and the baby be warm enough? Should he have brought some money in an envelope to give the grave-diggers? To the priest? He also had to empty his father's locker at the factory before the weekend. Then there was his father's house to close and empty.

Noah had made love to Ruth four times during the night before. He hoped Blanche and the people invited to the house after the funeral wouldn't stay too long. He wanted to be alone with Ruth again. He wanted to be with her before the day turned gray and it got dark.

He was holding Anne, breathing down onto the blanket folded over her face so she'd have the added warmth of his breath. Ruth's arm was looped through his. Fr. Bodnar was saying the final prayer at the head of the coffin. He was wearing a heavy black coat with the white alb sticking out beneath. The scarf around his neck was thick gray wool; he wore no gloves, holding the prayer book in his hard swollen hands.

" 'May the angels and the martyrs greet thee,' " he was saying. " 'And may you with Lazarus, once a begger, enter into the holy city, Jerusalem . . .' "

Few things happen when they really happen. Hearing the words, Noah realized his father was dead. He was giving him over to the care of others. He was commending him to angels and to martyrs, to Lazarus once a beggar. He was releasing his father from his own hands, into hands that would guide him into Paradise, away from Noah, forever. His father was no longer his; he was theirs. He gave him up. He let him go. He was gone.

Noah looked at the coffin set down against a heap of earth and snow. It should not be brass and lead. It should have been wood. Noah should have made it himself. It was too late now.

" '. . . and into Paradise,' " said the priest. He clapped the book closed and with a quick shudder pulled his elbows into his sides to huddle himself against the cold.

Off to the priest's right was Esther Overbaugh. Noah hadn't noticed her before. She was wearing a blue quilted ski jacket and big yellow mittens. In one hand she held a pair of red woolly earmuffs, in the other her car keys. She'd put on weight. She was looking not at the grave or at Fr. Bodnar but at Noah. She had come to claim his grief. It was hers by right; she had prepared herself for this moment years ago and now her time had come.

Noah kept his eyes fixed on hers a moment, then looked down at her earmuffs.

In the weeks that followed, Noah planned more than once to go to see Esther, to thank her for coming to the cemetery. He hadn't had the chance at the time because Ruth had started to cry into his shoulder and he'd taken her away to the car. But he knew it wasn't to pay a courtesy call. Since the moment he'd known his father had died, Noah's grief and his desire had been fused. He couldn't mourn without wanting Esther Overbaugh. She was the one he wanted to hold. It was her consolations he longed to receive.

Ruth, believing him to be only in mourning, accepted his moods and assumed she understood their cause. She asked him more often than usual to help with the baby, purposely going out so she could leave Anne with him in the workshop to cheer him up, to distract him from his sorrow. Other than that she made few demands.

After a week and a half, Ruth decided it would help if they closed up his father's house, cleared it out, and left it behind. They went to the cold linoleum rooms. Noah was standing at the sofa, touching one of the arms with the tips of his fingers. Here's where he'd brought Esther Overbaugh when his father was in the hospital after he'd been sideswiped on 202. Esther thought the linoleum designs were beautiful. Here's where he'd received her comforts and given her back his extravagant gratitude. Here's where he'd pledged to Esther if not his love, at least his grief, and he felt now that the debt had to be paid before he could find any peace.

Noah moved through the frozen rooms without taking off his coat. He heard Ruth clumping something into a cardboard box in his father's room. She'd gone right to work, stacking, piling, packing, throwing out, making choices, decisions. Noah thought he deserved a few elegiac moments, but he felt nothing so much as his desire for Esther. His mourning had been displaced. He resented that this farewell should be so lacking in dignity; that remembrance should be so rudely trampled on by an old lust. But there was nothing he could do about it.

He went to the back storeroom. Esther had never been interested in his carpentry so he'd never brought her here. He'd cleaned it out completely a few months before when he and Ruth had moved into the house with the stable, but the workbench was still there, sturdy, bolted into the walls. It was too low for him. When he built it he hadn't figured he still had more to grow. The surface was good solid beech. He couldn't leave it there.

On his way out to the car to get the tools, he passed through the living room. Ruth was sitting on the sofa, her feet up on a box of books. She was reading a copy of *Yankee* magazine and sipping some whiskey from a water glass. She was wearing three sweaters and an old pair of snow-pants. Her boots she'd left out on the porch and her shoes, sticking out from all that padding of snow-pants and sweaters, made her feet look small, which they very definitely were not.

Without looking up from the magazine she asked, "Do we want the rug? Maybe for Anne's room."

"Sure. It was always your rug to begin with."

Ruth nodded, took another little sip of whiskey and went on reading.

Going down the three plank steps from the front porch, Noah resolved his difficulty, and in the simplest way possible. He could desire Esther Overbaugh all he wanted, but that was where it ended. He'd do nothing about it. If that made for some difficult moments in his life, that was too damned bad. Ruth was his wife, he'd made her a promise, and he'd stick to it.

Besides, he'd just become aware of something he should have known before now. Ruth was good. His wife was a good woman. Maybe his passion for her had distracted him, had kept him occupied with other thoughts. But now, wanting Esther, he could see Ruth more clearly. Fortunate the man, he thought, who, probably without knowing it, marries a good woman. He himself was most fortunate, and if he didn't know it before, he knew it now. It was the sweaters, the feet on the box and the whiskey that did it.

When he went back through the living room with the tools, Ruth was rolling up the rug. "God, how I hate linoleum," she said. No woman could be better than that.

Noah's desire for Esther Overbaugh lasted until spring, then faded completely. He was allowed, beyond that, one month of unimpeded grief for his father, then that too faded and was gone.

II

$\underset{\text{N}}{\text{O}}$ the evening that Noah brought the children home from their grandmother's he found refuge from his need for Esther by slipping into Ruth's white flannel nightgown. Anne was in the kitchen more or less washing the supper dishes. Most of her time was spent lifting the suds out of the water so that the thousands of soapy bubbles would become a magical adornment to her arms and hands.

Danny was at the table, his services as dish-dryer needed only intermittently between Anne's reveries of splendor and romance. Not at all impatient, he would arrange and rearrange the salt and pepper shakers, the sugar bowl and the butter dish into all conceivable combinations, strategies in a game not yet invented.

In the living room, Joel in his inherited playpen would be exploring the vast wastes of the ceiling, charmed in particular by a pool of light in the far corner just above the lamp.

Supper, for the most part, had gone well. The onion Noah had cut up into the fried potatoes from yesterday hadn't cooked and was slippery, but the roast chicken he'd bought on the highway was crusty and good.

Noah had told Anne and Danny about the beauties of working with applewood. While he was talking he felt something out of the ordinary going on inside him. He was not inclined to either define it or locate it, but it seemed to be a part — yet not a part —

of his still untamed urge for Esther. It seemed a parallel want rather than an opposing force. It didn't cancel his passion, it co-existed with it. It had a life of its own.

Noah ignored it.

But while he was telling Danny and Anne how, just after he and their mother were married, he'd contracted for all the wood in the old Lonsdale orchard when it was being bulldozed by developers from Manchester, an impulse was introduced into his mind independent of what he was saying. He should go upstairs and get into Ruth's nightgown.

Noah continued his story, the children rapt because he was telling tales of ancient origin, before they were born, how he'd lost so much money on the deal he'd had to hire himself out to a builder in Hancock for a whole winter and work with the apple-wood only at night, and how it had made their mother laugh at him.

During the telling, the notion of the nightgown persisted. It was like a pleasing agitation that hinted of possibility. Possibility of what, he had no clue. But there it was, either take it or leave it: agitation, pleasing, suggesting something beyond itself. An invitation to put on the nightgown.

The children had laughed to know their mother had laughed. Noah laughed too, trying not to engage the notion that had lodged itself so firmly in his mind. It was absurd. It was completely contrary to his sense of himself. It was ridiculous and, if he thought enough about it, disgusting. To go upstairs and put on his wife's nightgown was unthinkable, even though he could now think of little else. He would not even explore the idea, however, nor would he try to trace it to its source. It was to be dismissed and forgotten.

By the time they were eating the leftover marble cake with thick slabs of Neapolitan ice cream from the A&P and discussing

Grandma's allergy to chocolate, Noah realized he had not only accepted the notion but had become eager to carry it out.

After he'd closed the bedroom door, he turned on the ceiling light and pulled down the shades, even the unnecessary one that shut out the upper branches of the maple just outside. The room, when he turned around, was a desolation, like a ransacked attic. Maybe because the light wasn't allowed to filter out, it cast a more stubborn and unrelenting glare on all the objects that shared its confinement. That there were no curtains on the windows didn't help. Ruth had taken them down to wash them the day before she got sick. But their absence was the least of it.

The bed hadn't been made for longer than Noah could remember. The bottom sheet, patterned with huge blue anemones, was rumpled and creased so that the flowers looked broken and beaten down. Pubic hairs that would have been brushed from the taut surface of a made bed lay curled in the ridges of the wrinkled cloth. Sawdust that had sweated out of Noah's pores in sleep, even after he'd showered and scrubbed, lay like a silt in the folds of the sheet and stains from his dreams stiffened the petals of the anemones as if they'd been spattered with droppings. A pair of corduroy pants were tangled into the tossed heap of blankets as if the wearer had escaped just in time to keep from being maimed.

On his way to the dresser, Noah yanked the pants from the blankets and let them drop to the floor. The cheap metal handles on the drawers — the old dresser had come with the house — rattled and clanked when he took hold and the drawer itself, when he drew it open, the slow rub of wood on wood, sounded like the long exhalation of what could be a final breath.

Noah looked over his shoulder to make sure the shades were still down, then took out the folded nightgown and flapped it open. It looked smaller than he remembered it. He put his head in from the bottom and began to search for the sleeves and the opening at the neck. Wrestling with all that flannel, he forgot whether he was trying to get in or get out. He was like a Halloween spook trying to fight his way free of his own shroud. There was even a moment of panic when Noah felt trapped, when he felt he couldn't find his way through, that there was less and less air.

Once into it, he found the fit somewhat loose except for the sleeves and under the arms. The length came to just above his knee. As if cold, Noah clasped the collar closed at the throat.

He glanced at himself in the dresser mirror. He looked foolish, like Noah Dubbins wearing his wife Ruth's white flannel nightgown. He leaned his head to one side and then to the other, looking, judging, almost preening. He turned away and looked up at the ceiling. The position of the beams and laths above the plaster was marked by bands of smoky gray like an X ray of the ceiling's ribs and bones. He waited to see if more information was to be imparted, but there seemed to be nothing up there beyond the reminder that he'd put off fixing up this particular room from the day they'd started buying the house ten years before.

He folded his arms across his chest because the nightgown had no pockets and he didn't like to let his hands hang down where they'd brush against the skirt. He sat on the edge of the bed, curious as to what he was doing and why he was doing it. No clue seemed to be forthcoming.

He wondered if he was supposed to sit in the nursing chair as he had the other time. He looked over toward it. Piles of clean laundry had been dumped there to wait for future sorting and had gradually been sat on so much they'd become an added cushion, almost a part of the upholstery itself.

Dirty clothes, mostly his, had been thrown on top, sat on, then mixed in when anyone would search for a missing sock, a clean blouse, a fresh towel. When Noah did the laundry now he would just dump in the whole load from the chair and then start the entire process all over again. He decided to stay where he was, on the bed.

He made a cursory check of his feelings, testing each one in relationship to the nightgown, to see how it matched: his lust for Esther, his impatience with his children, his dangerous debts, his fears for his wife, his desperation without her, his general bewilderment. Each emotion was put in juxtaposition or in combination with the nightgown to see if it blended or if it clashed, or if it related not at all. It was like trying to determine what should go with what he was wearing, as if his task were to select suitable complements and accouterments and come up with a satisfactory psychic ensemble.

But nothing matched. Wearing the nightgown seemed an isolated experience, complete in itself. It affected nothing and nothing was affected by it.

Here he was, sitting on the edge of the bed, Ruth's nightgown dutifully pulled down around his regular clothes. What was he supposed to do now? Something erotic? Something desperate? Masturbate? Break down and cry? Rage and rend the garment? Preen some more? Mimic feminine behavior?

Again he set each act up against the nightgown, but no relationship suggested itself. It occurred to Noah that perhaps some vacuum had been created within him and that the revelation, the understanding or whatever it was, could come if he would only yield to it; that he had been summoned to this place and insinuated into these circumstances for the visitation of either horror or of grace, but he must first become receptive.

He sat still for a minute — which was his idea of yielding, of being receptive. But he became bored. He got up and made the bed, putting on fresh sheets and pillowcases extracted from the nursing chair. Next he sorted the rest of the clothes, put away what was supposed to be put away and prepared a separate pile of what was obviously laundry.

He sat on the bed again in his "yielding" attitude. The top of the dresser was a mess. It was a clutter of baby-oil bottles, talcum cans, bottle caps, a squeezed washcloth, two spoons, a dried diaper, an assortment of combs, brushes, nail files, bills, a pair of under-shorts, ribbons and a clock that hadn't worked for three years.

Noah weeded it all out, making a throw-away pile of the dis-cards, including the clock, then put a clean diaper in place of a dresser scarf (because the dresser scarf had probably been used for a diaper) and arranged the surviving items neatly on top where they would be ready for use when needed.

Again he sat down on the edge of the bed, receptive. Then he tried the nursing chair now that he'd made it more comfortable. He glanced around the room. There was the pale rectangle, about two feet by a foot and a half, on the wall next to the closet door. It was the reminder of a framed picture taken away by the previous owners. Ruth, using Anne's crayons, had done a drawing in it, a comment of their failure to fix up their own room, a tribute to their willingness to let it stay the way it was because there were better things to do.

It was Mount Monadnock, the mountain that from a distance in the west presided over the town. In the picture it rose above a landscape of trees, a great heave of earth that Noah's father had told him was the burial mound for the last Indian brave in Hills-boro County. The spotted cow Ruth had drawn in the foreground kept the picture from being too solemn, always a problem, she'd said, with mountains.

The cow made Noah smile. He'd forgotten the picture was there. He got up, went to it, and kissed the cow right on the behind, a show of affection and sincerity.

Humming, he slipped out of the nightgown as if it were a work smock and he'd finished his job. It was when he was folding it to put it back into the dresser that he paused to consider.

He was feeling relaxed, eager to go downstairs to Anne and Danny and Joel. When he searched for the source of his present state, he knew immediately what it was. He had cleaned up the bedroom, or at least straightened it out. Work had always been the great restorer, especially work that brought order out of chaos. An exterior process that created an interior approximation. He should keep that in mind.

When he opened the drawer to return the nightgown to its rightful place, he began to reflect further. He had worn his wife's nightgown and he had kissed the cow's ass. There was lint on his pants and the taste of dust and old crayon wax on his lips.

He closed the drawer. On his visit to Ruth the next day he was, by Dr. Corrado's orders, to talk as openly to her as he could about the money problems they were having, about the possibility of giving up the house, about her going to the state hospital at Concord. She was supposed to be confronted with as much reality as possible, and all those possibilities were very real. He'd do that.

He would also take her all her nightgowns.

12

"NOBODY ever comes to see me," Ruth said. She and Noah were coming down the steps from the manor porch (called the portico by the staff in honor of its two-story-high columns). Ruth wasn't complaining about having no visitors. She was trying to explain why she'd walked right past Noah in the entrance room where he'd been waiting for her. He'd had to call her name.

She'd looked around and it wasn't until she saw Noah repeating her name that she went over to him and said, "Oh." She seemed startled, then tried to look pleased. "I didn't even see you sitting there." Her smile was one of embarrassment and apology but still she didn't seem to have recognized him. Before he could resent it, he excused it. He couldn't expect her to deal with everything all at once.

He wondered if he might kiss her. His rule had been to wait for an indication from her. So far, it had come mostly on days when she wouldn't be speaking, as if his kiss had been enough, or too much. Today no indication had come, no move of her face toward his, and he tried not to consider it one of the day's first failures. After all, she was speaking and that should be sufficient.

Then he remembered that her talking wasn't necessarily a sign of improvement. It had occurred to him on one of her mute days that it might be during the long silences that the real healing was taking place, that the slow crawl toward health absorbed her so completely that she had nothing left to spend on him. It could be that during those silent times when she seemed most ill she was actually working her way through the maze of her mind, intent, unheard.

This idea was a comfort until he considered the obverse. On days when she was responsive was she merely taking a respite from the task to which she'd so totally given herself? Had she come to an impasse or, even worse, had she given up and gone back to some known and more familiar place among the tangled passages she'd traveled so far? Was it simple nervous exhaustion that animated her on her "good days"? Could her responsiveness in actuality be a reflex caused by an uncomprehended impulse struck against a drawn nerve? Were the bad days the good ones and the good ones the bad?

Noah, in an exhaustion of his own, had given up trying to figure it out. When he was with her, he tried to be interested and patient, and any feelings or thoughts that didn't contribute to that were tossed away, squelched or, like the treatment given to a difficult child, sent off to be dealt with later in a manner stern, measured and superior, when he and the problem would be together, alone.

This cut across all the perplexities he felt when he came to see her and it allowed him to ignore his annoyance now at not having been seen, his hurt at not being recognized and his disappointment that she didn't want to be kissed.

"I know everyone has other things to do," Ruth was saying, "but it's nice to have someone stop by once in a while." With that, she put her arm through his and Noah decided not to mention that he'd been there the day before yesterday, that he'd brought her some tomatoes from the garden and they'd eaten them together sitting on the bench overlooking the lake, that she'd liked them and remembered the day she'd planted them. They'd also played Ping-Pong in the gym and she'd shown him the moccasins with Indian beads she was making in the therapy workshop, but if she'd forgotten, she'd forgotten and he should let it go at that.

Dr. Corrado had explained to Noah that sometimes her medicine or some part of her treatment might make her forget and it would be a waste of time to remind her or to insist that she remember.

Noah asked her if she wanted to go to the gym, to the lake, or what would she like to do.

"They don't play basketball until Tuesday," she said, which Noah took to mean they would not go to the gym even though basketball had never been a consideration before.

Noah used the turning that would start them toward the path to the lake as an excuse to press her arm closer to his side, as if steering her along. She didn't seem to mind.

Maybe it was his imagination but in spite of the mix-up in the entrance room, he felt she was better today. Then he realized why. The snarl of curls that had been clumped around her face by the hospital's "beautician" had been combed out. This could mean she was starting to take more notice of herself. Her hair reached down to her shoulders, a flow and wave of honey brown, a reminder all over again of a cutting of the best walnut, Noah's highest praise.

Her face seemed less gaunt as though she'd begun to sleep better, and her eyes, although they were still frightened and scornful, seemed to be getting back their clearer green as though she'd spent long moments looking at the trees.

And she had on her blue cotton dress, the one she'd bought last fall almost a year ago when she took Danny for his first day at school. Summer chores and outings, the gardening, the canning seemed to have shredded the last remains of a wardrobe she tended to ignore anyway and it was either get something new or wear a maternity dress. So she bought the blue cotton.

Simple and ample, it suggested movement inside itself. Noah could sense the brush of breasts and buttocks against the material, the twists and turns at the undefined curve of the waist. It offered hints of restlessness or of languor, it obscured and it revealed, it could be homely or elegant depending on Ruth.

Right now it was a bit prim because she'd pulled it in with a belt as if trying to restrain its more voluptuous instincts. But as far as Noah was concerned the attempt was not a success. She looked beautiful.

Ruth, talking too rapidly for it to be a symptom of improvement, was telling how Dr. Corrado always wore a tie even on the hottest days. It was then that Noah remembered the nightgowns. He had them in Anne's airline tote-bag slung over his shoulder. He'd meant to give them to her at the manor so they could be left there, but in the complexities of their meeting he'd forgotten.

Interrupting her in midsentence as she was telling him that Dr. Corrado never wore a plain-colored tie, he held the bag out to her. "I almost forgot. Here."

Not at all affected by the interruption, she said, "What're you doing, bringing me things for?"

"Open and see."

Ruth unzipped the bag and opened it wide. She saw nothing but a bulge of white flannel. Noah reached to take the bag back. "It's no big thing. I'll give them to you when we get back to the manor."

She pulled the bag away and tugged out one of the nightgowns. Holding it high in front of her, she looked at it as if it were something suspect. Then she smiled as if recognizing what it was.

"I didn't know if you needed them or not," Noah said.

Ruth lowered the nightgown and stuffed it back into the bag. Looking at Noah she smiled again and said, "Of course I can use them."

"I should have brought them sooner."

"Maybe. But at least you thought of it now." She touched his shoulder, something she'd never done since she'd come to Mount St. Michael.

Noah put his hand to her waist. He wanted to look right at her, into her eyes, but he was afraid of getting too close too suddenly. He didn't want to ruin the day.

But he looked anyway. He was supposed to talk about money.

Her eyes were looking directly into his and they didn't waver. At first he wanted to turn away or at least glance down. But, again, he didn't. Ruth's hand was on the side of his face, her fingertips gently touching the lobe of his left ear. Her smile was intimate and willing, her eyes steady but questioning.

It was a look he knew. It startled him to see it now. He could hardly have expected it. But he returned the stare, holding it so that what was passing between them could take its time, that it could linger at all the old way stations, the moment of challenge, the moment of possible rejection, the moments of repentence and forgiveness, of forbidden knowledge yet to be shared, of secret offerings yet to be made; that it could pause at all the known approaches to love, making their arrival more sweet, more fevered and, ultimately, more fun.

Ruth's hand moved away from his ear down to his neck. Noah began to press her toward him, but she resisted just slightly, but still looking at him.

Noah was worried that he might have frightened her. He didn't move. He searched her eyes, her face, to see if she was all right. He had no way of knowing how fragile her seeming health might be and, encouraged as he was by what was happening now, he was afraid he might do something wrong, a gesture, a touch, a word that would send her back to her illness, away from him, into a terrible suffering where he could do nothing for her.

"We go this way." Ruth had withdrawn from his touch, but only so that she could take his hand in hers. She leaned in the direction of the dairy and indicated with a tilt of her head the way they were supposed to go. Her voice was quiet and reassuring.

Noah held back. "Are you sure . . ."

Ruth slowly moved her head from side to side, hardly able to believe what he was saying. "Don't be afraid," she said. "We'll be all right." Then she pulled lightly on his arm.

He followed her, then brought himself up alongside. She was still smiling. She lifted her head and turned to look at him. This was another attitude he knew quite well. She was pretending to appraise him, a practiced way she had of teasing him, suggesting she might just change her mind. It was her way of mocking his sureness. It invited him to renew or continue his seductions. Ruth was making a sign in the code that only the two of them could read and it made him want to take her with him onto the ground right there and then.

To hold himself back he brought her hand up to his lips and kissed the palm as if her opened hand pressed against his face might be a restraint. Ruth looked at him sadly, letting him know that she understood and sympathized with his tenderness.

"So sweet," she said, shaking her head. Then she grazed her lips along his cheek and whispered, "I'm going to put it on and wear it for you."

Noah drew his head back. Ruth was looking off to the side, still smiling, but now the smile had become impudent, almost sly.

"That's why you brought them, isn't it?" She spoke again in a whisper, but it didn't sound like Ruth, or rather it didn't sound like Ruth talking to him, to Noah, to her husband. There was a note of privileged confidentiality in her voice as if she was speaking to someone she'd just met, someone who had no idea of what to expect from her. She sounded like a woman offering favors daring and undeserved.

Noah was about to suggest they walk to the lake instead, or maybe to the gym — basketball or no basketball — and play Ping-Pong. But he talked himself out of it. Her strange tone he told himself meant only that while she might be having one of her better days, perhaps her best one yet, she was still not completely well. She had hardly been miraculously cured overnight. He must accept momentary lapses and seeming regressions. Also, his sudden reluctance reminded him of himself as a teenager, a boy scared by opportunity. This, as much as anything, decided him to go on, all the way to the dairy.

Taking the lead, he said, "Let's just walk." He squeezed her hand lightly, his signal of concurrence in all that had been determined in the long looks, the coded glances.

The path narrowed and Noah realized that it wound not toward the dairy but into the wooded hills that bordered Mount St. Michael to the west. Holding Ruth's hand he led her on. Pine and oak high over their heads shadowed their way. A spring from the hillside to their right joined the path for a short way then found its downhill course to the ravine below. Here the path ended but they kept right on walking.

Giant boulders stood off among the trees like the remains of ancient animals that had slumbered so long they'd turned to stone. Layer upon layer of shed pine needles and fallen leaves softened their way and a crow emptied the woods of all other living creatures by calling far off and getting its answer from a still greater distance, like an echo coming back to them from beyond the farthest reaches of the woods itself.

"Are you all right?" Noah asked.

Ruth nodded, then whispered, "Wait here." She started up the slope toward a massive stone that stood in a clearing sheltered by the great spread of white pine that circled it.

"Where're you going?"

"Wait here." Ruth held up a hand to keep him from following, then she disappeared behind the rock.

Noah knew they shouldn't be here. He had let himself ignore the realities of their situation. As much as he wanted her and as much as she obviously wanted him, he knew he had to get her back to the manor or the lake or somewhere where they wouldn't be alone. A feeling of dread, of abandonment seemed to inhabit this place. No paths led to it. No one could see or find them ever again. No one knew they were there. He was alone. Ruth was alone. They were lost. They were doomed. That was what the crow had called, that was the answer that had been echoed back.

And yet it aroused him to be here in this separated place, where indeed no one knew they were. The secretness of it and his being there with Ruth spoke to the secretness of himself as if he really was a youth again to whom things could still be mysterious and forbidden. He felt urged to do secret things, things he might never have done before, or things that would become secret if he were to do them here.

Noah started toward the stone. "Ruth?" He sounded to himself as if he were going to ask her if she'd seen his socks anywhere.

She was naked behind the great rock, holding up one of the nightgowns as if trying to decide whether or not she wanted to buy it. Noah went toward her.

She had become skinny again, almost the girl to whom he'd returned the puppy. Her hips seemed not only to have slimmed but to have narrowed, her breasts not exactly shrunken but contracted and tensed. Noah knew what he would do. He would apply again the sculptor's hand, he would mold her back into the full woman she'd become in the years right after they'd married. Even the stretch marks, the small waved striations that her pregnancies had stamped onto her buttocks and her belly, he would knead into the smooth pale skin and give her back her soft unblemished flesh. He reached out his arms.

"Wait," Ruth whispered. "I'm not ready yet." For a moment, she struggled to put the nightgown over her head but then as he touched her it became a struggle to hold him closer, then a grappling to help him find someplace on her body where she could receive him at last. Together they worked in desperate innocence, in ignorance, knowing there was someplace to be found, frightened that it would not be found in time, each move a gasp of hope and despair, urging them on before it would be too late.

Then they lay on the rough dry leaves. Noah touched Ruth's cheek and soothed her forehead. He kissed her eyes and pressed his cheek gently against her mouth. But she didn't respond. She seemed to be watching him, warily, as if she wasn't quite sure she trusted him. Usually, after making love she was tender as if the act itself was mostly a frantic search for gentleness. He kissed her on the lips then drew back and looked at her. She was still watching him as if waiting for him to make one wrong move.

He thought of talking quietly to her about home, about the children, the baby, about the work he was doing. He searched among recent incidents and remembered he hadn't told her about the fireworks on the Fourth.

Family traditions had been kept up he told her, the picnic on Gedney's Island for Anne's birthday with the first watermelon of the summer, the annual trip to see the Old Man of the Mountain with steaks and french fries outside Franconia Notch, early raspberry picking on the lower slopes of Mount Monadnock — with the exception that this year there was a break in discipline and they'd eaten the entire yield with none saved for jam. And the Fourth of July fireworks in the parking lot of the school on High Street.

So he told her now about the great fountains of green and gold and silver, the sharp reports like sky bombs detonated in the dark, the whistles and the bursts of red then blue then silver again, the falling sprays of exploded stars dying in the sky.

His voice trailed off. He should not have said dying. It was the wrong choice of word. He had begun to see the fireworks again not as splendor now but as loss, each discharge magnificent but so quickly turned to embers, the light of each new burst illuminating the debris of the last as it slowly streaked down the night sky like great tears of dust, whole galaxies flowering into ashes, falling silently to earth, extinguished, forgotten.

Noah had stopped talking. He said nothing. They should not have made love. And Ruth had heard not one word of what he'd said.

The nightgown, never worn, was bunched under Ruth's left shoulder. When Noah tried to tug it free to make her more comfortable, Ruth shook her head, telling him not to. She turned and looked at a scrap sticking out near her ear. Holding it up to her eye, she examined it, rubbing it with her fingers, testing its texture.

She pulled away from Noah and jumped up as if she remembered an appointment she mustn't miss. Noah stood up, but she backed away from him.

"You didn't let me get dressed the way I was supposed to!" She sounded as if this had been a betrayal. She reached for the nightgown, not taking her eyes off him, as if he might try to snatch it away first.

Noah could think of only one thing. He had to get her back to the manor. Then he thought of a second thing. He must not try to get too close to her. And that was all he could think of for now.

He let her put the nightgown on and smooth it down over her stomach and her hips. He would leave her other clothes here and come back for them. It would be better not to touch them while she was there.

He let Ruth lead the way back. At the edge of the woods she stepped out onto the gravel path that led back to the manor and turned to him as if that was as far as she would allow him to follow her.

"I'm sorry," she said. She was looking off to the side, too ashamed to look directly at him. "You see, I never did that before. Except with my husband. But thank you for the nightgown. It'll be nice and warm. I shouldn't . . ." Without finishing, she turned and walked off down the path.

Noah didn't move nor did he want ever to move again. He wanted never to step clear of the woods, out onto the gravel path at his feet. She hadn't known him, she hadn't known who he was. The whole time he was with her she'd been with someone else, not with him.

Ruth turned where the path turned and was gone, taking the nightgown with her. And they'd never gotten around to talking about money.

13

WHEN the Diocese of Portland decided in 1875 to set up a parish and a church in Mattysborough it was assumed, as a matter of course, that the church would be named for St. Matthew, the tax collector who was surprised one day at his counting table and summoned in no uncertain terms to apostleship, martyrdom and sainthood. The choice of patron was obvious and it relieved the bishop of the necessity of arbitrating among the several immigrant factions that would make up the new parish as to which national saint would be their first intercessor.

Among those put forward were St. Columcille, St. Rémi, Our Lady of Czestochowa, San Pantaleone and, from the man who was to be appointed organist, St. Wolfgang, the patron saint of Salzburg, which would make the church, without its being detected, a shrine to Mozart. But if the choice was obvious, it was not without complication. Some of the town fathers were wary, anticipating the implication that the town had been named after a Roman Catholic church rather than the reverse. But the bishop persevered, arguing that it was a tribute to their community, a gesture of gratitude for the hospitality they had extended to the Irish, the Italians, and the Poles who had come to sweat in their mills and shiver in the shanties of the sub-town built especially for them beyond the bend in the river, the main street of which was called Overseers Drive.

Persuaded finally by the bishop's alternate proposal that the church be called St. Peter's, which would seem as if they had no saint of their own and were forced to borrow one from nearby Peterborough, the town fathers gave St. Matthew their blessing and the barrackslike church was built and the graveyard ready by the winter of 1876 to receive its first occupant, one Maureen Mahoney, beloved of John, b. 1850 — d. 1876. (The second would be William Mahoney, one month later, aged one month.)

The parish prospered, prospered in fact to such a degree that, within a century, the solid middle-class parishioners would derive a prim satisfaction from the knowledge that their appropriated saint was a man who had renounced tax collection.

Th next controversy was limited, years later, to the issue of extending the graveyard to the north side of the church or reserving the space for a parking lot. Very quickly, the future dead were relegated to a pleasant plot just outside the town, about a mile away, and the gravel fund for the parking lot was oversubscribed in no time at all. (As would be the asphalt fund ten years later.)

Now the graveyard, in the south and western fields, was a place more of serenity than of sorrow, so few within memory were buried there. It had become a practice, in the days of fasting, for families to picnic after mass among the stones, shaded by the maples and beech planted long before Maureen Mahoney had come to sleep forever within sound of their whisperings.

And so it surprised and offended no one when, with the institution of the Annual Summer Fair — scheduled, in charity, for the convenience of the summer people — the tables and stalls were, without discussion, set up among the stones in what was, after all, one of the most pleasant spots for miles around. Here one could buy home-woven cloth and handstitched linens, minor antiques like crocks, cabbage slicers, kerosene lanterns and coffee mills, ceramics so plentiful that they suggested themselves as Mattysborough's primary cottage industry, discarded but useful clothing, books read and unread, outgrown recordings and, of course, food: pies, cakes, cookies, breads; preserves, pickles, jellies, jams and marmalades. The fair, in other words, was the usual confluence of the humble (used clothes, books, records) and the proud (pickles, cakes, cloth) mediated by the cabbage slicers and coffee mills, which managed to be both.

This year, in an attempt to make the fair seem more up-to-date, it was suggested that it be billed as a flea market. The debate was serious but the proposition voted down, thanks to a coalition of those intending to donate used clothing and the Coopers who had offered their four unsold puppies for the raffle.

Ruth's usual assignment was the book stall, a job she volunteered for not just because she'd become a convert when she married Noah and wanted to prove her parish allegiance, but because she could then get first grabs at anything good, a dusty attic copy of Jane Austen or Willa Cather or Sara Orne Jewett that had been dumped at the rectory the week before.

This year, Blanche, unasked and without advance notice, took over the books. She simply appeared at seven-thirty in the morning, a full hour ahead of anyone else, waited in the car until Fr. Bodnar finished his mass and his breakfast, then presented herself at the rectory. "I'm here to do the books," she'd said.

She was the first one Noah noticed when he rounded the church, looking for Polly. He'd come to accept the offer of the money. The night before he'd dreamed that he and Ruth were in the Moscow airport, in Russia, and he had no way of getting them home. Another night, he'd dreamed of finding dimes and quarters on the grass outside the grange hall, a great litter of them waiting to be picked up. He'd been offered money, but had refused.

Now he couldn't hold out anymore. He had to keep Ruth at Mount St. Michael, whatever the cost. He'd made love to her and she hadn't known him. Dr. Corrado told him that the treatment

Ruth had had that morning might have disoriented her so that she might not know people, even her husband. The doctor also reminded him that the hospital could no longer wait for certain bills to be paid. And so he'd come to the fair.

Every year Polly did the hamburgers and hot dogs while Jean, with an authority derived from two visits to Mexico, dispensed gazpacho made from a receipe that had come with her Cuisinart. Noah had forgotten about the fair and called Polly's office (no answer because it was Saturday) and the house where Melissa, the cook, told him where Polly could be found and made him promise to remind Jean to bring her back some handstitched linen napkins if, late in the day, they went down below a quarter each.

It made Noah uneasy to see Blanche. He'd isolated his reason for being there, his reason for needing the money. It was so he could stop selling off his tools, so he wouldn't endanger his house. His concern was with property, with ownership, with the practicalities of business. He'd managed in his thinking to exclude all references to hospital bills, medical bills, doctor bills. He'd come to make a business arrangement, not to seek rescue from a personal calamity. He'd imagined his conversation with Polly as a brisk dialogue, abrupt, a quick compact between two men well versed, as the saying goes, in the ways of the world.

Now there was Blanche, doing Ruth's work, giving Ruth a presence he thought he'd left behind. All the energy he'd accumulated by thinking in terms of tools and real estate threatened to drain away, leaving him with little but his desperation to support his cause, a support which, in the world of business, was not the ideal prop for an already risky deal.

Noah wondered if he should put off his conversation with Polly. The office on Monday would be better; maybe a phone call would do it. He looked at Blanche. She was wearing her only hat and her best dress, the one she'd bought for his and Ruth's wedding. The dress was loose-fitting with long sleeves gathered at the wrists. Its color seemed inspired by rust. It looked like an orange dress that had corroded in some spots to black, in others to umber, to ocher, and in still others to a dirtied version of the original orange, a nightmare flower brought to mock the summer greens and golds of the cemetery, a portent of the autumn season not far ahead. Noah wondered the same thing now that he'd wondered at his springtime wedding. Was she doing it on purpose? Was she intruding a cynicism, a malevolence or even a prophecy to mar the event? Had she a private vision that could find utterance only in these hints of corrosion and decay? Most likely, Noah told himself now as then, it was the first dress on the rack at J. C. Penney's, it was inexpensive, it was made of a silklike material that made it seem appropriate for a wedding, and it fit. For Blanche the combination was sufficient to make purchase mandatory.

The hat was more festive, a navy blue straw with a rim too narrow to give her shade, and a cluster of what looked like dwarfed apricots clustered on the side. She had come dressed for church because this was the St. Matthew's Fair and she hadn't wanted to seem disrespectful. She'd known that women Catholics wore hats in church and news of the Vatican reforms hadn't reached her in time to keep her from searching out the hat again and perching it squarely and dutifully onto her head so that she would not be out of place at a Catholic gathering.

(At the wedding no one else had worn a hat but she'd interpreted that as a temporary dispensation prompted by the bride's previous nondenominational attachment.)

She hadn't seen Noah. She was too busy arranging and rearranging the books in varying patterns on the trestle table as if her task for the day was to search out a predetermined combination. Two men and a woman were examining her wares and each time one would pick up a book, Blanche would quickly shift the display into a new pattern as if a turn had been made on a kaleidoscope and it was her job to make sure the new design was at least equal in interest to the last.

To get to the hamburgers and hotdogs, Noah circled around behind Blanche, past the antiques and the jams and the jellies, brushing past the halted strollers, working his way through the clumps of people ambling along the cemetery paths, excusing himself when he had to squeeze between those evaluating pickles and those skeptical about the fine needlework that was advertised as having been done by hand. (Ruth had an attachment to her sewing machine that could turn out in minutes stitching that would have occupied her ancestors for more winter weeks than could possibly be counted on a single hand. She resented the attachment and had given it to Danny to play with, now an imagined nautical instrument that could create — not detect, but *create* — true north by being pointed in any direction he chose.)

Noah was greeted by his fellow townspeople. After his marriage to Ruth he'd been awarded honorary and retroactive respectability. His hand was shaken, his shoulder gripped, his back slapped, patted and rubbed. The blind girl's pig wasn't forgotten, merely downgraded from "a vicious and unforgiveable act" to "an understandable accident." Mrs. Consagra, his third grade teacher, pinched his ear, Peggy Cannon kissed his cheek, Kate Coble squeezed his right biceps, Mrs. Wasachek brushed his hair back from his forehead and Miss D'Arezzo pulled his nose and shook it as if playing with her poodle.

He was told he looked well; he was told he looked peaked. A spot was scratched off his shirt making the hair on his chest itch. A crumb, real or imagined, was brushed from his lips, a fly from his neck, and he was made to turn around twice so that Mercedes Walbridge could judge for herself if he was getting enough to eat.

Community exchange was not limited to the living. Graves and tombstones were pointed to and pointed out. "You remember

Molly Hennessy." "Oh, Molly, yes of course." "And Emmett — the uncle — you remember him." "Emmett? Is he here? Where? Oh, there. Yes, Emmett." "Rose Harrington, isn't she here?" "Somewhere I think but I'm not sure where." "Isn't that Harry's aunt?" "You know, I think it is. The one with the curly hair." "Kinky I think you'd call it."

Polly, decked out in a white apron and a chef's hat, was poking a slippery hamburger into its bun. After handing it to a man wearing a limp silk sport shirt covered with palm trees, he began rolling the hot dogs over on the grill and jabbing the hamburgers as if prodding them to hurry up and get done. "What you gonna have, what you gonna have?" he called, his high choked voice ill suited to the hawker's cry.

At the table next to him was Jean wearing the official apron advertising the Paris edition of the *Herald Tribune*. Her hands were thrust into the front coin pockets where they were either playing with the change or scratching her stomach. "Gazpacho hot, gazpacho cold, both at the same time, both for the same price. Cool the body, warm the blood. Hot cold gazpacho. Cold hot gazpacho."

Fortunately, Noah had, without realizing it, made some necessary preparations for the task at hand. On a trip to the mill he'd told Polly he probably shouldn't have interfered with the entertainment the night of Banana-nose's retirement party. Polly professed not to know what he was talking about. If Noah hadn't asked Cory to sing more songs Polly himself would have done it. The boy had been terrific.

Then Noah'd met Jean one day at Mount St. Michael when she was leaving after a visit to Ruth. He apologized for having been rude. Jean said she'd loved it. When would he do it again? Soon she hoped, but not now. She had to run. She had an appointment for a pedicure in Concord. Noah'd wondered again if her toes looked the same as her fingers. Why hadn't he looked the night of the party when she was running around in her bare feet? Because it didn't really interest him was the answer and he let it go at that.

Noah stepped up to the grill. Without looking up, Polly said, "Hot dog or hamburger?"

"Nothing, thanks."

"What do you mean, nothing?" Polly looked up. "Noah! Jean, look, it's Noah."

"Why so it is," Jean said.

"How's it going?" Noah asked.

"We're making a million," said Polly.

"Good."

"What's your pleasure?"

Noah glanced at Jean who was staring into the vortex her stirrings had made in the gazpacho pot. "Can I talk to you a minute? In private?" he asked.

Polly looked at him as if he suddenly couldn't remember exactly who he was. Then he reached out and slapped his upper arm. "Sure."

They walked toward the entrance to the church, a small shed built onto the long low building, a wind barrier where the congregation could stamp the snow or mud from their boots and not track it down the main aisle. Instead of going inside, Polly and Noah stopped in front of a stained-glass window just to the left of the shed where they could be overheard only by St. Patrick who was too busy pointing a couple of snakes in the direction of Manchester to care what the two men might say.

"They want me to have Ruth transferred to the hospital in Concord," Noah said. Because this was a business meeting, Noah made sure he spoke in a very matter-of-fact way as if he was about to ask Polly the road directions. His truer impulse was to fall to his knees, clutch at Polly's shirt-sleeve and beg that he be allowed to keep his wife near him. He would like to have clasped his hands, squeezed them white and raised them in supplication. He wanted to cry and cover his face in shame, to bow himself low in the dust and wait for Polly to raise him up. This was Ruth he was talking about, his children, his family and his home.

Except that it wasn't, not really. This was business. Who would lend money to a man so much in need? Desperation showed a want of capability. No competent man would get himself into such a pickle, and who would give money to an incompetent?

Polly nodded his head, indicating that he knew how to get to Concord.

"Dr. Carrado thinks it helps to have her near home so I can go see her." Noah was pleased that he'd thought to bring in Dr. Corrado, an authority whose recommendations could not be put aside lightly. It gave weight to his cause. Noah got another idea. "And not just see me," he said. "It's important she see her friends." He'd managed to implicate Jean. He felt inspired. "People Ruth likes and trusts." Then, as shameless as he ever wanted to be in his whole life, he came right out and said it. "Like Jean." He paused. "Like you."

Noah wanted to throw up. Why hadn't he honorably thrust himself into the dust? He stared at Polly, too aghast at his own hypocrisy to go on. He knew he should shrug or make some gesture common among the indifferent, the unneedy, but his loss of scruple and honor had immobilized him. If he made a move, surely it would be to hang his head in shame; if he made a sound surely it would be to groan in disbelief at the words he'd spoken.

Polly seemed to mistake his paralysis for an admirable reticence, for an intelligent transfer of the matter into his, Polly's, more capable hands. He slapped Noah's arm, the apparent equivalent of a Masonic handshake that indicated a transfer of burdens, a relief from worry, an invitation to resume at once the pleasures and privileges of the earth that were his by right of brotherhood with the man who'd delivered the fraternal slap. It was a gesture of benevolent arrogance and smug heartiness. It was for Polly an assumption of responsibility. For Noah it was a rite of relinquishment, and he was too stunned to disrupt or disclaim it.

He heard Polly outline the specifics of the loan. He nodded at the stated conditions, giving assent, acknowledging them to be fair and reasonable. He kept saying "Fine," "Good," "Fine" — as if he were evaluating cuts of beef that were passing by on a conveyor belt before his eyes. "Fine." "Good."

When the conference was over, Polly slapped Noah's arm again and motioned him back to the table. They would make it official in his office on Monday. So brief had their meeting been that the hamburgers were still raw. "Have one," Polly said, opening a bun and poking around on the grill.

"I think maybe I'd better get back to work. I left Cory alone in the shop and I don't like to do that too often."

"Nice kid, Cory. Reminds me I got to get him come sing another party I'm giving next week. Toddman Spencer's birthday. I'd invite you too but it's going to be dull. Except for the kid. You mind?"

In reflex Noah was tempted to protest, saying he'd need the boy in the shop all next week, day and night, and the week after, but he realized Polly intended this to be one battle he wouldn't lose. Well, it would have to be between Cory and Polly from now on. Noah couldn't go on protecting the boy forever. He was withdrawing from the field, abandoning the boy to the smirks and snorts that his innocence so justly deserved. Also, Noah's mission of the moment wouldn't allow for any antagonisms between himself and Polly.

"No, I don't mind," Noah said. He almost added, "Why should I mind?" but couldn't bring himself to be quite that craven no matter how much he needed the money he'd come to ask for.

Polly shoved a hamburger into a bun and held it out. "To the honor and glory of St. Matthew."

Noah accepted.

"You want mustard? Relish? Ketchup?"

"Ketchup."

Looking around, Polly began mumbling, "Ketchup, ketchup. It was right here. Who took the ketchup? Jean, have you seen —" He stopped. Jean, still chanting "Hot gazpacho cold, cold gazpacho hot," was spooning the last of the ketchup from a thick cereal bowl into the pot in front of her.

"You took the ketchup!" Polly said, disbelieving, as if she'd given away his last pair of dungarees.

"Oh. Sorry. Here." She handed back the empty bowl, reached down into a straw bag leaning against the table leg, brought out a bottle of gin and upended it into the gazpacho, counting, "One, two, three, four, ooops!" She screwed the top back on the bottle, put it down into the straw bag and took up her chant with a new note of innocence. "Hot gazpacho cold, cold gazpacho hot. Cools the body. Warms the blood." She stirred the pot, lifted out the ladle and sipped.

"God, that's good!" she said. She turned toward Noah. "Want some?" She raised the ladle to her lips again so that she could stare directly at him over the rim. The invitation was inevitable. She was mocking him again, teasing him because he was without his wife. Testing him, daring him to make the next move, the same as she had done the night of the party, the same as she'd done years back when she told him he could fuck her anytime he wanted to.

He said now what he'd said then, only more quietly this time. "No. But thanks."

"Oh stop being so serious. Have some." She held out the ladle she'd been sipping from, looking directly into his eyes. She wasn't mocking him. She was making a very definite offer.

Noah shook his head no. "I have to work. Gin's not a good idea."

"Then I shouldn't have put it in. Otherwise you could have had some. Sorry." She spoke more gently than he could ever remember her having spoken before as if regret carried with it the gift of repose. He'd never known Jean Thibideau to regret anything; she'd never been this calm.

"Well," Noah said, "maybe half a cup won't make that much difference."

"No. You have to work." Her voice now was strong and steady, the voice of authority, the voice of dismissal. The moment had passed. Regret, repose, both gone. She was a woman in charge. "First thing," she said, "and you'll be losing an elbow. And it'll all be my fault."

"Half a cup won't hurt."

"Nope. Absolutely not. Not for —" and here she paused, became quiet again and said — "not for anything." Then she smiled, pleased with herself for having controlled the entire exchange, leading him first this way, then that, and now discharging him, but not without the intimately spoken "anything" which kept the situation unresolved. It would be resolved, perhaps, another day. A day, she seemed certain, that would be of her own sweet choosing.

"Whatever you say," he said.

Jean bowed her head, smiling again, congratulating him for having seen the situation so clearly. She then called out, "Cold gazpacho hot! Hot gazpacho cold!"

"Hamburgers, hot dogs! What're you gonna have?" Polly cried. They were finished with him. They were calling out for their next victim.

Noah took a bite of his hamburger. Grease and blood dripped down onto his shirt. He took another bite. More grease, more blood flowed down. He began to make his way back through the fair.

At the antiques table just ahead, he saw two teen-age girls showing each other the items on display, giggling and bumping each other with their hips. They would be about fifteen, both a little plump, one with her hair pulled severely back into a bun, the other's hair crimped and straggly from not having been dried after a swim. They were both wearing white tennis shorts the better to show off their bronzed legs. One wore a cut-off T-shirt to keep her tanned midriff cool; the other a white blouse with frills that made up for the severely bunned hair. Each time one of them would lift something from the table, a lantern, an old crock, they would both shriek as if the object were a joke crafted especially to induce hilarity.

That would be Anne in a few years, all her solemnity dispelled, ground up by giggles.

"Don't forget our meeting on Monday!" Noah heard Polly call. He turned and held up his hamburger in salute. A stream of grease rolled down his arm, into his sleeve. He rubbed his arm against his side to absorb the grease into his shirt, pleased with his casual and crude solution to the problem.

Instead of finishing his hamburger on his way to the van, he'd stop and enjoy it. He liked the idea of taking time out to do nothing but eat a hamburger. He leaned against a locust tree, wiped his mouth with his arm and took a big bite. It was the best hamburger he'd had in his life, juicy, a real taste of beef. Polly should be proud of himself. Noah would remember to congratulate him. He wished now he'd accepted the gazpacho, gin or no gin.

The girls had moved on to the preserves where pickled beets and canned green beans brought them close to collapse and, when the one with the cut-off T-shirt held up what looked like a jar of raspberries, the one in the frilled blouse brought her hand up to her mouth to stifle a scream as if she were being shown a collection of grasshoppers.

Noah looked back at Jean ladling gazpacho into a cup and sipping it, then he looked again at the girls, the two best friends. The girls were Ruth and Jean. They'd been this foolish, this giddy, this free. Why had Ruth hoarded none of it against these days of her trouble? Why hadn't Jean? Was there no way these girls could be warned, no way they could be counseled to put in reserve some fragment of this freedom, to store it against the coming seasons?

It was, Noah knew, impossible. To be spendthrift was itself the treasure. To squander unheeding, that was their riches. Nothing could be spared or stored or kept. It had to go. To cling to it would mean that it had never been.

Two paths away, at the clothes table set among the headstones of the Fitzgibbonses and the Fitzsimmonses, the girls were holding skirts and dresses to themselves, to each other. One had put on a pair of elbow-length gloves. Nothing could escape their enthusiasm, nothing could evade their foolishness.

Perhaps, Noah thought, the world would be different for them. Perhaps this joy would last them forever. It seemed so limitless. Surely the laws would be suspended in their favor. Noah began to believe it possible. He began to feel that the glooms and despairs of the world, at least the world around Mattysborough, were about to be dispersed, that these two girls with their bright and giddy presence had come to proclaim a new era in the town.

Now they were reading to each other the names of the dead as if releasing them into joy, now they were offering each other ceramic pots and sculptures, objects of such comic power that they had to punch each other to express their mirth.

Noah had been wrong. There was no hope for them. They would have to go unguarded to whatever waited, just as Ruth had gone, and Jean, and Noah himself; just as Anne and Danny and Joel would go, unremembering, ignorant of mirth and freedom, undisgraced by giggles and giddiness, alone, abandoned even by what they once had been.

Blanche, too, had seen them. She was smiling, watching them eagerly, expectantly, like a spectator at a game, hoping she would soon be invited to play.

It was time to go home. Noah began to circle again around the graves so he wouldn't have to talk to Blanche, to tell her why he was there. When he got to the three birch trees that shaded the graves of Maureen and William and now John Mahoney too, he looked back for one more glimpse of the girls. He looked among the tables and the stalls and along the paths between the graves, but couldn't find them. He saw instead the traffic of his townspeople moving among the heaped and piled stalls. He saw Jean eating a hot dog and Blanche shifting the books on her table. He noticed that balloons, bright pastel colors, pale greens and pinks and yellows and blues, had been tied to the tables, to the statues in the cemetery, on the crosspiece of a crucifix, on the stone wrist of an angel.

These were the girls he'd seen; these were Jean and Ruth. They had become bright air of many colors, they held aloft the tables, the stalls, the stones. They raised up Noah's spirit.

Before getting into the van, Noah thought of taking one more backward look, of looking for the girls again, but he decided against it. Instead, he asked that they who had refreshed his soul, who had raised up his spirit, for just those few moments, already gone, he asked that they be blessed forever.

14

Noah had told Anne and Danny he had to go to the bathroom, but when he got to the upstairs hall, he went into the bedroom instead. After he closed the door he sat down on the bed and squeezed his hands down between his legs. If he hadn't given the nightgowns back, he could put one on now. But he'd given them to Ruth.

He'd felt so hopeful that afternoon, at the fair. He'd expected to feel that way for a long, long time, especially since he'd finally settled the matter of the loan with Polly. He'd told Cory he'd be home with the children, that he wouldn't need him until Monday. He'd wanted the evening alone with his family. But now, moments before, downstairs, he had wanted to break Danny's arm. He had even told him he would break it.

"Tear that card and I'll break your arm," Noah had said.

They'd been playing five-hundred rummy. Blanche had taught Anne and Danny how to play and they in turn had taught Noah the day after Ruth went to Mount St. Michael. Danny had made a discard, the five of clubs, but when Anne reached for it, he grabbed it back.

"Wrong one! I slipped. I meant this other one." He put down the three of diamonds.

Anne cried "No!" and the argument was on: laughing insistence from Danny trying to persuade his sister to enjoy the idiocy of his error; repeated requests from Anne, secure and humorless in her rights; Danny shuffling his cards back and forth trying to make the five as anonymous as possible, just another card in a spread of eight and therefore of no value whatsoever. Firmer demands from Anne. The offer from Danny to let her have it if she could pick it out from the others in his hand. Anne's appeal to Noah. Noah's quiet reminder to Danny, "You put it on the pile." Danny's whimpering plea. Anne's reach for Danny's cards, Danny's quick withdrawal. Anne's renewed plea for her father to intervene. Danny's accusation that Anne cheated in adding the scores.

"Give her the five so we can keep playing," Noah had said.

Danny jerked the card from his hand and slapped the others face-down onto the table. He tightened his jaw and bit in his lips to show that he was about to expend great physical effort. Then he took the five of clubs between his thumbs and index fingers, ready to tear it in two.

"He's going to rip it up," Anne cried, terrified that her brother was about to commit an act that would damn him forever.

"Tear that card and I'll break your arm."

Noah looked right at Danny until his son's eyes met his own. The boy's lips were still tucked into his mouth, the card still pinched between his fingers. The boy widened his glare to show he was serious about the card.

Noah didn't repeat the threat. He simply went on looking into his son's eyes with a calm that only power can afford. The boy brought the card up closer to his face not, Noah could tell, from increased defiance but as one final test of his father's sincerity. Noah kept his face immobile.

Danny retreated even farther into the grotesque, hoping a fierce face might strike terror in his father's heart and at least equalize the contest. He bulged his eyes and opened his mouth to bare the scalloped line of his tiny white teeth. Sucking in air, he made an inverted hiss like a spitting cat. Then he gave in. He lowered his eyes and put the card onto the discard pile.

Anne picked it up.

Noah stared at his hands, pressing them deeper between his legs, hunching his back and drawing his shoulders forward. He would have done it. He would have taken the bone in his two hands and snapped it. He knew he could make the break with no difficulty at all, so frail did he know his son's arm to be. A firm grip, and snap. Not even a cracking sound, just a snap. A quick little chirping snap like the bone of a bird.

Noah could see Danny's face. No fear or even pain, no horror at all. Just bewilderment. Bewilderment that his father should have done this thing to him. Noah saw him look from the dangled arm into his father's eyes, then at the arm again, puzzled, unable to understand.

Then the actual pain began to rise, a single shaft let loose, about to shatter its way into the brain. Then the cry would come, still not a cry of pain. A cry of knowledge. He would know now what had been done to him and who had done it. His father had done it. Noah, his father, had done it.

Noah got up from the bed. He went to the closet and opened the door. He shoved aside the hangers on the rack that held his after-work and Sunday clothes, his corduroy suit and the herringbone jacket he'd bought the winter before last. His fingers worked along the crossbar, flicking away his woolen shirts, his heavy mackinaw. There was no nightgown, he could tell there wasn't.

He clicked past Ruth's red woolen suit and a bright yellow blouse, slowing when he came to the green linen maternity dress that dated back to Anne, then moving slower still when he saw the gray-blue and the dark maroon she'd worn for Joel. He stopped completely when he came to the pink that had been her best for all three pregnancies. He looked at it, then worked his way back to the green linen.

Almost feverishly he yanked it off the hanger and slipped it over his head like a man about to be discovered naked in some compromising place. Quickly he smoothed it down over his thighs, breathing heavily as if from some great exertion. Then he became calm. He'd rescued himself just in time. He was safe.

But safe from what? He sat on the bottom edge of the bed and looked at himself in the mirror on the closet door. There he was, wearing Ruth's lime-green linen maternity dress. It was sleeveless and fitted high around the neck. He hadn't zipped it up the back so there was no pull in the shoulders. The front bunched out, his shirt underneath not quite filling the space provided for Ruth's swelling breasts. His lap was layered with wide folds of stiff green, his huge hands resting quietly among its ridges like beasts tamed by the peace of their surroundings.

If he didn't look so absurd, he'd be disgusting. Still, his feelings were not unpleasant. But he had no idea where the satisfaction came from. He took off the dress, then put it on again, working the cloth slowly down over his shirt, over his pants, trying to trace its effects. He felt a hint that he was becoming invisible. Some kind of obliteration was going on, but it was nothing he could get a hold on with any certainty.

Then his head emerged and he saw himself in the mirror again, as silly as before. *Invisible* was obviously not the right word. Never had he been more evident.

He turned his head away from the mirror, then quickly back, as if to see if his image was still there. It was. Undeniably. He stared at himself. The expression on his face was one of calm appraisal, a judgment of the dress's size and style, his look not much different from the one he'd seen when he bought his raincoat the previous Easter. If anything, he seemed to be hedging toward approval.

Anne knocked at the bedroom door, timidly. "Daddy?" she called softly.

Still looking at himself in the mirror, Noah answered the one way he knew would stop her from opening the door. "I'm getting ready for bed." There was no panic in his voice. What he was feeling now was a quiet bewilderment.

Danny laughed at the absurdity of what his father had said. "It's not time for bed."

"You won the game," Anne said.

Danny intensified the news by making it sound like a surprise. "You won the game!"

"When I added it up —" Anne began, but Danny interrupted, again raising the pitch of their tidings. "She added it up!"

". . . it turned out you got five hundred and three."

"She made a mistake before." Danny laughed again as if error was always an amusement.

"So you're the one won." Now Anne herself managed a light laugh.

Noah said nothing. He raised a hand slowly to his chest, feeling the texture of the linen, trying to convince himself that he was actually wearing the dress. His fingers moved back and forth on the fabric like the lazy scratch of an old itch.

No sound came through the door until Anne said, "I didn't have hardly any points at all and neither did Danny."

Noah knew from the rising waver in her voice that she was pleading for her lie to be believed, that he must answer her and save her from the shame of her deceit.

Shame was what Noah felt himself, but not because he was wearing his wife's dress. He'd begun to forget he had it on. He was ashamed that his children should feel the need to woo him with flatteries and with lies. He was ashamed to think that he himself might have made it a stipulation of his love, and, worst of all, he was ashamed that they would so abjectly and so needfully give in.

Before Noah could speak, he heard the clumping and shuffling of shoes on the floor just outside the door. "Doodle-doodle-doodle, bam-bam. Doodle-doodle-doodle, bam-bam. Wheh-wheh-wheh." It would be Danny flailing his arms and stomping his feet, declaring an intermission, after which, refreshed and regrouped, he and Anne might take up again their faltering campaign to get their father back downstairs with them.

"Doodle-doodle-doodle —"

Through the noise, Noah heard Anne softly ask, "You ready for bed yet?" He was about to call out the hearty "Almost" that would give him time to take off the dress when there was a thud against the door followed by Anne's "Stop it!"

"Wheh-wheh-wheh —"

Noah stood up, pulled the dress over his head and thrust it in among the clothes jammed on the closet rack. Another thud, this one against the wall, still the stomping and singing. What had started as an entertainment was now a taunt, Danny's silliness aimed now at Anne, mocking and ridiculing her for her hypocrisy and her lies.

"All *right!*" It was Anne appropriating her mother's phrase, her mother's intonation, a proclamation that all patience had come to an end and that the consequences would no longer be her responsibility.

Just as Noah was about to open the bedroom door, it was crashed aside and Danny came stumbling backwards against his father's stomach. Before the boy could spring forward, Noah reached his arms around him to stay the rebound. Anne, in the same instant, flung herself against her brother, grabbing at his face.

Danny shot out a fist that was collapsed back against himself by the force of Anne's rush.

Noah widened the circle of his arms to include his daughter. Too closed-in to swing their fists, the children continued to nudge each other with blunted punches, squirming in their father's hold.

Because his arms were occupied, Noah lowered his head to come between them, to try to separate them from each other even as he held them. Down in their midst, he caught the scent of Danny's hair, a musty sweetness as if some sticky candy had been decomposing in its wilds for at least a week. And from Anne the clean smell of Palmolive soap and the sour bubblings that Joel had deposited on her T-shirt earlier that evening.

Danny's fist knocked against his father's cheekbone and Anne boxed Noah's right ear. Then they stopped. Noah raised his head, scraping the bristle of his chin against Danny's arm.

Now that the wiggling had ended, Noah could feel the beat and pulse of his children's blood, an unsynchronized tapping against him, broken and hectic rhythms like the heart's equivalent of chattering teeth. Their heaving breath strained against his arms, contracted, then strained again. Stiffly they drew back their heads as if getting them into position so Noah could easily knock them against each other as no doubt he would.

Noah knew he should say "That's enough of that" in the gruff voice that was standard for a situation like this. But he wanted simply to stand there, holding them, feeling the quick chatter of their blood, their breath straining against him. Or he wanted to bow his head again into the midst of his flailing children and catch again the scent of soap, the sweetening must, the trace of sour vomit, and take to his cheek, to his chest, to himself, the fury of all their blows.

Anne leaned her head against him, too weary to do battle any more. In the voice that asks to be told a story or sung a lullaby, a voice too careworn to plead, she said, "Come play cards with us, will you, Dad?"

Noah agreed.

Downstairs two more games of rummy were played. After the baby had fallen asleep in his crib and Danny and Anne had gone quietly to bed, Noah picked up around the living room, washed the coffee cup and the Coke glasses, read a little in Anne's science book from last year, savoring the delay until he would go upstairs again where he knew the dress was waiting.

15

OLD Dr. Corrado had all but disappeared into the upper branches of the apple tree. Noah held onto the ladder just above the fourth rung and pressed it hard against the trunk of the tree so the doctor wouldn't fall. Level with his eyes were the bright orange socks Ruth had mentioned.

Because the doctor always wore a black suit — wool in winter, poplin in summer — he was like a mutant of the red-winged blackbird with the russet band now relegated to the ankle instead of the wing. As he worked his way up among the branches, the quick colored flash came and went like a signal, but a signal of what Noah couldn't guess. He wasn't sure in the case of either the blackbird or of Dr. Corrado whether the orange was meant to warn off or to attract, whether it was an outbreak of vanity or a mechanism for survival. He considered it could be all four and that his dealing with the doctor was supposed to take each into account. This did little to bolster his already wavering courage.

He tried to listen to what the doctor was saying, something about its being against the nature of the apple to be marketed in any unit less than the bushel. But Noah couldn't concentrate. Were the orange socks Dr. Corrado's equivalent of the dresses? Had he somehow been able to reduce an aberrant compulsion down to an acceptable eccentricity? The socks were said to lend the doctor personality and charm, a potential disgrace distilled to a quaint characteristic.

Perhaps the doctor would give Noah the necessary prescription and the dresses could be set aside in favor of, say, a certain kind of baseball cap to be worn at all times and in all places (backward no doubt), or a belt of exotic substance with an elaborate buckle depicting the burning of Nome, Alaska. Or a pair of orange socks. Anything that would achieve the effect the dresses achieved, but without the attendant threat of shame and dishonor.

If Noah could not be relieved of the impulse, then let the impulse at least be given a form more acceptable both to himself and to the world in which he had to live. The idea of a yellow baseball cap with blue piping and visor had a momentary appeal but it was nothing he could get a firm hold on.

He'd mention all this to Dr. Corrado when he brought up the subject of the dresses. Maybe the socks indicated that the doctor would be sympathetic, even knowing. Perhaps this was what they signaled and Noah had interpreted the signal correctly. But he had no way of being sure.

The doctor moved up a step, then another. He was standing on the top rung of the ladder, completely lost among the upper branches. The socks were out of sight and Noah began to hear what Dr. Corrado was saying. His voice trembled with both age and indignation. "Whoever heard of buying six apples at a time, or four? That's for oranges, not for apples. The apple is the first bounty of the earth. It cannot be doled out in numbers. It has to be by the basketful. It's even wrong to sell them by the pound. A pound is too small a measure for the apple."

Noah had asked Dr. Corrado for a special appointment. For the past week, at least once a day, he had worn one of Ruth's maternity dresses. At first he wore the dress only in the bedroom, usually at night. Then he ventured out into the upstairs hallway after the children were in bed. Once he'd gone into each of their rooms to watch them sleep. Two nights ago he wore one downstairs when he went to the kitchen and ate a hard-boiled egg. He'd eaten the egg right there at the kitchen table, sprinkling it with salt and pepper, with the light on, wearing the pink serge that had been Ruth's best from the time she was pregnant with Anne.

On one level, putting the dresses on worked. He'd become calm, he did his carpentry with concentration, even with some of the old pleasures. Wood had become buoyant again. He'd forgotten how light wood was, how working with it could lift the spirit. He was content to be at home in the evenings with Anne and Danny and Joel, enjoying them again, available to the wonders and surprises they never failed to bring, amused and moved by their intense little bodies wiggling and working their way from the day into the night.

He no longer had sneezing fits on his way home from his visits to Ruth.

And memory had become bearable. Throughout his life with Ruth he thought he had been having experiences that it would some day please him to remember. They would nourish him and sustain him. But a trick had been played. Each experience had been transformed not to nourishment but to stone. What he'd been gathering to himself, even hoarding, were stones, stones of sorrow, each burden proportionate to a previous joy, weighing him down.

The dresses did not reverse the transformation nor did they dissolve his bitterness. A trick had still been played and he drew no sustenance from stones. But in his new-found patience he could appreciate the perfection of the ploy, its symmetry and balance, and his own complicity. Noah Dubbins, ardent and gullible collector of stones.

And with the dresses he seemed able to control his urge to see Esther Overbaugh. He was, in plain fact, coping. He was doing exactly what he'd pledged to do when Ruth got sick. He was holding his family together and he was staying faithful to his wife.

On another level he saw some problems. The dresses were, to say the least, a departure from his usual conduct. They could mean he was cracking up. Except that he had been cracking up before he started wearing them. Now he seemed fine.

But who would believe him? Who would accept him in one of Ruth's dresses? No one. He couldn't accept it himself. (It might amuse Ruth if she was well, but only up to a point. Then she'd probably begin to wonder.) But it would frighten his children, scandalize his neighbors, sicken his friends and give Blanche the perfect reason to take the children from him. Maybe he hadn't gone Greek, but he'd certainly gone peculiar.

The decision to talk to Dr. Corrado had been made just the night before. Noah had gone outside to Ruth's garden, in the dark, to dig around the roots of the beans. He was wearing Ruth's blue-gray dress, the one with the three-quarter sleeves. He knew the garden by heart, where the cabbages were, where the beans began and the tomatoes ended, where the green peppers were, and the basil, the carrots and the beets.

Shadowed by the back of the house rising behind him, he moved slowly forward, like a blind man, the wide skirt brushing the tops of the plants as he dug with a trowel in the soft earth, turning it, breaking the clumps with his fingers, the only sound the slow fall of the soil or the light chink when he hit a stone, or the rustle of his hands down among the plants, the brush of the dress against the leaves.

When he reached the end of the row, he stood up straight, not moving, the trowel held down at his side. He could see the outline of the trees along the river and the rise of the stable roof against the sky. He was listening. He was waiting for the sound of branches snapping. What he heard was the traffic on the distant highway sounding like surf, far off. A night plane blinked and winked its way across the sky, trying in the most outrageous way to catch the attention of the stars.

Then Noah heard a stirring near the catalpa tree. He looked but could see nothing in the dark. The stirring stopped. Still he listened and waited. Then he realized he was standing there waiting for the deer. His coming to the garden had been an invitation, an enticement, for the deer to return, to come again. It was the deer to whom he would make his appeal. It was to the deer that he would address all his perplexities. And it would be from the deer that he would receive the revelations that would reconcile him to the mysteries that were rising up all around him.

Noah continued to listen, to stare toward the trees. Then he dropped the trowel and went inside. He'd made up his mind to talk to Dr. Corrado first thing in the morning.

Dr. Corrado said he'd meet him in the dining room at Mount St. Michael. They would have some coffee together and talk about whatever it was Noah wanted to talk about. When Noah got there, the doctor was at the serving table scowling at a baked apple. He was wearing his inevitable black suit and a pale blue shirt with cuff links that were replicas of an old Roman coin. His necktie was a design of maroon shapes on a field of dark blue like a microscope slide of paramecia swimming in a dark fluid, commemorative perhaps of his early days in medical school.

In a rare concession to the August day, the doctor's suit coat was open and the tie swayed over the baked apple like a divining rod uncertain of the presence of whatever it was supposed to locate. Dr. Corrado reached twice for the baked apple and twice pulled back.

Noah saw the cuff link, the face on the coin. It had the same high forehead as Dr. Corrado, the same well-angled nose, the same generously formed mouth, the same dip between the lower lip and the pointed jaw. It could be Dr. Corrado twenty-five years younger, before time had hollowed his cheeks and sunk his eyes deep into his skull. There were other differences too. The man on the coin seemed wearied, resigned and indomitable; Dr. Corrado himself was animated, frantic and humane. It was as though time had taken, along with his empire, his repose and had given him in its place, in his seventy-sixth year, the energy and anguish of youth. He had been changed from a monarch to a crone. Maybe Dr. Corrado wore the cuff links to remind himself of the good old days when he was younger, more dignified and didn't wear orange socks.

When Noah shook his hand the doctor let out a slight "Ah!" as if a small broken bone had been dislocated by Noah's grip. Noah was about to apologize when the doctor, waving a dismissal over the baked apple, said, "Let's get out of here. I know something better."

On their way to the orchard, Dr. Corrado began his harangue about apples. It was late summer, why hadn't the price gone down? He was almost hoarse with derision. Noah thought he'd let Dr. Corrado finish what he had to say before he'd mention the dresses.

In the shed Dr. Corrado rummaged fiercely through the stacked baskets, half-bushels, looking for the sturdiest one, preferably with two handles and unsplintered sides. He told Noah he could take the apples home for the children. He'd give him a recipe for apple butter. He chose a basket with only one handle but perfect in every other way except for a few dried leaves caught in the weave at the bottom. Dr. Corrado carried the basket; Noah carried the ladder.

In the orchard, Dr. Corrado chose himself to climb the tree. Noah would stay on the ground and steady the ladder. When Noah started to protest, Dr. Corrado reared his head back and stared at him, unable to believe he was about to be opposed. Up he went, taking the basket with him, discoursing on non-apples, apple-shaped produce that was meant to simulate the real apple and stimulate a memory of what an apple had tasted like. There he was, pulling the fruit from the branches as if he were milking the tree, and still Noah had said nothing about the dresses.

Noah's first fear was that at the least mention of the dresses, Dr. Corrado would begin proceedings to have the children taken away from him. If that were the case, Noah would simply silence him with a single blow to the head. Or maybe fall to his knees and beg for another chance. He wasn't sure which.

Next came not so much a fear as a vision. He would say the word *dress* and Dr. Corrado, before Noah could continue would throw up his hands and scream "Aaaaah!" like a movie spinster scared by a mouse. Then Noah himself, panicked by the "Aaaaaah!" would scream too. This would further terrify Dr. Corrado who would scream again, sending the two of them off in opposite directions, hands raised high over their heads, screaming, running as if each was being pursued by his own separate mouse.

Noah heard the scrape of leaf against leaf and the crack of a twig as the branches were tugged downward, then released as the apple let go. It was the sound of a restless bird worrying the branches, distressing the leaves.

"When was the last time you saw a worm in an apple?" Dr. Corrado asked. "It's almost unheard of. All the spraying, all the cultivation. Tell me, just tell me, when was the last time you had an apple and you took a bite and there was a worm in it? I'll bet you never did. Not someone your age."

Noah didn't want to answer. He wanted Dr. Corrado to come down from the tree and calm himself. All morning Noah had had the feeling he was being held off by a barrage of words, that Dr. Corrado was not just energetic but hysterical, afraid that Noah might ask or say something he didn't want to hear. Could he have guessed about the dresses?

"No," Noah said, "I don't remember any worms." Dr. Corrado, satisfied, said nothing. The time had come to mention the dresses. Noah stepped back from the ladder and lifted his head up toward the tree as if preparing to address some god dwelling in its branches.

"Doctor —"

No sooner had Noah said the word than he heard the cry, "Aaaaaah!" The ladder began to wobble. Another loud "Aaaaah!" came crying out from the upper branches. Noah reached over to steady the ladder but his arm brushed against the vertical support and pitched it sideways. Instinctively Noah raised both arms to catch Dr. Corrado, now looking as if he were intensifying his supplication to the god up in the tree.

But no Dr. Corrado fell. Instead a hailstorm of apples came pelting down onto Noah's head, onto his shoulders, onto his arms. One hit him on the forehead, another on the right cheek. When he was hit on the mouth, he closed his eyes.

Still he heard no Dr. Corrado fall. When the last apple bounced off Noah's ear and all was silent, he opened his eyes. There were the orange socks and the black shoes swaying in front of him like those of a man hanged. Dr. Corrado was holding onto a branch, trying to work his way hand-over-hand toward the trunk of the tree.

"Just let go. It's not that far," Noah called up to him. Dr. Corrado let go, releasing the branch. Like the spring of a catapult, it sent down another bombardment of apples, and the basket too. Then came the doctor, passing before Noah's eyes — his legs, torso, shoulders, head — his jacket and his tie flaring up like an unopened parachute — then the arms, the hands grasping the air. The doctor had landed among the apples and they kept rolling out from under him.

Noah grabbed him by the arms and tried to yank him toward himself to keep him from falling. They wrestled, the two of them, each trying to balance the other. Noah clutched the sleeves of the doctor's coat and Dr. Corrado dug into Noah's shirt trying to hook his fingers into an opening between his ribs.

After dragging each other almost down to the ground, shouting brave encouragements, and pulling each other back up with desperate shoves and tugs, they managed to steady themselves. Noah was looking into Dr. Corrado's eyes. The man was terrified. It was as though in his descent from the tree he had seen some terrible truth that he must try to keep from Noah. Noah let go of the sleeves and the doctor released his fingers from Noah's ribs. Dr. Corrado drew his opened hands away only a few inches and held them there as if asking Noah to keep a distance between them.

"Doctor, I —" Noah wasn't sure if he was about to apologize for letting go of the ladder or whether he was going to mention the dresses, but the doctor stopped him before he could start.

"Your wife is mad," the doctor said, his anguish as immediate as if Ruth's insanity had at that moment been revealed to him, on his way down from the tree. "She may always be mad. What do you expect me to do?" He started backing away as if begging Noah not to hit him, not to hurt him more than he was hurt already. "She could be insane the rest of her life. I don't know. I don't know anything. Everyone else, they know. They know everything. They know about drugs and chemicals and shock treatments. They know about snakes and charms and saints that cure. But I, I don't know about anything. I swear to you I don't."

What had been terror now became despair. "And the worst is, I'm the best there is. I say it to you in all modesty. If I can't help her, no one can. I'm doing the best I know how, but more than that I cannot, I cannot tell you. Except to say the words, the words we all use. But are they the right ones? Maybe you can tell me. You know her better than I do."

"What words?" Noah asked. He wanted to hear them. He

thought maybe one of them might be an identifying sound, a word with the power to hold "Ruth" in its meaning. Then he would know the word and could have some means of possessing her. If, in her madness, she was no longer "Ruth," maybe there was a new word that would define her or summon her as the word "Ruth" had summoned her to his mind the day he'd read it on the flyleaf of Willa Cather's *O Pioneers!* "What are they?" he said.

Dr. Corrado started with *schizophrenic* and worked his way through *postpartum depression* and kept right on going. By now he was pelting the words at Noah like accusations, like a series of indictments for crimes she'd committed. None of them could Noah apply to Ruth. Never could she be any of the things the doctor was saying she was. She was still who she was.

"Unhinged! Deranged!" the doctor, in his despair, called out.

Noah listened to it all. It seemed a series of horrible vilifications directed at his wife, like blows upon her body, like lashings across her face, her eyes.

Noah must have made a move toward Dr. Corrado because the doctor held up his hand to warn him to come no farther, to get no closer.

"She's mad!" he said. "She's crazy. Insane! Don't you understand?" He backed off some more, stumbling on the apples, struggling to keep his balance. "Crackers! Cuckoo!" With each stumble he blurted out another word. "Daft! Nuts! Loony!" He began waving his arms, not just to catch his balance, but to shoo Noah off as if he were a wayward chicken. "Unbalanced!" he screamed, then turned and ran down the slope toward the manor.

"Oh yeah?" Noah shouted after him. "She's Ruth! You hear that? Ruth!" He picked up an apple and threw it at Dr. Corrado but missed. The doctor, without looking back, continued his dash down the hill, his arms flung out, his jacket flying out behind him, his necktie flapping over his shoulder in a wave good-bye.

With each call of the name, Noah threw another apple. "Ruth! Ruth, godammit, she's Ruth!"

Dr. Corrado's bright orange socks flickered in the grass like licks of fire poking at his feet, making him run.

"Ruth! Ruth!" Noah kept yelling until his voice broke. Then he dropped to his knees and said the word one more time — "Ruth?" — looking down at the ground as if searching for her hidden among the apples.

16

AFTER Noah had guided the van onto the shortcut that led toward the town of Sharon, his conscience left him. It simply dropped away as if an iron ball he'd been wearing around his neck had fallen off into a convenient abyss. Its last trace was a vague question, whether the weight had been a mark of bondage or a talisman worn for protection. But it no longer mattered. His conscience was gone and he had no wish to get it back.

Away from the lighted highway he could see the night sky through the black trees that arched out over the road and he could feel beneath the wheels the stones and sudden potholes of the crumbling asphalt. Up and around the barbed wire that fenced off the woods sprang an underbrush of young trees, maple, birch, and pin oak. Ignoring the wire barbs, they spilled out toward the road, brushing the side of the van, wishing Noah well and trying to bring him luck.

Noah was bent on seduction. The seduction of Esther Overbaugh. He'd made up his mind that afternoon during his visit to Ruth. For the past week he'd been trying with all his might not to wear her dresses. He'd succeeded, but without their calming influence he found himself at the mercy of other impulses he could do without. His visits to Ruth, especially since the afternoon of the nightgown, made him sexually desperate. He had vowed fidelity, yet the impossibility of making love to his wife had thrown him back into his old adolescent panic when he had been so afraid he might *never* be with a woman that he retaliated with a determination to be with one at any cost.

Determination, of course, was not synonymous with achievement. And here again he was thrust back to his youth. Was he going to be successful or was he going to fail? With Esther there should be no doubt of success, but then why was he so worried? He tried to reassure himself. He thought of the last time he'd seen her, when she was brushing something from her shoulder just outside the kitchen door in the bar. He picked his way through memories of her high school comforts. But it did very little good. For all the reassurances he gave himself, he still asked — like the boy he'd been — would he win the yearned-for prize or would disgrace and humiliation be heaped upon his head like a scattering of dung and ashes?

He even had an image of himself: his shoulders hunched to support chunks and clumps of hardened cowpie, flakes of it shot through with undigested straw strewn into his hair, the just reward for a man so bold, so needful that he would dare to think he could seduce Esther Overbaugh; Esther Overbaugh who had never heard of such a thing; Esther Overbaugh appalled at the very idea; Esther Overbaugh stunned, then horrified, then rising up in rage and wrath, reaching for the miraculously handy dung and ashes placed nearby on a table that resembled, to Noah's mind, the one used at high school graduation for the athletic trophies and the music awards.

The van bounced off a rock torn up out of the ruined road, then lifted off the edge of a pothole as if it were about to pole-vault its way to Sharon. He'd put too much air in the tires. No, he'd picked up too much speed and had better slow down. But his panic wouldn't let him. And besides, he'd just felt a nudge of conscience, a hint of wrong against both his wife and Esther too, a possibility of guilt and remorse, the weight beginning to materialize again around his neck.

On he sped, now through unhedged fields and under a wide sky. Apparently the acceleration helped. The weight dropped away again before it could take on substance. It had been jolted right out of his psyche by the tumult of bewildered lust and adolescent panic.

It wasn't that Noah had no conscience to begin with, nor was it that his sexuality was unsubjected to moral scrutiny. He was not avoiding judgment nor was he squelching scruples. It was just that he simply couldn't contain need, determination, panic, and conscience all at the same time. And since need, determination and panic couldn't be separated, since they were an indissoluble unity, it was conscience that was crowded out, not by choice but by nature, not in considered defiance of the moral law but in helpless subscription to the law of nature. Conscience would have its moment. But later, when his psyche would be less cluttered. Nothing was going to cancel his decision of that afternoon.

He and Ruth had been playing Ping-Pong in the gym. Noah began having sexual fantasies he could do nothing about. He was being careful, in the game, not to hit the ball too hard, and Ruth was returning it with even greater care, both of them playing as if the object of the game was not to best an opponent but to keep the ball moving back and forth without interruption. Ruth was wearing her coat and what she had on underneath Noah had no idea.

That bothered him enough, but even more were the calls and shouts from a basketball game at the far end of the gym behind him. They bounded and rebounded off the walls and rafters, sporadic eruptions that began to sound as if the players were actually spectators at some turbulent sexual display and in their stirred-up state were calling out to each other to witness the cause of their excitement.

One on top of the other the calls would mount, then mumblingly withdraw only to build again, straining to a higher cry of disbelief and arousal. Some sounded as though the demonstration was almost unbearable in its provocations and they were begging for release; others sounded as though they were caught up so completely that they had abandoned themselves to a blind rush toward their own disintegration.

Then would come another respite of mumbling, of murmurs being slowly, then suddenly heated. Now the shouts would come, the cries and calls as if the players were at the same time fending off and yet urging forward an inexorable climax.

Noah kept the careful Ping-Pong volley going. He wanted to turn around but he didn't. Perhaps the metronomic rhythm of the Ping-Pong ball would calm him.

But then he hit harder than he'd intended and Ruth missed. She put her paddle down as though that finished the game. She looked up at the gymnasium windows, tracing with her eyes the pattern of the protective mesh as if preparing a judgment on its design.

Noah went and put the paddle into her hand and gave her the ball. He looked at the far end of the gym. He was too late. The basketball game was over and the players were busy toweling their hair. He should have looked sooner. He'd missed it all.

"You serve," he said.

Ruth looked across the net, down the length of the table, then up again at the windows. Noah went back and carefully took the ball from her, then served from his side. One of the basketball players called out words Noah couldn't understand. Others yelled back what sounded like agreement, an enthusiastic concurrence in the merits of what they'd witnessed.

"Ruth? Ready?"

It was only after his third serve that Ruth returned the ball and another volley was begun. Noah played with forced attention, the ball going back and forth, back and forth, back and forth. Now it seemed to him that he and Ruth were teasing the ball, testing its endurance and its patience, that they were being cruel and malevolent. He deliberately missed and pretended dismay over his clumsiness.

The ball rolled under the table back to Ruth's side. She stared down at it, then crushed it under her sandal. Looking over at Noah, she said, "I didn't want it to get all over my coat."

On the way back to the manor they walked side by side, not touching. The elms thrust themselves up over the path, putting them into a welcome shade. Noah reached down and pulled up a weed. It squeaked as it slipped out of the rooted stalk. He twirled it between his fingers, watching the whirl of its tiny wheat-like shoots, more like feathers than kernels of grain. He put the stem into his mouth between his front teeth. He wanted to go back to the gym, to see what the basketball players had seen.

Ruth hadn't paused and now she was a few paces ahead. Noah took the weed from his mouth and reached it out so that its tip brushed against her neck just below the right ear. She kept on walking, without the slightest reflex to show that she felt anything at all.

Noah gave the weed a slight twist so that the feathery seeds spun off her skin, then touched again like a pesky insect. Ruth acknowledged nothing. Noah withdrew the weed a little and lifted it higher so that the tip lay just inside her ear. He turned the stem so it would stir slightly. When Ruth gave no response, he stirred the weed again and waited, keeping just behind her.

When he saw her raise her head just a little, not, it seemed, to free herself from the torment of the weed but to accept it more completely, he stopped walking and stood where he was. Ruth went on alone and Noah watched her go, the dappled light of the sun through the elms falling soundlessly against the back of her camouflage coat like soft blows that she readily bore. One sandal strap had come loose.

So that he would not throw himself face-down on the path and tear up, with his teeth, with his mouth, the stones and the earth, he let the weed fall from his hand. After it had touched the ground he decided he'd better go to bed with Esther Overbaugh.

17

Noah wanted to flop over onto his back and rest, but when he tried to draw away, Esther didn't raise her shoulder, so he had to pull hard to get his hand out from under her. It was like drawing a cork from a bottle and when the hand *did* come free, Noah's whole left arm shot out, banging his knuckles against the wall near the bed.

His right hand came free after three quick tugs, the final one forcing him to grunt. Esther neither moved nor spoke. As if getting ready to do push-ups Noah braced his flattened hands against the mattress, stiffened his arms and raised himself, suspending his body over her like a sheltering canopy. The air cooled his chest, and he could feel the matted hairs uncoil from his flesh one by one like sprung wires.

He raised his head and stretched it back, moving it from side to side, hearing the cartilage in his neck crinkle like cellophane. He was about to lower himself a little so he could roll over onto his side when he realized he wasn't quite free. His left ankle was twisted down under Esther's right foot. Noah thought of asking her to lift it but he didn't feel like speaking just yet. And besides, he didn't consider it appropriate for that to be the first thing he'd say. He didn't want to hurt Esther's feelings.

Actually, he didn't want to rouse any emotions in her whatsoever. He would have been pleased if she remained what she seemed to be at that moment, an inert conformation of pillowing flesh hardly visible in the light that spilled from her kitchen two rooms away. Silence, Noah hoped, would indicate ecstasy tamed to a contentment beyond speech.

Slowly he lowered himself back onto her and gently brushed his nose against her neck so she wouldn't think he'd forgotten her. Esther languorously tilted her head toward him as if trying to clamp his nose between her jaw and her collarbone. Noah escaped by letting his nose seek out the nest of her ear, scratching itself along the way on the tiny prongs of a metal and glass earring that had been set into the lobe like the replica of a scab.

He rested his nose inside the bowl where the wax one turn deeper into the whorl gave off an odor of chocolate. It was a comfortable smell and Noah decided to take a brief respite before trying to get his left ankle out from under Esther's right foot. He liked having his nose tucked away for a little bit. It meant they had gone the distance from the passionate to the cozy.

He didn't feel guilty. Apparently his rationale for being with Esther was valid enough for even his unconscious to endorse the adultery. After all, he'd done it for the sake of his children and for the sake of his wife Ruth.

His nose still tucked into Esther's ear, his left ankle still trapped under her right foot, Noah lay quiet a moment then said, "Esther?" His warm breath returned to him from under the hollow beneath her jaw.

The voice that answered was firm. "Don't go falling in love with me."

Noah's impulse was to take his nose out of her ear and say, "Don't worry, I won't," but he felt that simple courtesy required that his assurance be not too quick and not quite so much at the ready.

To fill in the time until it might be polite to give her the promise she'd demanded, he repeated the original whisper, "Esther," only this time he put an "oh" in front of it to distinguish it from the first time he'd said it.

"Don't go falling in love with me I told you!" As she spoke, her moving jaw created a corresponding movement inside her ear so that it seemed the tip of his nose was being munched on.

As if in obedience to her injunction Noah pulled himself away completely, using the roughness allowed to the rejected to free his ankle, and the abruptness permitted to the disappointed to slide his nose out of her ear and bury it in the pillow at her side.

His left arm still lay across her breasts. He'd wait for one more warning, certain it would come. Then he could draw the arm home to his side and, after a respectful moment or two, get up, get dressed and leave without being confronted with his own real lack of feeling.

Esther couldn't have been more helpful. She was allowing him to present his indifference as restraint. He could leave quickly with some little show of reluctance and it would seem like a forlorn retreat from a battle he had been decreed by Esther herself never to win.

He kept his arm in position, waiting. His hand fell limply down the slope of her far breast; his wrist lay over the nipple. He could feel his pulse, slow and measured, pressing the tip, releasing it, pressing it again, as if enjoying some erotic play on its own.

Afraid the pulse might start sending messages through the blood that would complicate the present simplicities, Noah began slowly to draw his arm to his side. But just as the palm of his hand was sliding across the mound of her breast, Esther placed her own hand on top, staying its retreat.

Without applying any pressure, she kept it there. "Don't feel bad," she said. "It's just I can tell when somebody's falling in love with me." Her voice was low and there was a note of complaint, of annoyance that she was so continually subjected to what she considered an inconvenience, men falling in love with her.

Noah turned his face away from her, not just to get his nose out of the pillow but to get off by himself so he could think a little. Where did Esther get the idea he was falling in love with her? Had his performance been so superior that she had mistaken it for the real thing, for actual love?

Noah was pleased. It had never occurred to him in all his days and nights with Ruth that he was, without having known it, a great lover, that his marriage and his easy fidelity had robbed the world of his unique offerings, and that he had selfishly confined gifts that belonged more rightfully if not to the world at large at least to the women in and around Mattysborough, Damora and greater Keene.

His vanity swelled and just as he was about to consider some specifics that might support this new theory, Esther reached over and put a hand on his shoulder. "It's just I don't like to see people suffer," she said. "All you guys, just because I like you doesn't mean it's okay for you to go and fall in love with me."

She began to rub and caress his shoulder, perhaps to mitigate the harshness of her accusation against all you guys. "I should have warned you before, but I was afraid maybe you'd think I was conceited even thinking such a thing, that you were probably going to fall in love with me. But I should have warned you anyway. What you think of me, if you think I'm conceited or not, it doesn't matter just so long as you don't fall in love with me."

Hers, then, were the unique offerings, not his.

She kissed his shoulder and moved her hand up into his hair, letting her stubby fingers spread out like forest creatures foraging for seeds and nuts. Her nose was against his neck and she began to whisper, "Promise me you're not going to fall in love with me. Okay?"

She put one leg up over his thigh and pulled herself closer to him. Her lips were rubbing up and down against his ear as she spoke. "If you promise, I'll let you again."

Noah didn't answer. Her arm was down across his stomach as he lay on his side and she gave him a quick jerk toward her as if to force out a reply. "Okay? You want to? Again?" She jerked him one more time, a squeeze that almost made him gasp.

"I don't think I'd better," said Noah, setting his whisper at the same ardent pitch as hers. He started to shift toward the edge of the bed so he could get up, but Esther held him that much tighter, clamping her leg even more securely across his thigh. Her right hand moved up to his chest where it could press firmly against the breastbone. Her left hand began to emerge, fingers first, from his hair. Noah wondered if she was going to get a grip on his eye sockets.

She kissed him behind the ear then pulled away as if afraid to let her lips pause against his flesh. "Promise me is all you got to do." To stifle a whimper, she put her mouth against his neck, pressing her lips hard against the tendon that stretched down from his ear. Then she pulled his whole body closer as if for no other purpose than to stop herself from saying more. Sounds still came as she repeated the words, "Promise, promise, promise," stifled but desperate to be heard whatever the obstacle.

"I promise," Noah heard himself say, his voice low as if he were taking a solemn vow.

With a long sigh, Esther took her mouth off his neck, lifted her leg away from his thigh, raised her hand from his chest and took her fingers from his forehead. She collapsed backwards onto her side of the bed like a weight relieved of itself.

A sense of deepest loss came over Noah. The pledge he'd given to Esther was something he had no right to give. He told himself that all he'd done was promise not to fall in love with her, but this did nothing to lift his sorrow. It was the depth of the promise, the totality of it, that made it wrong. A pledge that complete should be made only to Ruth.

The promise itself was incidental; it counted for nothing. What did count was the coupling of his own profound response with Esther's anguished need to hear him say those words. He wanted to get up, go home, but his sorrow made it impossible for him to move, as if Esther had extracted from him his strength as well as his pledge.

"All you guys," he heard her say, "just because I try to be nice." She then began to list the reasons why men fell in love with her. She had what they wanted. She owned the place. She worked like an ox. She had two cars. There was also something about her having gone to school in Massachusetts, grades five through seven.

Her enthusiasm grew as she spoke, her wonder expanding with each new example as if she'd find such excellence impossible to believe if she hadn't witnessed it with her own two eyes. She was ninth generation. She read books, the thick kind.

As she went on, Noah's sorrow began to lift. It was as if her enthusiasm was infectious or her chronicle of achievement appealed directly to his spirit, raising it to greater and higher heights. She was telling him that she knew the secret ways of perfumes and that her taste in clothes was impeccable and enviable. Noah stopped listening to the words themselves and heard only the rising pitch pointing the way to exultation.

He was filled with joy. And he knew why. He jumped up from the bed. Something good was happening. He had no way of explaining it, but he felt something was happening to Ruth, at this moment, while he was standing there in Esther's bedroom. Ruth was getting well.

Some special grace, some sudden blessing was being given to her and she would be all right again. Noah could see her standing at the side of her bed, silhouetted against the window of her hospital room. She too had been roused by the knowledge that something fine and good was happening to her. Noah saw her turn away from the window and look at her bed. He knew she would not throw the blankets to the floor, she would not tear the sheets. She would touch the pillow gently with her open hand.

Noah was standing up straight, waiting. The light from Esther's kitchen hit against his eye, creating a blind spot. To better see his vision of Ruth, he jerked his head to the left. What he saw now was Esther's rising form, coming up from the blankets. She was kneeling on the mattress, wading heavily toward him on what looked like the stumps of her legs. She crossed to his side of the bed, still reciting her litany of the virtues that had tempted so many men to love.

"I know when I'm supposed to cry and when I'm not supposed to cry. I let myself be tickled even when I want to be by myself," she was saying. Her right knee got caught in one of the blankets and she fell forward onto her hands. "I laugh when I'm supposed to laugh because I'm understanding," she said. "I understand all about everything. There's nothing I don't understand about."

She stopped in front of him. By the soft light from the kitchen Noah could see planted in front of him her heavy form, the pink of her flesh making her look like a hairless sheep dog. She raised her head, exposing the breasts slung down between her arms like an extra set of muscled legs that couldn't quite reach the bed. Her belly swung low, brooding over the rumpled blankets. Her buttocks rose up behind, dignified and calm, like a reserve pair of breasts kept in readiness should they be needed.

As if it were a quiet flow of tears, her hair fell down along her cheeks and her eyes were looking at him, resigned and mournful, but with a fullness of love that made him catch his breath so he wouldn't have to cover his eyes.

The full vision of Ruth that Noah had expected to see, her moment of new-found grace, had been preempted. Instead he saw the sad face of Esther Overbaugh. He looked at it, then reached out and took it in his hands and drew himself toward her. He began kissing her, tumbling her sideways onto the bed.

"And I've got this great sense of humor," she said, resuming her litany. "I laugh at anything."

Noah was curled at her side, his knees against her thigh, the top of his head against her cheek. He had pulled his hands in toward his groin and had lowered his chin to his chest. But now he slowly straightened himself and pressed against her. He kissed the hair that lay along her cheek, then brushed it away and kissed the puffy flesh beneath.

"You went and did it, didn't you?" she asked.

"Yes," Noah whispered, trying to burrow his mouth down into her cheek, to sink his entire face into her flesh. Contrary to her commands, he had gone and fallen in love with Esther Overbaugh and wanted now to seep down and disappear forever in the soft welcoming flesh.

"No!" she said. "You can't! You mustn't!"

"Yes!" he whispered, "Yes!" Then he began to laugh. At first he thought it was because some gigantic joke had been played on him. Then he realized it wasn't that at all. He was laughing because, at that moment, he was beginning to fill to overflowing with a great and growing joy.

18

J EAN Thibideau stood patiently next to Noah at the old band saw that had been called back into service after the surrender of the new. She was waiting for him to finish his cutting so she could get his approval of the pieces of wood she herself had just cut with a simple coping saw. She'd been allowed into the shop to make a small corner shelf for Ruth's room at Mount St. Michael but she was not permitted the use of the power tools. Once Noah would approve the cutting she could begin nailing the pieces together.

It was, of course, against all rules and regulations for her to be there. But she had given Ruth a bud vase — with the arrangement that a single flower of the florist's choosing would arrive each day. This, Jean decided, would require a special shelf. She further decided she should make it herself, and what could be more logical than that she should make it in Ruth's husband's shop? And she'd have Ruth's husband to show her how.

Noah refused. He was not running a hobby shop. Jean never asked again. She merely came every day and either worked in the vegetable garden, saying hardly a word (it was for Ruth she was doing it) or did the laundry or straightened out the back hall or made a jambalaya and left it in the oven to be reheated. She weeded the driveway and the sidewalk and painted the deck of the front porch and the three steps leading down.

Danny and Anne hadn't noticed the fresh paint and had come running into the house, ignoring the stickiness on the bottoms of their shoes until halfway up the stairs in a race to the bathroom. Noah got most of the footprints off except those on the rug. He painted out the marks on the porch and the front steps before Jean could see the damage and decided to let her come into the shop to make the shelf.

Waiting for Noah's attention, she ran her finger along the edge of one of the pieces as if she had honed a knife and was testing it for sharpness. Thoughtfully, furrowing her forehead far beyond the need, she angled the two sections together to make sure the fit was perfect. It was. Then, softly, as if closing a book that had moved her profoundly, she folded the two sections together and examined the symmetry, again running her finger reverently along the edge she'd just sawed.

As far as Noah was concerned, she was pretentious and a fake. But still, he had to admit he liked her, grudgingly but sincerely. Of course he could do without the sex ploys and the coy tauntings. After all, he wasn't completely unsusceptible. But he liked her. She was usually cheerful and she put on a good show. He often wondered which came first, the blithe manner or the seemingly vacant attitudes behind it. His guess was that the manner came first and the attitudes after. This, in turn, had made her outspoken. Not necessarily honest, merely outspoken. A thing was said not because it was the truth or because it expressed what she really felt; it was said because it was daring, contrary or unexpected.

And who was to say whether this created Jean was inferior to the original? Given a choice, both Noah and Ruth opted for the Jean that was. They knew themselves the beneficiaries of the sacrifice she must have made when she gave up the ordinary for the extravagant, when she surrendered the honest for the interesting.

She was, after all, not just a fake; she was a work of art. Energy and imagination, intelligence and stamina had been brought to bear, and when Jean tramped the world in her oversized boots, the imprint left behind had the stamp of independence and originality — fine qualities if you're not quite up to courage and truth.

It was no wonder, therefore, that when Jean came today to make the shelf, she arrived, perversely, not in Polly's cast-off flannels and a moth-eaten sweater but in a paisley print silk dress, spiked-heeled shoes and a string of pearls with earrings to match.

Noah found himself glancing at her hands, the delicate touch, the fine long fingers. She would touch him with those fingers if he'd let her.

Here he was in painful need of Esther who now refused to see him because he'd "gone and fallen in love" with her, being subjected to offers from Jean who attracted him not in the least. Maybe if he gave in to Jean it would straighten itself out. His lust, unpredictable and irresponsible, might — given the chance — make the switch from Esther to Jean. The trouble was, his lust, unlike his love, wasn't blind. He had, to his complete surprise, been captured in part by Esther's amplitude. By comparison, Jean's physical perfections seemed stingy.

Also, one of Esther's allures was that she acted the way she felt, she never "performed." Jean, Noah expected, would be dazzling. But it wouldn't be from passion. It would be from pride. She would be too proud to be anything but the best he'd ever had. And he'd be aware, from first to last, that he was being treated to a display, not to a desire.

But what was wrong with a good display? If it couldn't fulfill, it could at least distract. What was stopping him? She was standing right there running her fine delicate fingers along the cut edge of a piece of maple. He was being stupid. He was being selfish.

Wisdom, then, was having an affair with Ruth's best friend, the wife of the man to whom he owed more money than he could ever repay. And generosity was forcing himself to be unfaithful to his wife with a woman for whom he had no attraction.

Noah gave up. He finished cutting the board and turned off the power. Jean, standing there, was distracting him with her patience. As a matter of fact, she'd been distracting him all morning with her silence and diligence. Instead of pestering him and carrying on a no-end conversation yelled out over the power tools, she'd gone obediently to the corner he'd set up for her and had worked away with a concentration that annoyed him. He was sure it was a performance of concentration, not concentration itself. It demanded to be noticed. "Look at me concentrating." "Look at me working seriously." "Look at me not pestering you." "Look at me too involved with my work to even think for a single moment about making love to you."

"Did I do it right?" she asked, frowning down at the wood.

"Perfect. You want me to show you again how you use the vise for nailing it together?"

"Nope. Not necessary." ("Look at me being terse.")

When Noah started up the saw he realized that the silence hadn't come from Jean alone. Cory, on his side of the shop, wasn't singing, not a single note all morning. Noah looked over. The boy was sanding the shelves for yet another dry sink. His lips were puckered shut and he was eyeing his work with a determined indifference. ("Look at me not minding that you let her into the shop. She's a witch and nobody could ever go for her. Would they?")

As Noah watched, Cory leaned with the block sander onto the wood, moving slowly up and down the board to show that he was faithful to his task no matter what burdens were being heaped upon his blameless back. It had been bad enough when Jean came over and did the laundry. ("She didn't empty the lint catcher. And Anne's sweatshirt still has the root beer on it.") Jean's weeding he minded less, but the jambalaya was dissected on his plate before he ate it, the ham bits separated from the shrimp, the rice from the peppers, all as if Jean had made a mess that it was his duty to straighten out before it could be safely eaten. The porch painting exasperated him so much that he was speechless except to say whenever he had the chance, "Look at the rug. Just look at the rug."

Now Jean had been allowed into the shop. Cory was hurt and Noah understood. He was tempted to let the boy use the band saw, but there'd already been enough exception to professional discipline for one day.

Noah considered mentioning to Cory that he'd be singing the day after tomorrow at Jean's, at the birthday party for Toddman Spencer, thinking it might promote some fellow feeling between the two, but he figured the hell with it. Cory should learn to take care of himself. And if the boy chose to be displeased, he should be allowed to be displeased. If he wanted to feel abused, let him feel abused. Jean wasn't doing anything that should bother him to begin with. Except, of course, be there.

Maybe Noah would take Cory fishing on Sunday, just the two of them out in the boat. That, he was sure, would make amends for everything.

Cory moved his hand over the wood to feel how smooth it was. After rubbing back and forth three times to make sure he'd missed nothing, he dusted his hands on the bib of his denim apron and came over to Noah. "Should I take Joel with me to fix lunch?"

"Lunch already?"

"It's late. After one." He paused ever so slightly then said with just a touch of emphasis, "I was working so hard I forgot."

He went over to the playpen and reached down for the baby, gathering a blanket and the toy skunk into his arms at the same time. When he got to the screen door he turned to Noah and said in a loud whisper, "Does *she* get lunch too?" He jerked his head in Jean's direction.

"Lunch would be lovely," said Jean not looking up from her work.

Cory looked to Noah for verification. Noah simply said, "Of course she gets lunch."

"There's not enough," Cory whispered.

Jean's voice sang out from her corner, "Share and share alike I always say."

Cory touched his cheek to the baby's forehead as if it were Joel who would be deprived by the scarcity. "Well," he said indignantly, "I'll have to open some more peaches Ruth canned but I don't know what she's going to say when she finds they're all gone."

"Ruth cans peaches so we can eat them," Noah said quietly. "Don't worry. It'll be all right. She won't blame you."

"Well, all right I guess." Cory turned quickly, flaring the blanket in a swirl around him and went out. Before he got halfway to the house he was singing "Yellow Submarine" into the baby's ear, the song sounding like a terrible complaint lamenting the living conditions of Liverpool in the sixties.

Between cuttings Noah could hear Jean's tap-tap as she nailed the shelf together. Then he heard nothing. He did another cutting and found himself listening, but still hearing nothing. He was determined not to turn around, not to "Look at me not making any noise."

He put another board to the saw for a lengthwise cut. Jean came to his elbow.

"Get away when the power's on!" he yelled.

The power went off. The saw slowed, then stopped, halfway through the board. Jean was standing next to him.

"Turn it back on," Noah said.

"Don't trust Polly," she said. Then she flicked the power back on. The board, unheld, went flying back and sideways like a rampaging propeller, slamming against the wall just above the baby's playpen. It struck with such force that a hole was knocked into the wallboard and, if it hadn't been for the insulation underneath, it probably would have knocked right through to the outside clapboard.

Noah reached over and pulled the switch. The saw began to wind down. Jean stared at the gash in the wall, then at the playpen where the board had landed. She went to the workbench near where Noah was standing, took off the pearls, put them on the bench, then began unclipping her earrings.

"You know what could have happened," Noah said.

"Let it be a lesson. Don't have anything to do with amateurs." She rattled the earrings in her cupped hand then rolled them out onto the bench like a pair of dice, but didn't bother to look at the results. She went and picked up the splintered board from the playpen. "Sorry about this. Tell Polly to give you another one just like it and send me the bill." She tossed the board off into the corner where she'd been working. The reverberations knocked a hammer off the bench.

"Done it again. I'd better get out. Sorry to miss lunch. Ruth's peaches are an old favorite." She started toward the door, stopping to kick into the air the mound of sawdust beneath the bench. "Just like the beach at Acapulco! Whee!" She kicked it again.

"What were you telling me about Polly?"

"I already told you. Don't trust him."

"I owe him money. Did you know that?"

"I suspected. And I never suspect wrong." With her shoe, she began pushing the sawdust back into a pile. "Lots of money?"

"Lots."

"Pay it back. Fast."

"I can't."

"You've got those, for starters." She nodded toward the necklace and the earrings on the workbench.

"No, I don't," Noah said.

"You want to bet?"

"What are you trying to do?"

"Stick my nose in other people's business."

"Well, stop, will you?"

"Okay," Jean said. "If that's the way you want it." She started out but Noah grabbed her by the arm. She looked at his hand, then at his chest, then at his mouth, then at his eyes. "About time," she said.

Noah let go.

"Ah," said Jean, "it must have been true love, it was so brief."

"Come on. Tell me. I know you're trying to help, so do it, will you?"

Jean looked right at him. "Esther Overbaugh's been Polly's pet sow for the past five years. Did you know that?"

"No."

"I didn't think so. But now you do. So act accordingly."

"How much do you know."

"Everything."

"How?"

Jean shrugged. "I have my spies."

"Esther?"

"Possibly."

"Esther told you about herself and me?"

"Possibly."

"And she told Polly too?"

"No. Polly doesn't know anything. And it's got to stay that way. That's what I was trying to tell you. Don't go blabbing about it to Polly of all people."

"Esther," said Noah, "she won't see me."

"Pity."

"Because of Polly? Is that why?"

"Can you imagine? The two of them, together?"

"No."

"Don't. It's disgusting. I imagine it all the time."

Noah picked up the pearls and the earrings from the bench and held them out to Jean. "Here. And thanks. I guess."

Jean ignored the outheld hand and headed for the door. "Put these back on," Noah said.

"It's too hot out."

Noah held the pearls in his fist and raised it toward her. "I don't need any more problems."

Jean stopped at the door but didn't turn around. "Okay," she said, her voice hard and firm. "Here's another solution. You want to go with me? To Mozambique? Madagascar? Marrakesh? Leave it all behind? Just go? You and me? Want to?"

"No."

"Then shut up."

She pushed the door open, went outside, then turned to face him through the screen door. "I suppose you're wondering why I got all dressed up in my silks today. Well, I'll tell you." With that, she stepped back and flipped up her skirt. She was wearing nothing underneath. "That's why," she said. "Now you know."

She turned quickly, knocking Cory with her elbow. He was standing there with the baby in one arm, holding a serving spoon with chunks of potato salad on it. Jean took the spoon from his hand, lapped it with her tongue and handed it back. "Thanks for lunch."

When she got to the driveway she turned around again. "Don't go giving Esther Overbaugh those pearls," she called. "Polly'll recognize them." She swung around and, before going on, raised the back of her dress, bumped her bare behind in their direction, then dropped the skirt and continued around the side of the house.

Noah watched her go, staring after her with amazement. What he'd seen in just that moment had weakened, then conquered him entirely. Jean Thibideau's behind had achieved what all her other charms had failed to do: he'd become a convert, he subscribed fully and willingly to the common consensus that she was indeed the most beautiful woman in town. His captivation was complete. He couldn't help it. He'd phone her later. He'd tell her he'd work with her in the shop if she wanted to come back that evening. She would be dazzling. And he, too, would contribute a little dazzle of his own.

Then, very quickly, he told himself he'd do no such thing. He didn't even bother to give himself the reasons. There were plenty, if he ever needed them. He could list them later.

He turned back to the shop. There was Cory, still looking at the spoon, wondering how it got so clean.

19

NOAH strolled right down the middle of the dirt road because he wanted to reclaim it as his own. It led into the woods, then to a clearing that looked out toward the mountain. From the clearing itself a few short stubby roads, all dead-ends, went back in among the trees and it was there that Noah had made what he considered his first conquests, going back to the blue Pinto he'd bought when he was sixteen.

In the beginning he parked as deep into the woods as he could go and still not get the car stuck in the ruts and ditches that marked the ends of the roads. But before he was eighteen and owned a Camaro he was parking boldly at the crest of the ridge with the valley sloping beneath him and the mountain itself in full view straight ahead.

As he walked now, stones and pebbles crunched beneath his shoes, the sound grinding out above the empty fields on either side of the road. Overhead the night sky was clear and black, each star hard in place as if it had been nailed into position and would never move again. In the field to his right, the last of the hay had been freshly mowed and the bales, strewn at random in the cut grass, looked in the shadows like dropped supplies for a forgotten army that would never come.

Noah was restless. It had begun that afternoon. He'd worked on a cedar chest even though he had no order for one. He just felt like working with cedar. The dry sinks could wait. That evening he asked Cory to stay with the children. The boy had been quiet since the day last week when he'd let Jean into the shop. Probably he'd overheard the talk about him and Esther or, possibly, he hadn't recovered from the sight of Jean Thibideau's bare behind.

Noah had meant to take him fishing, but there'd been no time. When he asked the boy the previous Monday how his singing went at the party he turned his head away and said in a near-whisper, "They gave me ten dollars." And when Noah asked how many songs he'd sung, the boy shook his head to ward off the entire subject and Noah didn't pursue it. It must have been brutal. The boy hadn't wanted to speak much above a whisper all week. Still, he'd readily agreed to stay with the children. Maybe he was beginning to forget the party, to forget Jean, and take up again the tasks he'd been so eager to perform earlier in the summer.

At first Noah thought he'd go to Rosie's on 202 and see what was happening, just to get away. Maybe someone from the lumberyard would be there and they could do nothing in particular together. Or maybe he'd meet some woman who only wanted to talk. Or he could even play the pinball machines, another arena of forgotten triumphs.

But Rosie's would be loud. And the crowd on a Saturday night would be too young. He was thirty-two now and they'd all be kids.

He could go to the movie but when he got to the one theater in town, it was nothing he felt like sitting through. Maybe an evening with Blanche and the dogs, just being in the old rambling house, talking in the kitchen about Ruth, about the children, watching the smoke from Blanche's asthma cigarette, hearing her cough. But he didn't feel like any of that either.

He settled for taking a walk. It seemed to him the good thing to do, to stroll the deserted streets of Mattysborough, to hear family sounds from the houses set far back from the sidewalks, the low murmur of a voice on a porch, the muted clatter of dishes being washed, the tin sonorities of a TV set, an upstairs window closing. To feel the night breeze pass him by on its way to somewhere else, the slight stir of the leaves overhead like the gentle scatter of mice in the eaves. The tobacco smell of cut grass, the damp odors coming up from the river.

He would stop on the bridge and listen to the waterfall upriver near the old firehouse. Then he would walk back home.

Noah stayed in the middle of the road even though one of the tire ruts or the fields off to the side would be easier for walking. He hadn't intended to come this far but once he'd started out he'd just kept going, not thinking, not noticing the sounds and scents he'd thought would please him. On the bridge he'd slowed down to listen to the waterfall but hadn't actually stopped. He would go now only to the edge of the woods, to the far end of the fields, then turn back. He wouldn't walk all the way to the clearing.

As he neared the edge of the fields, a shape came out of the woods and moved slowly toward him down the side of the road. He hadn't seen it until it was completely free of the trees behind it. It had two heads, a couple clinging to each other, stretching their limbs after being cramped in their car. He remembered the need.

He didn't like being seen walking alone toward the clearing. By common consent, it was reserved for people together, particularly those who had no place else but their cars. It wasn't that they might think he was a spy. He was ashamed to be alone. It suggested a defect, an inability to get someone who would have come with him.

Noah moved to the side of the road and looked down at his shoes as he walked. The couple passed him by on the other side, the whisk of denim against denim louder than the grind of the pebbles beneath his feet. They paid no attention to him.

Now he would have to go all the way to the clearing before turning around. Otherwise it might seem he was following them. He started to step back into the middle of the road but changed his mind. After three more steps he stopped. He looked back over his shoulder. The couple had cut into the field, still with their arms around each other, slowly moving among the bales of hay, climbing the gentle rise of the field itself as it sloped slightly up toward the woods that bounded it on the horizon.

Noah watched them. From what he could see in the light of the stars they had separated but were holding hands. He turned back and started walking again toward the woods.

He stopped once more. He felt uneasy. He crossed over to the other side of the road. After he'd walked a few more steps he realized he was afraid. He looked ahead at the woods. There was no one there. Even if there was, what difference did it make? He couldn't possibly be afraid. He'd go to the clearing, turn around, and head home.

When he got to where the road disappeared into the trees, Noah realized why he had come here and where he was going. He would walk toward the mountain and beyond it; he would keep on walking and never come back. He was leaving Ruth and his children, the town of his birth; he was going away, leaving for good. He would be alone, solitary forever, without even himself.

He would mourn. He would mourn the loss of his wife and his children. But he couldn't mourn for them until he'd lost them, until he'd left them. Now he would leave. Then he could mourn.

He would pray for them. He would pray for them because they were alone in the world, without his protection. But first he had to withdraw that protection. He was withdrawing it now. Then he would be able to pray.

When he'd get to the clearing, he would walk down into the

ravine below, then across the valley floor. He would climb the mountain, cross it, and keep right on going. He wouldn't look back. He would be gone forever.

He entered the woods, the road a tunnel through the trees, the clearing straight ahead.

There were no cars in the clearing, not even one for the couple he'd seen head out across the field. He walked to the edge where the steep descent down into the valley began. Beyond the next ridge was the mountain. He looked at its massive bulk, the dip just before the rise of the southern peak where, when he was a boy, he had been told there was a volcanic crater. He stared down at the pine and oak in the valley at his feet; he lifted his head and saw the Milky Way stretched to the north and west, looking as it always did, as though it might let fall a rain of ash onto the town of Contoocook.

None of this was real. All shapes and forms, all sounds, all scents, were merely distractions, diversions from the truth that was revealed to him now. Horror ruled the world. Horror brooded over a meaningless earth and had taken note of Noah Dubbins.

He was in despair. It had come at last, severing all connections with the world and everything and everyone in it. It nullified the pact of mutual acceptance between himself and the earth. The most jealous god of all, despair allowed only itself. It required neither worship nor submission. They weren't needed. It had what counted, possession.

The mountain was permitted to exist and the trees, because they were ineffectual. God himself was allowed, but only because he was powerless. Salvation, hard-fought, hard-won, was not withdrawn, it was merely made incidental and beside the point. Everything that could tempt Noah from his despondency, all his senses, all his faith and hope, all his goodness, these could continue without impediment. He knew the night air to be fresh and the mountain to be a comforting hump set fondly on the horizon. He knew his children were splendid and that to work with cedar had its rewards. Ruth was beautiful and always would be. All this was true, and he was allowed to know it. But he also had to know that it had nothing to do with him, that it all meant nothing.

He stepped toward the ridge that led down to the valley, looking only into the distance. Then he stopped.

He'd seen the mountain move. He'd seen it shift as if it were about to rise from an old and timeless slumber. It would rear itself toward the sky, monstrous and dumb. And he would have to see it.

There was a shudder in his blood. He felt it rising to his throat, into his mouth. He tried to hold it back, but it fluttered against the root of his tongue like a trapped and panicked bird. Now the mountain would rise up. It would be Esther, it would be Hippolyte Thibideau, obscenely coupled; it would be Ruth and the grounds-keeper. They would move with gutteral groans, devouring each other whole with growling mouths. It would be a giant unearthly crow shrieking, spreading out its evil wings, screeching the deaths of Anne and Danny and Joel. He would have to hear it; he would have to see it; he would have to watch; he would have to listen. Horror would rise up, brute and obscene, merciless and honest.

The mountain moved again.

Then Noah heard his howl. He heard it rise above the fields, the woods, the cry of a man thrown into scalding water. He threw his hand across his mouth but his teeth bit down and he howled again. Then there was silence, all the world suspended, no breath, no motion, no stir. Noah waited, listening. Nothing.

Then it was himself he heard, chattering over and over again like a child shivering with the cold. No words were formed. He had no idea what he was trying to say; a prayer or a promise, he had no idea.

He silenced himself and stared toward the mountain. It didn't move.

He must go home. He started back through the tunneled woods, back along the graveled road. He had been spared. He had not crossed the mountain; he had not gone forever. Horror had risen up in his path, forbidding his advance. Now he was heading home.

The chattering of unformed words came one more time, but more subdued, as Noah trudged toward the town. It sounded like a low mutter of thanks and praise. When he passed through the mown fields he looked up at the sky, the stars, still nailed hard in place. Far to his left along the wooded horizon, the Big Dipper touched down onto the tops of the trees as if it had been placed there by a kind and careful wife.

20

THE pantry floor was littered with jars, boxes, cans, bottles and old paper bags. On the counter were the dishes — plates of varying sizes and patterns, the saucers and the soup bowls. The glasses and cups Noah had put on the drawers he'd pulled out. He hoped he wouldn't knock them off. The serving bowls and empty mason jars he'd put in the old flour bin for the time being and the spices and condiments were lined along the windowsill.

He'd already scrubbed the shelves and put down fresh liner. Now, looking over the mess he was supposed to fit back, he wondered what he could throw out. Throwing out was surely a part of the operation. And besides, some of the smaller jars had been around so long they were covered with a layer of grease and furred with a light dust as if they were evolving into small animals.

Noah picked up a spice tin and rubbed it with his thumb. The label read "Basil." He pried off the top and sniffed. It had the smell of a meadow in the late afternoon. The tin was almost full. When had Ruth used basil, and for what? He snapped the lid back on, put the tin onto the windowsill and wiped his thumb on his thigh.

The feel of silk reminded him that he was wearing one of Ruth's old maternity dresses, the light blue she bought when she was having Danny. Like the linen one, it was sleeveless and had the zipper up the back. Unlike the green, however, the blue had a more defined waist so that it fit a little snug across the chest.

His only reason for wearing it instead of the more comfortable lime-green linen was that he didn't think he should wear the same dress all the time. He was, after all, involved with Ruth's dresses in general and not the linen one in particular. Within his compulsion, or whatever it was, he had been given a range of possibilities and he took from this what relief he could. Whatever else, he wasn't in a rut.

It was two weeks since he'd gone to look at the mountain. Since then he'd allowed his impulse unimpeded satisfaction. He put the dresses on without protest whenever he felt urged. Or, if that wasn't feasible at the moment, he made plans to do so at the first opportunity. He was taking no risks.

He didn't even ask questions any more. It seemed to Noah that he had gone to the oracle and said, "My wife Ruth is ill and without her I don't have the patience and strength I need to have. I want to keep my children, but I can't if I'm going to be cruel. I want to be faithful to my wife, but my lust has led me to another woman. I have debts and no money. Tell me what I have to do if I'm going to get through all this until my wife comes home to me."

And the oracle had said, "Put on one of your wife's dresses from time to time."

But when Noah asked the next question, "Why should I do a thing like that?" the oracle became silent and spoke no more. So Noah did just as he'd been told — even warned — to do. Since the night in the clearing he took no chances. The best he had been able to do was to consider that, in some way, he was asking for Ruth's protection, asking her to shield him — probably from himself, from the violent self that had led him, years before, to the killing of the blind girl's pig. His work and his love for Ruth had rescued him, but now he'd been thrown into a time of testing. And so it seemed only natural that he would turn to Ruth for rescue again, to beg her help and her protection. The dresses, perhaps, were the shielding he'd asked for. He didn't really know. But then, when he'd gone to the oracles he hadn't asked for knowledge, he'd asked for help. The dresses did their job and he had to be satisfied.

Noah looked at the smudge he'd made with his thumb on the skirt of the blue dress. He rubbed it, spreading it out, then decided to let it alone. He'd have to try some cleaning fluid later since he didn't want to take the dresses to the cleaners.

He was wearing the dress at this hour of the afternoon not just because he was alone with Joel in the house while Cory, along with Anne and Danny, was off on a field trip, but because he was worried that he might begin to feel uneasy. He was going to hijack a truck of lumber for Hippolyte Thibideau later in the day — a truck on its way from Pennsylvania to Montreal — and he didn't want to start feeling peculiar when there'd be nothing he could do about it. It was like making preparations for a journey, taking precautions that anticipated possible difficulties, like eating a bigger lunch or going to the toilet before leaving the house.

As for the hijack, he'd agreed to it without a moment's pause. Polly had come to Noah at the shop two days before. It was not a particularly hot day but Polly in his denim regalia and white shirt was soaked through as if he'd just come up from the river. His voice, when he spoke, was even more high pitched than usual, sounding like a man struggling not to say "uncle" when his index finger was being bent back one jerk at a time.

When Polly mentioned the hijack, Noah thought he might be putting him purposely into danger because he'd found out about himself and Esther Overbaugh. Noah wanted to watch him closely, to see if he could tell how much Polly knew, but he had trouble looking directly at him. This wasn't because he was worried about a confrontation, but because this man was the preferred recipient of Esther's favors. It was a subject he'd like to avoid.

When Polly had come into the shop, Noah, so he wouldn't seem worried, pretended to a calm that went beyond even *his* usual laconic ways. The only change he could notice was that he was being more polite. He offered Polly a chair without realizing until he was halfway through the sentence that there was no chair in the shop, nor had there been since the time when Ruth would come and read to him while he worked through the night, to be with him even when he couldn't come to bed, a practice that had ended when the children came. Fortunately, Polly refused the offer of the chair and got right down to business.

"I'm in trouble," he had said, "and you're the only one I know who can help me. The only one I trust to even talk to."

He went on to explain that he himself had accumulated debts that had to be paid, quickly. He hinted that he'd taken loans at extortionate rates and that his lenders were impatient and powerful. He knew that he could, if he wanted to, take Noah's house and shop and tools, but there was no time to make sales, to run the money through the market. And besides, it was something he'd said he wouldn't do anyway. Unless he absolutely had to.

The "interests" to whom he was indebted had indicated that they would be somewhat pacified if Polly would deliver, for reworking into veneer, the shipment of black walnut that would be coming through the territory soon. It could be hijacked and delivered to a specified mill near the Massachusetts border. The interests had given him no choice; he had to do it. If he didn't . . .

Polly said he'd hijack the truck himself, but he could be recognized by the driver. He was not unknown in the industry. There'd be no danger for Noah even though, of necessity, a gun would be involved.

He, Polly, had come to Noah's rescue. Now Noah must come to his. The veneer, in the market price, would equal almost the amount of Noah's debt, but in reward, Polly would cancel the entire amount. And there would easily be future loans once the present trouble was over. Polly was certain he could continue to be of help if it was necessary. But Noah must help him now.

Noah said yes.

"What you'll do is stop the truck somewhere around North Village. It'll be slowed anyway because they haven't repaired from the washout last spring and it's single lane to begin with."

Polly was squatted down in the corner of his office, turning the combination to the safe where he kept the gun Noah would use. In his denim, he looked like a humpbacked bluebird that had molted its tail feathers. But his voice was less constricted than usual, lower a pitch or two, as if the bent index finger had been released and his lungs had relaxed down from his neck to at least as far as his collarbone.

Noah would have preferred silence. He wanted Polly to get the gun and hand it over, then talk. But Polly went on.

"You know what to do. Wave him down like you need help. Block him off. Give him space to stop. You know how to gauge it." Polly rubbed his fingers on his pants leg just above the knee, then tried the combination. He seemed to be cracking his own safe.

"What if he doesn't stop?" Noah asked.

"He'll stop."

"What makes you so sure?"

"You look like a good man. And you look like a man in trouble. He'll stop."

"And if he doesn't?"

Polly stood up and thought a moment, not looking at Noah. Then he spoke as if he had worked his way through a puzzling philosophical problem, step by step. "He'll stop because you'll make him stop," Polly said. He paused, reflected, then went on. "But without letting him see the gun. If he sees the gun, he'll keep right on going. So you don't show the gun. You just stand there. You don't move out of his way. You stand there so he can't get past. And you go right on standing there. So he'll stop."

Polly thought it through again, testing it for error, then, obviously finding none, he squatted down again next to the safe. Noah got a quick picture, himself flattened out on the road with a lumber truck loaded with black walnut heading safely for Montreal.

Polly rubbed his fingertips again and began slowly to try the combination one more time. "Once you get rid of the driver you go on to Penacook so you'll be going east too. Then make your left, loop around back through Marlow and Stoddard. Go south to just before Winchendon, then make your turn back north and head for the mill where you'll make the delivery."

He put his ear against the door of the safe as if trying to hear if anyone was inside listening. He began telling Noah to make sure it was the black walnut he was hijacking and not a load of poison oak. Noah didn't say anything.

By now, Polly was hugging the safe, one arm around it, the other working the combination, his ear pressed to the door, as if amorous persuasion might get the safe to yield its treasure. The more intractable the combination proved to be, the more ardent Polly became, and the more ardent he became, the more patient he seemed, as if he not only expected but preferred a long wooing. Noah started wondering if this was what Esther preferred in him, but he made himself stop.

Now Polly was talking about the mill near Massachusetts being tooled to roll the veneer the moment Noah would make the delivery. His voice was getting lower as if the assurance of readiness was really a plea to the safe, asking its cooperation so that plans could move forward.

When Polly began to tell about where the truck should be abandoned after the delivery, Noah was no longer listening. He was staring at the walls, upright boards of cherry wood fitted together in tongue and groove fashion, without nails. They went from floor to ceiling of the office like an extended wainscoting, an extravagance that would interest only a lumber company.

Noah kept staring. Maybe it was the neat fit that held him, the skillful work, the wood beautifully preserved. He looked along the grooves where the boards joined. He was expecting them to part; he was waiting for the walls to open, to reveal something he was supposed to see, something secret or forgotten.

There had been wainscoting in the kitchen of the house on Pine Street where he'd grown up, but it had been nothing like this. There, the grain had been false, painted on, a tan swirl over a cream colored base meant to resemble the painter's idea of wood. But here, in Polly's office, this was real.

Noah continued to stare, waiting for the walls to part. Polly, still down on his haunches, was talking about the relief he'd feel when the hijack was over and done, the words obviously meant for the safe, like the promise of a suitor for better times ahead.

Noah, not hearing, was watching a burial at sea. Cloaked figures, silent, at night, a bound and shrouded body on a plank tipped toward the waves. He heard no splash. The memory ended before the corpse hit the water.

Noah stood up. This was all a mistake. He was not supposed to be here, in this room. He must tell Polly it was all wrong.

Polly's cheek was pressed against the side of the safe as if it and he were posing for a photograph. He was talking now about the excellence of the gun inside. Noah sat back down. He was in the wrong place. This was the wrong time. He'd been meant to go to sea, but a long time ago. He'd seen these walls on an old sailing ship, below deck, not much bigger than a cubbyhole with a single bunk built along one side. The walls were upright boards of cherry wood fitted together, tongue and groove, without nails. He would have come aboard as a boy, about eight, and he would have served into manhood. He would serve faithfully, die young and be buried at sea, not deeply mourned, but honored and well remembered, for a time anyway.

Of course none of this was true and Noah knew it. Sternly, as if speaking to Danny about to have a tantrum, he told himself that his father had taken him to Portsmouth when he was eight. They'd boarded an old sailing ship stopping at the island Navy Yard. He'd seen a room no bigger than a cubbyhole with a bunk in it. The walls were upright cherry, tongue and groove. The rest was his imagination and he'd better stop. Right now.

No! He had been misplaced. Some accident had misplaced him in time and in space. During some moment of divine distraction, more than a century had been skipped and, in partial correction of the error, he had been set down in a room of upright cherry wood boards. He had been put here, in Hippolyte Thibideau's office, when he belonged at sea, long dead.

Noah stood up again. He wanted to protest. He felt like a man wrongly imprisoned. He was not where he was supposed to be. It was all a mistake. He would demand his release. The deck rolled beneath his feet, the sail billowed out over his head. He tried to catch the wind so he'd have the breath to call out his demand.

But there was a rending of sail, a clear tearing of cloth. The wind was stilled, the deck no more than the pine floor beneath his feet, the rent sail reduced to the split seam of Polly's dungarees. Noah looked toward the corner of the room. Polly, squatting alongside the safe, straining for a closer embrace, had burst through the seat of his pants. At almost the same moment, the combination clicked and the door swung open.

Noah looked at the cherry wood walls, trying to catch again the deck and the sail, his cubbyhole room or even the tilted plank that would have given him a clean burial at sea, but there was nothing he could reach or hold onto. He scanned the boards from floor to ceiling, from ceiling to floor, searching along the grooves for some hint of possible escape. But there was no way out.

The gun was weighing down his hand. He looked at it where it lay slapped across his open palm, a .45, drab green as if it had been carved from a young tree, probably apple before its first yield.

Polly, strutting back to close the safe, was telling him that the clip was in place and he should be careful. As he walked, his patterned cotton undershorts showed through the split in his pants, a design of blue diamonds set in perpendicular bands of gray and maroon that reminded Noah of the wallpaper Blanche had put up the year before last in the sewing room.

Noah put the plates back onto the pantry shelves, and then the serving bowls. The cups he hung on their hooks and he stacked the glasses on the bottom shelf where Anne — and very soon Danny — could reach them without having to stand on a chair.

The boxes, bottles, cans and jars were more of a problem. He'd throw nothing away because he had no way of knowing what each meant to Ruth. He might toss out something she treasured or needed. Everything would have to stay until Ruth herself decided otherwise. All he'd do is wipe off the grease and the dust.

It was when he was cleaning the tin top of the baking powder can, fascinated by the silver shine he was giving to the embossed word "Calumet" that he heard the back door slam and Blanche's voice calling, "I could use some help with this separator if you're home!" Her footsteps couldn't be heard because of her cough, but the cough was getting closer.

Noah reached to close the pantry door, but hesitated for a fraction of a second. Maybe he should just go right on shining the letters on the baking powder can and let happen what might happen. Maybe it would mean little or nothing to Blanche to see her son-in-law, her daughter's husband, in one of her daughter's maternity dresses. Maybe she would understand better than Noah himself and explain it all to him with a puff on her cigarette and a cleared throat.

For Blanche it might not be difficult, but it was too difficult for Noah himself. He closed the door and began pulling the dress over his head.

The serrations of the zipper caught his hair and it hurt when he yanked the dress loose from his head. "I'm in the pantry." He tossed the dress onto one of the upper shelves.

There was a crash of cans and jars being kicked over when Noah opened the door. There amid the saucers and soup bowls stood Blanche in her slippered feet, holding an old portable milk separator from the days when she'd kept a cow. Danny had found it in the cooler at the back of her yard and she'd promised he could have it once she'd cleaned it up. It looked like a miniature washing machine of the old drum style, made of aluminum. Blanche was waving it over the kitchen table as if it were a space ship circling for a landing.

"It didn't used to be this heavy," she said.

After making room for it at the expense of the sugar bowl, the salt and pepper shakers, a box of Quaker Oats oatmeal and a milk carton, she put it down, coughed, took the cigarette from her lower lip and turned toward Noah. "You'll have to take it up to his room for him. I —" She stopped and jerked her chin down toward her chest to give her farsighted eyes a better view of him. "Taking out the pantry," she said, bringing her chin back up to its usual position, tipped slightly upward. "Making the downstairs bathroom, huh?"

"No, just cleaning the shelves."

Blanche pulled her chin in as if another farsighted glance was necessary to confirm the truth of what he'd just said. Apparently she was satisfied, because the chin thrust out again and she took a puff on her cigarette.

He held out the baking powder can and the cloth to offer added proof if she thought it was necessary. Blanche pushed past him so she could look at the pantry for herself. Noah covered the top of the can with the cloth as if to conceal the lettering. This made him feel nervous, as if he was hiding something, so he deliberately took the cloth away, exposing the lid, the lettering and the polished tin.

"I should have brought some wallpaper to line the shelves with," Blanche said. "I've got some cream-colored with brown vines. Or if you want, some yellow with big green lotus leaves left over from the dining room. Look nice even if you can't see it flat on the shelf. Sometimes it's enough to know it's there."

"I went and got some plastic liner. Thanks."

"I could bring it tomorrow."

"No. The liner's okay."

"Boring if you ask me. How about painting the whole room while you've got it all pulled apart? Some blue enamel left from the window frames. I could start tomorrow. Before you know it, I —" Again she stopped.

She had been looking around the pantry, appraising in her mind's eye the effect of blue enamel, and now she was looking up at Ruth's dress crumpled on the shelf above with some of the skirt draping down. Blanche pulled her chin in, then thrust it outward, the head movement of a pigeon strutting. When she yanked on the skirt, the dress came falling down over Noah's head. He pulled at it, as if it were a net thrown over him, getting his ears caught in it, then his hands and arms, tangling more of it over himself instead of getting free.

He heard something being knocked over and then felt something wet splash onto his shirt and down the front of his pants.

"Hold still," Blanche said. She unwound the dress from around his head and lifted it off his shoulders. "You went and tipped your scrub water all over yourself." She started to rub him with the dress but it kept bunching up in her hand. "You better go change. And what made you think you could clean anything with a rag this big? It goes all over the place. You've got to tear it up smaller."

With that, she pulled at the top of the dress and ripped the front down to the waist. Then she continued along the sewn line of the waist until she'd separated the top from the skirt. She threw the skirt at Noah. "Here. Tear it into four. You've got enough rags here to clean the whole house. Except silky like this isn't the best you can do. Doesn't catch the dust the way it's supposed to."

When she saw that Noah wasn't tearing the cloth or even using it to wipe the scrub water from his shirt and pants, she grabbed it back and went to work on it herself. "The blue enamel's almost the color of this." With a single tug she rent the skirt right down the middle and held out the opened cloth as if to display something that had been concealed before. "You don't think this'd be a pretty color? And with some green wallpaper I've got for the shelves? Blue and green? The trees and the sky? You can't do much better than that for a combination of colors."

She gave the skirt another rip, tearing it in two, and handed half to Noah. After she'd given her piece one more tear, she let the cloth fall to the floor onto the heap of rags she'd been so busily building. "Baby awake?" she asked going out of the pantry and starting toward the living room.

"I haven't heard him."

"Well, I'll just give a peek." Blanche rolled some phlegm around inside her lungs so it wouldn't require attention while she was with the baby, then went down the hallway.

Noah looked down not at his wet shirt and pants but at Ruth's torn-up dress that lay heaped at his feet. Blanche had ripped the dress so savagely, so unfeelingly. It seemed she had done it without pity, without minimal human regard.

Why Blanche should waste her pity on an old worn-out dress he had no idea, except that the dress itself had an association with his sorrow and his fortitude. It was the emblem of all that was being endured. It was the source of his patience and his fidelity. It was the proof of his willing submission to mystery. And Blanche had reduced it to a pile of rags.

"Anything you want me to take to Ruth later?" Blanche called from the living room.

"No. Nothing."

In the living room she was sitting in the overstuffed chair with Joel on her lap. She'd attached the suction cup of one of the baby's rattles — a clown shape of strung colored beads — onto her forehead so that it stuck out and dangled down in front of her face like a creature sprung from her brow.

She bounced the baby on her knees and the clown danced in the air, clouded in the smoke from her asthma cigarette. Joel seemed more interested in the smoke than in the clown and it was the cigarette he reached for. Leering and saying, "No, no, no," Blanche shook her head not in disapproval over his choice, but to activate all the more the clown's dance and distract the baby from the burning herbs pasted to her lower lip. Just when Joel had started looking at the clown again, a coughing spasm took hold of Blanche's lungs. Greater clouds of smoke rose up to shroud the clown.

As Noah went up the stairs, Joel seemed rapt at the spectacle, his grandmother's heaving breast, the rolling rumble of the phlegm, the billowing smoke and the beaded toy that danced helplessly, all for the entertainment of his grandmother's nose.

Noah continued up the stairs. He would not only change from his wet clothes, he would put on another of Ruth's dresses and come back down when Blanche was gone. He could continue the work he'd been doing. Before hijacking the truck, he would make up for the outrage the blue dress had been subjected to.

He heard the wheezing cough, a warning, a plea not to do it, telling him he'd chanced enough for one day. But Noah paid no attention as he went along the upstairs hall to his room.

21

He wasted no time. Because he was soaked through with the scrub water, including his socks, he stripped off all his clothes, rubbed his skin with the dry part of his shirt, then threw the shirt to the far side of the bed as if he were discarding it for good. The closet door was open and he went straight for the lime-green dress. It was crushed into the tight press of the overcrowded cross-bar. He pushed the other clothes aside with his forearm and pulled the dress free without even bothering to take the hanger from the rack. As soon as he withdrew his arm the other clothes sprang back to claim this new fraction of space, trapping part of the skirt in their sudden crush. Noah had to give an extra jerk before the dress was completely free.

When he lifted it so he could stick his head through the top, he remembered that his impatience was not with the dress; he had no reason to pull at it and yank it the way he was doing. Nothing was the dress's fault. He was acting no different from Blanche when she'd ripped the blue one to rags. And besides, what was his hurry? He certainly wasn't going to go trooping back downstairs with Blanche still in the territory.

To slow himself he resorted to the easiest means available. He heaved a sigh, drawing in all his exasperation and then letting it out in a more purified form as if his lungs were a natural filter, refining his cruder emotions.

He looked at the dress held limply at his side. He knew he'd resigned himself to asking no questions, especially after he was informed that no answers were forthcoming, but surely he was entitled to some small glimmer of understanding or insight. Why should he be left in such absolute ignorance when he was the one, the single one, being put through all the trouble?

Noah was about to claim it wasn't fair, but as soon as the idea began to form itself in his mind, he was aware of the absurdity of his demand. He'd been ready to go into a tantrum because he had judged some aspect of his situation "unfair." What more worthless cry could he make than a cry for "fair"? It was a word whose echoes had no end, that reverberated through all a man's life until it was finally absorbed into the laughter of the gods.

Where, for him, would fair begin? And where would it end? What was fair to Ruth in her illness? Fair to his children, fair to Noah himself with his own mother's desertion? Ultimately "fair" meant only one thing: never to have been, never to have been born at all. That alone would be "fair." And that Noah would not accept, not for himself or for his children or even for Ruth, with all her suffering.

He put the thoughts away. He had given up the demand for knowledge. He'd made his bargain and he'd stick to it.

He looked at the dress, wondering what it had done to be brought into this complicity that compromised his life, to be made an artifact to the mysteries into which he'd been drawn. As usual, no answer.

He slipped the dress over his head, then slowed the movement, holding off its fall down around his body. The linen was coarse but sturdy. Noah waited, then began lowering the material slowly. His face veiled by the cloth, he could see only a blurred green light through the weave. He felt the scratch of the linen against his arms, against his sides. He closed his eyes because he couldn't focus on the cloth when it was that close to his face.

He was obliterating himself; he was taking himself out of the world. He was ceasing to be who he was.

The dress slid down over his body and he pressed it to his hips. It had been death. It had not been the shielding he'd thought it might be. It had been a destruction of himself. Was it death then that he wanted, an end to himself forever? Had this been the plea the dresses made?

He lightly touched his fingers against his chest, feeling the weave of the cloth and the bones beneath his flesh. Then, he thought, what he had been tempted to that night at the clearing, the temptation to leave them all and never come back, it was a prompting that he was repeating to himself again and again, each time he put one of the dresses on.

Slowly he moved the tips of his fingers against the cloth. And slowly, new promptings began to come to him. Yes, it had been a destruction of himself that he'd sought. But it was not obliteration he'd been asking for. It went beyond that. He had asked not for death but for change. He'd asked to be allowed to go out, like a character rehearsing a play, and come in again, ready for another try. He'd asked to be given a new chance, as if a wish for death was really a plea for the resurrection.

He began adjusting the dress along the curves and contours of his body. He shifted the waist into position, making sure the tab of the zipper was lined up with the base of his spine. Could he, Noah, in those few seconds, putting on the dress, could he have passed through the grave? Had he died and been raised up, changed? Is that what the dresses meant, in their grotesque and humiliating way? Resurrection? Death and resurrection? Was he being given a glimpse of the ultimate blessing, a promise that the curse would pass and that he and Ruth would rise up, changed, and blessed forever? It was impossible, and yet Noah wanted to call out, "Let it be so! I beg you, I beg you. Let it be so!"

He reached back over his shoulder to zip the zipper up. It was like getting a hammerlock on himself. He couldn't find the zipper tab. He felt like a wrestler struggling with a stubborn and crafty opponent.

It was at this moment of contortion that he saw Danny stretched out along the length of a branch in the maple tree outside the bedroom window, watching him. They looked at each other. Noah finished zipping the dress, then didn't know what to do with his hands so he rubbed them against his whiskers and brought them together under his chin.

Danny had begun to inch back along the branch, carefully, as if he were about to turn and start scrambling along the bark. He didn't take his eyes off his father. And Noah felt that if he himself made a move Danny would fall from the tree.

He watched the boy's slow backward crawl. When Danny touched the trunk of the tree with his foot, he tapped it several times to make sure it was there. Convinced that it was, even though he wouldn't turn to look at it, he let his legs drop over the sides of the branch and, sitting up, eased himself backward toward the notch, his hands keeping hold in front of him as he went.

"Wait there," Noah said in a quiet even voice. "I'll come and get you so you won't fall."

When he reached back to unzip the dress so he could change into his own clothes, Danny twisted himself around suddenly and grabbed the branch above him. He hoisted himself up and began climbing.

"Danny!" Noah called. He went to the window. Danny had moved to the other side of the tree, away from the house, and was working his way through the branches, sometimes climbing farther up, sometimes letting himself down as though he was lost among the leaves.

"Danny!" Noah called again. But the boy continued climbing, crawling through the branches, down and up, dipping them with his weight, making the leaves rattle as he brushed through them like a panicked bird.

Noah reached again for the zipper but couldn't find the tab. It would have to wait. On his way down the stairs he could feel his genitals swinging and flopping against his legs under the dress but there was nothing he could do about it now. He was listening in dread for the crack of a breaking branch outside.

In the living room Joel was hitting the rattle, knocking it against his grandmother's face. Blanche, in turn, rewarded each hit with a puff from her cigarette as if it were the bang of the clown against her nose that produced the smoke. Without interrupting their game, Noah rushed past the room.

At the kitchen door he kicked aside the jars he'd put outside the pantry. In the back hall he stepped into a pile of garden tools and scattered them down the cellar steps. When a fold of the dress caught on the screen door, he jerked it free, making a rip in the side. He ran through the vegetable patch feeling the explosion of ripe tomatoes under his bare feet.

He turned the side of the house just in time to see Danny swing down from the lowest branch of the tree, drop to the ground and start running toward the street.

"Danny! Wait!"

The boy stumbled but kept on running.

Noah went after him. He wouldn't be convinced that his son was safe until he touched him, until he held him, until he could feel his breathing against his chest. He ran to the street. Danny was nowhere. Noah looked in all directions, then ran along the front of the house, looking across the street, then into his own driveway.

He went back to the yard, to the tree, to see if the boy had circled around ahead of him and climbed again. "Danny," he called.

He got no answer. Danny wasn't there. Noah wanted to lean

his head against the trunk of the tree, to rest, to close his eyes and wait, as if he were playing a game of hide-and-seek. But he heard a sound behind him.

He turned around. Blanche was standing in the tomato patch, Joel in her arms, the rattle still dangling down from her forehead. She seemed about to say something. Her mouth was open. She kept it that way, then closed it, slowly, as if she was afraid it might make a noise.

"I'm sorry," Noah said, "but I've got something I have to do."

He walked past Blanche toward the shop. Mrs. Driscoll next door was watching him over the hedge, but he kept right on going. The time had come to return Ruth's purse. He'd stolen it and the time had come to make restitution, to settle all accounts at last. Besides, something might happen to him during the hijack. He could be arrested, he could be killed. The purse was Ruth's and she should have it.

It was hanging on a nail just inside the door. He took it down. Blanche was gone from the yard and wasn't in the house when he went back upstairs for the gun. He took it from the drawer and put it in the purse. He couldn't change from the dress. There was no time. The truck was on its way. And he wanted to be wearing it. He wanted Ruth to know — to see — how much he needed her. She'd been spared enough.

On his way to the van, the purse slung from his shoulder, the wide skirt of the dress accommodating his stride, he saw Cory come running up the driveway.

"You see Danny?" he called. "He was with Anne and me at —" He slowed to a walk but kept coming toward Noah, slower and slower.

"Look for him at Mrs. Driscoll's. He might be there." Noah climbed into the van and slammed the door. Cory came alongside, grabbing onto the glass of the partly opened window like a drowning man clutching the side of a lifeboat. Noah started the motor anyway.

"Don't let Mr. Thibideau see you," Cory pleaded. "He already thinks you do things with me we're not supposed to. He almost said so at the party and I told him, no. I even told him it was Esther Overbaugh you've been going to see. I told him how all the women, they want you. How even his wife didn't have any pants on. But he won't believe if he sees . . ."

The van began to move but Cory continued to hold on, running alongside until it was going too fast. Making the turn from the driveway onto the street, Noah could see the boy running toward him, waving, calling. It sounded like "Will you be back for supper?"

22

THE van stopped, lurched forward about three feet, then another two, then one, like a fit or hiccups. Finally it came to a halt in among the bushes that bordered the hospital parking lot. Noah considered backing out into the lot but thought the hell with it. If the van wanted to barge itself into the bushes, let it barge itself into the bushes.

Barefoot, he stepped down onto the ground. He worked the skirt of the green linen dress in rapid rubs against his thighs to make sure he was covered, then reached into the front seat for the purse. He hadn't checked the contents but he expected everything was there. He had to hurry. He slammed the door of the van and stepped clear of the bushes.

The pebbles scattered on the asphalt of the parking lot pressed into the soles of his feet, sticking to the skin. Every few steps Noah had to raise a foot and brush it clean, trying all the time not to break his stride. Some of the tarred stones stuck to his hand. He wiped them against the side of the dress. If he took smaller steps his feet wouldn't come down so hard but he made himself move at his first determined pace, forcing the stones deeper into his feet.

Jean was with Ruth. They were sitting together on the bench above Fern Lake. Jean was reading to Ruth and Ruth seemed to be listening. He was glad Jean was there. It served her right. With her quick words and mock seductions she'd taunted his bewilderment. To her he was the dumb carpenter, fair game for teasing. That she would see him humiliated in his wife's dress didn't matter. What mattered was that she know at last that mystery had touched him and that he reveled in this display that contradicted her assumptions of his simplicity. What Jean did with the knowledge, what interpretation she gave it, was of no importance for the moment. It was important only that the knowledge be given.

Noah was far down the path that ran along the lake but he could see that Ruth's head was tilted just a little to the side, away from Jean as if she was giving the words special consideration. If this were so, if she was actually concentrating on the words, on the story, it meant this was one of her good days. It stopped Noah on the path, this sudden hope, like a twinge of the heart. He tried to look closer, straining his eyes, forcing them to work beyond their usual limits, not caring if he never saw again. This he would see.

He jumped off the path in among the ferns so he could cut directly across the lake. His feet sank into the cool mud but he kept on moving, sucking his feet back up, bending his body into the ferns as he went, still looking up at Ruth.

She hadn't moved her head. She was still listening. Noah was tempted to call to her, to raise his hand and signal his coming, but he didn't want to disrupt her concentration, nor did he want to disturb the sweet arc of her neck or the tender tilt of her head.

He was down at the bottom of the lake and the mud pulled harder at his feet. To force himself forward he lowered his head and butted it into the ferns. It meant he had to take his eyes off Ruth but now he didn't mind. He was sure of his path that led straight to where she was.

He pressed the ferns down in front of him, trying to pave the top of the mud, but the fronds were slippery, almost worse than the mud itself, and Noah fell to his hands and knees. The purse in his right hand was punched down into the ooze. He pulled it up and, planting one hand against a clumped root, raised himself to one knee, then managed to stand up completely.

He wiped his hands on the dress and looked down at the soiled front, the rich black mud smeared into the linen. He looked at his hands, at the purse. He wanted to wipe them some more but not on the dress. He reached out for some ferns but after the slightest touch he brought his hands back. Let the mud stay where it was. He had no time to waste.

He raised his head again to look at Ruth. Now he was close enough to see that the tilt of the head was not a gesture of concentration after all, but a drawing away, the beginning of a movement that, when completed, would bring her to her feet so that she could look down at her best friend with a scorn so absolute that Jean would probably be silenced forever.

But Jean was no longer reading. She was standing, looking at Noah as he worked his way through the ferns. The book was still in her hand, open at her side. Noah curled his fingers into the palms of his hand as if the feel of mud might give him renewed strength. As he trudged up toward the shore, Jean didn't move except to slowly close the book as if the story had ended.

Ruth was still seated, but now her head had straightened. Her hands were clamped onto the edges of the bench, her body reaching forward a little as if she were preparing for flight. She stood up. Noah watched as her arm rose from her side. She was waving. She was waving a handkerchief at him, at Noah.

"Noah!" she called. "Noah! Up here! Here I am!"

She kept on waving, stopping only to bring her arms out in front of her as if, even at the distance, she could help steady him in the mud. She brought her hands to her face and smoothed back her skin, then combed her fingers through her hair. She waved again, a quick flapping of the handkerchief, impatient, worried he might not make it to where she waited.

Noah, raising the purse up high, waved back. Mud from the purse dripped onto his nose and into his hair. He waved again then stepped out of the ferns and started up the grass embankment. Ruth started toward him but Jean put a hand on her arm.

"Here I am," Ruth said. "I was afraid you'd fall again. When did you get so clumsy?"

At that, Noah's muddy feet slipped on the grass and he fell. Ruth began to laugh, throwing her head back to point the laughter at the sky.

"Well," Jean said, "I guess *this* certainly explains a great deal, *doesn't* it."

"Go away, Jean," Ruth said. "Noah's here. He's here to see *me*."

Jean started to say something but changed her mind. She carefully put the book down on the bench as if it were something that might break or bite. Still saying nothing, she turned and walked away, looking up at the trees to show that nothing extraordinary was taking place. She was even humming.

Noah went to Ruth. He tried to say something but he had no breath. His chest heaved up and down, the linen scratching his skin. All he could manage was an extra heavy exhalation formed around the word Ruth.

She was no longer laughing. She seemed about to let her face settle back into the haggard scorn he'd seen so often. He breathed her name as clearly as he could, trying to stop her retreat.

It worked. She smiled. Her cheeks rose, her eyes brightened, her lips filled. "You look awful," she said. "You're all muddy."

"Ruth. You're beautiful today."

"I know." She licked her lips to complete the picture of her perfection.

"I brought you your purse."

He held it out to her. It was smeared and caked with mud. She looked at it, puzzled at first, then took it.

"Wait," Noah said. "Let me get some of the dirt off."

"It's all right. It doesn't matter. Let me get you clean first." She shook open the handkerchief she had in her hand and reached toward the mud on Noah's face. He pulled back.

"You'll get it all dirty."

Ruth paid no attention. She began rubbing his forehead. "You know what I'm going to do when I come home?" she said. "First thing, before I even go into the house? I'm going to go swim in the river. I don't care how cold it is. I'm going to make myself clean. Wash off everything."

Noah looked at her as she worked away at his cheeks. He wanted to speak, to explain to her about the purse and the dresses. He wanted to tell her about the stones of sorrow and Esther Overbaugh. He wanted to tell her about death and resurrection and about how she'd shielded him. But words were not his way. And he had no breath. His opened mouth was dry but still he wouldn't close it. He was waiting to see if the words might come anyway, breaking through the bones of his face, exploding his nose, spattering his mouth into the air.

But the words didn't come. All he could say was her name, again and again, more a breath than a word.

"Are you all right?" Ruth asked. She pulled back and looked down at his feet, bare and muddy, then let her eyes travel slowly up his body. "You got mud all over my green dress." She drew back farther. Noah watched the flesh on her face begin to go slack, the lips to draw down again, the eyes go shallow so that there would be no room to receive his gaze, room only for the contempt that had begun to gather there. She was leaving him.

"Don't go," he whispered. "Please don't go."

"You stole my purse," she said.

"Yes. I stole it."

He saw the old scorn rising in her like blood. He looked down at his hands. He saw the mud cracked along the creases of his palms. He saw the smeared dress, the filthy legs, the blackened feet. He was afraid he might start to sneeze, but before any eruption came, Ruth slammed the purse against the side of his head.

"No," he said. "Don't. Please don't. Don't go."

Obscenities, some sharp and clipped, some garbled, spilled from her mouth. Noah tried to reach her arm, to hold it off, but the purse had forced dirt into his eyes. Ruth knocked her head against his chest, pushing him against the bench. He stumbled and before he could get his balance, she gave him a shove. He slipped to the ground.

She was on top of him, grinding the purse into his face. He closed his eyes and turned his head away. She began tearing at the dress, ripping it away from his chest. The obscenities and curses became slurred and she began making the lisping, hissing noises, her breath forcing its way over and around a swollen tongue. He felt her writhing and struggling on top of him. He put his arms around her to hold her while she drowned.

Two attendants lifted Ruth away from him. She wasn't resisting. She seemed to feel they were there as rescuers, that they had saved her from a fall or picked her up after a meaningless stumble.

Another attendant stood nearby looking at Noah. Just behind him stood Dr. Corrado and Jean. The doctor was disheveled, his suit crumpled, his hair mussed, his tie askew as if he'd been asleep in a flower bed when they'd come for him. Jean had her hands on her hips. Her expression was bland and blank, the look of someone whose vindication is so complete it needn't even be noted.

The attendant took a step toward Noah. He jumped up and backed away. He looked at Ruth who was dabbing the mud from the purse onto her cheeks.

"Ruth?" he said, then turned and ran. He ran first down toward the lake, then along the bank to the path. Without turning to see if he was being followed, he ran to the parking lot. The mud on his feet made the stones less sharp.

23

THE *sumac* alongside the road hadn't started to turn red yet and since Noah was wearing the green dress, it was the perfect cover. He stood back among the leaves, looking through them as if they were the slats of a venetian blind. He'd see the truck when it got to the top of the hill. This would give him plenty of time to get out and flag it down. It shouldn't be too long from now unless the driver was eating a seven-course lunch. The truck had been parked outside the Mountain View Diner four miles back, just as Polly had told him it would be. Noah's van was safely hidden in the brush off the abandoned road to Hancock and all Noah had to do was wait.

He had one problem. When he'd parked the van, he couldn't find the gun, the .45. He was sure he'd brought it with him when he went to see Ruth. Someone must have seen it on the seat of the van in the parking lot at Mount St. Michael and taken it — another accounting he'd have to give sooner or later. He couldn't worry about it now. It was too late. He'd decided what he'd do, even without the gun. He'd step out into the road as if summoning help. He was prepared to move directly in front of the truck if he had to. Once in the cab, he'd use his own strength. He wouldn't need a gun. He had the strength of his wrath and his despair and his shame. He'd overpower the driver, pitch him out the door and drive off.

Noah stared through the leaves, first toward the top of the hill where the truck would come from, then downhill and off to the east where the countryside sloped down to a valley planted with corn or given over to pasture. Far beyond the fields were a barn with a silo, a farmhouse with outbuildings and a corncrib. Past that, more fields and pasture stretched toward the woods that covered the distant hill. Above that there was only the sky. No one was working the fields, no animals grazing, no birds, no breeze. There was just the view itself, motionless under the afternoon sky.

Then a solitary cow appeared on the slope of the far pasture and made its slow descent, ambling with a measured majesty as if its sole purpose in life was to walk now, for Noah's benefit, this length of pasture, through this field, toward this barn. The cow completed the view. What Noah was seeing now was something perfect and fulfilled. He continued to watch the cow, aware that he had come upon a moment singular in his life.

A deep yearning came up from within him, making him wish the cow would never reach the barn, that the moment would never end. Then it occurred to him that he was being given a final gift, a vision of earth perfect and complete, a signal that it was all about to end, that from now on, nothing would be the same, that what he was seeing now was a final glimpse of the beauty and the gentle wonder of the world.

He took a step toward the road, toward the downslope that led to the valley, then pulled back again into the trees. He'd heard a noise grinding off to his right. The truck was at the top of the hill. It was coming down slowly because of the weight of its load and the potholes in the road itself.

Noah wondered if he'd really step in front. He looked once more toward the fields and the farm. The cow was still lumbering slowly toward the barn. He looked again to his right. The truck was halfway down the hill. Noah, without a pause, stepped out onto the road and raised his hand.

The truck stopped. Noah could see a man peering at him through the windshield, over the steering wheel. When Noah jumped up to open the door to the cab, the man said nothing, just stared, stunned. Noah knew he looked peculiar with the torn and mud-stained dress, but he wished the man would say something, anything. It was all Noah could do to keep himself from looking again for the cow. But he couldn't look. He had business to do.

He climbed into the cab. The man was still gaping. Noah would have no trouble overpowering him. He was muscular but short, like a bantam cock. He couldn't be more than five feet two or three. Having made this evaluation, Noah forgot the cow and concentrated on the man. His black hair, freshly combed back with water, sworled into a great wave that might give him an added two inches in height, but it wouldn't make much difference. He wore a T-shirt with the already short sleeves rolled up to his shoulders. There was a tattoo on his right arm that looked at first like an armorial crest, but was actually, on further inspection, the insignia of the Peugeot automobile, a blue lion raised on its hind legs seen in profile, its front paws — more like spread talons — held out to different lengths in the posture of a prizefighter. Except for a scar cutting into his upper lip, the man had perfect features expertly scaled down to his size. Only the wave in his hair and the muscles in his arms were out of proportion.

"I'm only going about five miles up the road, to the overpass," Noah said.

The man nodded and started the motor. Pushing down on the clutch, shifting, turning the steering wheel, clutching and shifting again, the man worked with all the authority and grace of an exacting jockey. The truck moved slowly down the road.

Noah felt something on the seat under him, something bulky and hard. He shifted his weight, but whatever it was, it was still there. Noah squirmed once more, then reached down under him and knocked it down onto the floor. It was a gun. He looked over at the man.

"Don't let it worry you," the man said. "Just kick it over to my side and forget it." His voice was high, like Polly's, but raspy as if he'd been chewing sand.

Noah gave it a slight nudge closer to the man, but not so far over that he couldn't reach down suddenly and grab it. He barely believed his luck, as though the gun had been put there just to give him a second chance. He'd count to ten, then reach.

When he got to eight the man said, "You just saved some poor son-of-a-bitch's life. Did you know that?"

Noah said nothing. The man took a quick glance in his direction, then faced front again. "Can you understand what someone says when he talks to you? I mean, *capisce?*"

The man had obviously taken Noah for an escaped lunatic and, by some interior logic, assumed that Italian was a lunatic's native tongue. Noah decided to explain nothing.

"Well," the man went on, "if you do understand, you saved somebody's life. And would you believe it, I was the one going to kill him? Shoot him, square in the face with that gun down there."

Noah couldn't help noting that an unusual amount of gunplay in what was supposedly tranquil country had been scheduled for that day, but he kept his silence.

The man tried unsuccessfully to clear the gravel from his throat, then went on. "I owe this rich bastard runs the lumber mill a chunk of money — a big chunk — and this was going to square the debt. I seem to gamble more than's good for me, the horses mostly. And he tells me, the rich bastard, he tells me if I shoot this guy he sets up for me, I don't owe him money anymore."

Noah began to understand, but not completely. All he had for the moment was a memory of Polly's noncommittal stare when Noah had come to Banana-nose's party, intercepting their fun, defying them all to laugh at Cory. He knew there was more to it, but it wouldn't come to him immediately.

"But now I'm not going to do it," the man was saying. "I'm not going to shoot the son-of-a-bitch. We'll see him somewhere right along here, but I'm going to drive right by like I never even saw him."

He took another quick look at Noah. "I take you for a sign," he said, speaking matter-of-factly as if he were telling Noah about some minor idiosyncrasy, his voice less raspy. "When I first saw you, out there in the road, I thought you were my Aunt Rose died when I was fifteen. I thought it was my Aunt Rose come right out of the woods to warn me. To tell me not to do it. Don't go killing anybody. She was like that, my Aunt Rose. Strict. That's why I stopped when I saw you. I had to. She would have caught up with me if I didn't. So now I'm not going to kill the guy. Or anybody else. Because it's like my Aunt Rose came to me and told me I dassn't. We're like that, my family, mostly from my mother's side."

Again he looked at Noah. "My Aunt Rose, she wore her hair halfway short, just like you. And her clothes always got themselves a little mussed up. And she hardly ever wore her shoes, just like you. Except she was all right upstairs, in her head, no offense. Just strict, that's all."

Leaning a little toward the windshield, the driver kept looking from side to side expectantly. "We should see the guy right along in here unless he changed his mind. Thinks he's going to hijack this truck, carrying a gun. I'm supposed to be ready for him, with that gun there on the floor. Shoot him while he has his own gun, all loaded and everything so who'd there be to know I didn't have the right to do it. Self-protection. Say what you will about the rich, they know how to think."

Noah had a quick vision of pulling the truck into Polly's driveway, calling out to him to come collect his hijacked lumber, then flinging the dead body of the punk gambler at his feet. But the vision went as quickly as it had come and he let it go.

And besides, the man had more to say. "The guy screwed the rich bastard's fat-ass girl friend, then even insulted his wife. Something about she showed him her snatch and her ass. I never really got it all straight. All I know is he's supposed to get shot for whatever he did. Rich people, they don't futz around."

Noah wanted only to go home, to harm no one, to give no trouble to anyone in the world. He'd ask the driver to take him to his house. If he refused, he'd grab the gun and force him to do it. He'd heard enough. If the man refused, he'd shoot him, kill him, throw him out on the road and drive the truck home.

Then he remembered that he wanted to harm no one. He'd ask, then see what happened. "Would you," Noah asked, his voice low and quiet, "would you drop me off in Mattysborough? I live there. You make the next turn. I'll show you the street."

"They expecting you? I mean, is there someone there to take care of you? I mean, be there with you?"

"It's all right. I'm expected."

"Well, okay. Sure I'll take you wherever you want to go. If you're going to be all right when you get there."

"I'll be all right."

Noah, when he got out, offered the man the necklace and the earrings Jean had left on the workbench. They'd help pay off the debt that had almost made him a killer. At first the man refused, then took them and wished Noah luck, thanking him again for bringing the message from his Aunt Rose.

After the truck drove off, Noah realized he should have warned the man not to offer the necklace and earrings directly to Polly but to sell them first. He ran toward the street and called after him, but the man merely reached out his muscled arm and waved.

Noah went into the house. The children were gone. No one had bothered to close the front door. He walked through to the back, shedding the dried mud as he went. He called no names. He didn't look to see what they'd taken with them.

Standing in the backyard he could sense Mrs. Driscoll next door looking down at him from an upstairs window. Only a few threads across his left shoulder kept the dress from falling down around his feet. He gave it a light tug and let it slip to the ground, a whispering against his skin. He stepped away from it and walked a few paces toward the thicket. He heard no sound, not even the river.

He turned and started back toward the house. Before he got as far as the old clothespost a thought stunned him like a hammer blow. He, Noah, had done all this himself in order to achieve this moment. He had driven them all away so he could be alone, solitary forever, without any of them, not Anne, not Danny, not Joel, not Ruth. Somewhere in his knowing soul he had conspired to bring himself to this present desolation.

He turned to the river. One hand shot up and outward, raised to the thicket and the trees. This charge, this judgment, was not true. He had done what he had done for them, for his children, for his wife. To this he swore. He swore that he did not want to be alone. To believe that he did was a last temptation and to this he would not yield.

He turned and went toward the house. On the single stone step he sat down and looked out at the horizon of trees on the far side of the river. His final vigil had begun. Soon the deer would come, this time not to bless, but to judge. And Noah was ready to hear.

He waited. A branch snapped down near the water. There was a rattling of leaves down along the bank, coming closer. Noah stood up. He heard the sharp break of a single twig and the brush of leaves. Ruth, naked, emerged from the thicket. She had her arms wrapped around her and was shivering in the cold.

"Ruth . . . ," Noah whispered, afraid she might turn and run if he made too much noise. She didn't move.

"I told you I'd swim in the river and make myself clean before I came home. Well, I've done it. I told a man in the parking lot I lost my car keys. He gave me a ride. And now I'm home." The words came like a pronouncement, defiant but afraid.

Noah started toward her. She pulled her hands away from her shoulders, releasing herself from her own huddling. Both arms went down to her sides, then she raised her right hand. She was holding the gun, the .45, pointing it at Noah.

"Where'd you get—"

"You wanted me to kill myself, didn't you?"

"Kill — ? Never —"

Noah started toward her again but she tensed her arm and tightened her grip, leveling the gun right at him. "Isn't that why you put this in my purse? And brought it to me? So I'd go and blow my brains out?"

"No."

"You did! And here's the gun I was supposed to do it with."

Noah took a step toward her. She reached out the hand holding the gun. Noah stopped, then continued. He caught the scent of river water on her body, the smell of wet sage and goldenrod. He saw where a branch must have scratched her arm and there was a wet leaf pasted to her side. "Give me the gun," he said.

"Yes," said Ruth quietly. "You do it." She held out the gun. "Go ahead. You shoot. I can't."

Noah took the gun. Ruth started to take a step back, but stopped. She was looking at him with eyes so exhausted that they seemed to beg for sleep. Her whole body was slumped with surrender, the shoulders rounded inward toward her breasts, her arms dangling down as if she'd released them from their sockets and wanted never to raise them again. In her nakedness she was completely forlorn, abandoned, and all that had been beautiful seemed repugnant to him now, as if calamity had been a shameful violation practiced upon his wife and had made her repellent and unclean.

He could shoot her. He was ready to do it.

Then she took the one step back and slowly raised her shoulders, straightening her body. With one hand she smoothed the damp hair back from her forehead, then brought the arm gently down to her side. Now in the final light of dusk Noah could see her face. She'd lifted her head to the imperial height that had held it high on her first days at Mount St. Michael. She was no longer forlorn. The old look of scorn and grief that her madness had given her had come again as if she were finally seeing what it was that she had pitied, what it was that she despised. She had found at last the object of her mourning and the cause of her contempt. And with this face of sorrow and disdain she looked at Noah, at her husband.

Noah lowered the gun. Her look was for him and he had earned it. He had, in all his writings and turnings, come to deserve her scorn and to claim her grief. He had worn the dresses and taken the gun from Polly's hand. He had wanted to break his children's bones and give all his love to Esther Overbaugh. He had stolen his wife's purse. For this he deserved her scorn.

But he had accepted humiliations and bewilderment; he had

surrendered to mystery; he had faced horror and cried out to the hard nailed stars. Now he could claim her grief.

It ended here. What had seemed an arduous and tormented journey had been the true path that had led him here to Ruth. All that he had done and all that had been done to him prepared him for this moment. He was ready now to take her scorn. It belonged to him and it was precious. He was ready to take her grief, it was his and he was worthy of it at last. He had been given a way to touch her madness and now they met.

Noah fell to his knees and bowed his head toward the ground. With the yearning of all his years heavy upon him, yet bearing him up, he wanted to touch his wife with his lips. Bending lower, murmuring his sorrow and his love, he began with her feet.